LAND KILLS

Nat & Yanna Brandt

LAND KILLS

A Foul Play Press Book
THE COUNTRYMAN PRESS, WOODSTOCK, VERMONT

First Edition
Copyright © 1991 by Nat and Yanna Brandt

All rights reserved. No part of this book may be reproduced in
any form or by any electronic or mechanical means including
information storage and retrieval systems without permission in
writing from the publisher, except by a reviewer who may quote
brief passages.

The characters, places and institutions depicted in this novel
are wholly fictional or are used fictitiously. Any apparent
resemblance to any person alive or dead, to any actual events or
places, and to any actual institutions, is entirely coincidental.

Library of Congress Cataloging-in Publication Data

Brandt, Nat.
   Land kills / Nat & Yanna Brandt.—1st ed.
      p. cm.
   "A Foul Play Press book."
   ISBN 0-88150-209-X
   I. Brandt, Yanna. II. Title.
   PS3552.R3233L36   1991   91-22651
   813' .54—dc20   CIP

Text design by Dede Cummings / I. P. A.

A Foul Play Press Book
The Countryman Press, Inc.
Woodstock, Vermont 05091

Printed in the United States of America by Arcata Graphics

10 9 8 7 6 5 4 3 2 1

To brother Herbert

ACKNOWLEDGEMENTS

The authors wish to thank Bill Murray of Berkley & Veller/Greenwood Country Realtors of Brattleboro, and the staffs of the following Vermont agencies for their assistance in the research for this book: the Fish & Game Department in Roxbury, the Medical Examiner's Office in Burlington, the state police barracks in Brattleboro, the Natural Resources Agency in Springfield, and the Environmental Conservation Department in Waterbury.

LAND KILLS

PROLOGUE

*T*HE LEAVES WERE *still wet from night frost. They fell from the trees singly, lazily, except when a gust of wind whistled through the hillside. Each time the wind blew, the trees moved in chorus with it and great swarms of leaves rushed downward, hurly-burly, creating a crowd of colors. The sun, just coming up, began to pick out the reds and yellows in the highest branches. As it did, the entire countryside became a kaleidoscope of color.*

Between the sudden whirls of the wind, it was so quiet that the crowing of a rooster from the other side of the hill could be heard. So quiet that the man was afraid that someone in the farm there would hear him as he let out great gulps of air. Lugging the body into the trees was difficult enough; the coat snagged on broken limbs, a boot was pulled off by a rock, the stockings shredded from the ragged ground. Now, going uphill, the strain was more pronounced. Every so often, the man stopped. Breathing deeply, he would swallow and inhale, swallow and inhale, until he caught his breath. Then, tugging the body by the arms, he would resume dragging it behind him as if it were a travois.

An orange ribbon was tied to the branch of a maple tree where he came to a stop. Below it, almost hidden by the undergrowth, a lead pipe protruded from the ground. Its end was pinched. The man dropped the arms and stood back. A shower of leaves came down around him as the wind cut through the trees. Some of the leaves fell on the body. The man looked up, trying to gauge from the foliage in the surrounding trees how long it would take for them to cover the entire body. Then he looked around once more before starting to make his way down the slope, stepping gingerly around boulders and fallen trees.

Leaves continued to fall on the body. Soon the huge blot of blood on the coat was covered and as the blood dried, leaves stuck to the coat.

Off in the distance, the crack of a rifle broke the stillness. A buck bounded up the hillside past the body, its eyes wide with terror.

ONE

Welcome to Vermont. Crossing the border from Massachusetts on Interstate 91 on a half-filled bus, Mitch Stevens smiled to himself, contented. Broad meadows appeared on both sides of the highway in between verdant hills. Everything natural seemed green, a lush, rich green, against which red barns and blue silos stood out in colorful relief. And so much land looked unsettled. Mitch had to restrain himself from jumping off the bus and just walking, all alone, across a meadow, feeling the summer heat and perhaps a gentle breeze, smelling the land.

Within a half-hour he would be in Southborough, and with that thought, he could feel his stomach tighten. He was taking on a heavy responsibility. When he had called Ham to accept his offer, he had realized how much his friend depended on him to keep the newspaper going. Mitch suspected that Ham's illness was a lot more serious than he had indicated.

It was a long time since Mitch had run a newspaper

and a very different one at that. As city editor at the *Trib*, he had had a full staff of reporters and his job had been to inspire them and keep them working at top capacity. Now he was walking into a small town he knew nothing about, to work on a small newspaper with a staff he didn't know. The conventional wisdom was that a reporter wasn't much use to a paper for at least six months because that was how long it took to meet people and make connections. Mitch would be on the paper for only two months. Suddenly, the risk, the insanity of the whole enterprise hit him.

Mitch realized something else was making him nervous, something he had pushed to the back of his consciousness, but that kept crawling up to needle him. Jack Reed, the department chairman, had applauded Mitch's summer plans and prevailed on him to bring along one of his students as a summer intern.

Jack had been so taken with his own idea that he had even pried some money loose from the journalism department to pay for the student's room and board. Ham approved the idea and so did Mitch, in principle. It was only when he started to consider whom he would pick for the internship that he began to have doubts. Should he give it to the best student in his class who didn't really need the opportunity and would probably be offered the best available job anyway? Or should he give it to a talented student to whom the internship could really make a difference? For Mitch there was no contest; he'd select the student it would help the most. But when he looked over his class, the likeliest candidate was Rachel, and Mitch had genuine reservations about how the young woman would interpret his choice. He did not look forward to fending off Rachel's amorous advances without the protection of Val's constant presence. Every year, there was always one female student who developed a crush. Sometimes they were quite aggressive about it, showing up at his apartment in the middle of the night, claiming some emergency. Val was very good at putting out the fire. She would answer the door, firmly tell the girl that Mitch was asleep, going so far as to offer her milk and cookies. It usually did the trick. Unlike many of his colleagues, Mitch did not find the attentions of these young women stimulating either to his ego or his libido. His old newspaper buddies would probably accuse him of early senility. But Val's intoxicating sensuality was quite enough for him.

Mitch finally decided to offer the internship to Rachel, but not without lengthy discussions with Val and some residual anxiety. He had trepidations about Rachel's arrival in a week but he kept telling himself that he was a mature male with a grown son; certainly capable of handling the situation.

Mitch stared out the window. The vistas were uninterrupted, the landscape unchanged and unspoiled. How different from the lower Connecticut River Valley where the only vestiges of the past were the large tobacco drying sheds alongside the highway and the fields beside them strung with white mesh to protect the shade tobacco from the sun. It suddenly seemed to Mitch that he had been there just yesterday as a cub reporter to do a story for the *Tribune* on an average day in the life of a migrant-worker family. The growers were none too happy with his story—especially the complaints about wages and living conditions—and for a while he even got threatening letters. I wonder if things have changed, Mitch thought to himself. I wonder if the tobacco farmers still rely on migrant workers. I wonder if . . . it would be great to do a follow-up story.

Mitch stopped himself. He wasn't going to Vermont to muckrake or prove how great a reporter he was. He was going there to help out a friend and maybe, if he was lucky, find that perfect piece of land that he and Val had been talking about for years. Now that Val's career as an actress had taken off and they didn't have to cough up tuition for their son Ken's college education anymore, he and Val could finally think about buying some land and building a vacation home. He tried envisioning what it would look like—a Colonial, a Saltbox, a Cape Cod. Val was adamant. She didn't want someone else's house. She wanted to build from the ground up. It would be a place they planned together. It would be all theirs.

His thoughts were abruptly interrupted as the bus pulled into the Southborough station. "Bus station," Mitch mused, was a euphemism. The station consisted of an old trailer set out in the middle of a lot strewn with garbage. There was a pervasive smell of urine from a portable john. It was outside of town, along a highway strip filled with gas stations.

Mitch got out of the bus and waited while the driver unloaded the luggage. It took the driver about five minutes. And in another minute Mitch realized his luggage was missing. When he questioned the driver, the man just shrugged and told him it was not his responsibility and to go see the clerk in the trailer.

"Can I help you, mister?" The clerk looked at Mitch with a blank stare and little interest.

"I made it, but my luggage didn't. And what puzzles me," Mitch was making an effort to be polite, "is that I watched the driver load the luggage on the bus."

"Oh, that's okay then." The clerk started to walk away.

"What do you mean, that's okay? My luggage is not here and the bus has left." Mitch was trying to maintain a calm facade and beginning to lose the battle.

"That means it will be on the next bus."

"How can you be so sure?"

"Well, they probably took your bags off to make room for packages. It happens all the time. Now, don't you fret. Your bags will be here on the next bus, you can count on it."

"And what time does the next bus arrive?"

"At two A.M."

"And what am I supposed to do until then?" Mitch couldn't keep the sarcasm out of his voice but the clerk didn't seem to notice or care.

"That's your business, mister. But it'll be on the next bus as sure as I'm standing here. The driver'll put all his packages and bags for Southborough in here. You got no cause for worry."

"Well, I'd like to be a little surer than that, if you don't mind. Could you please call New York and make sure they put my luggage aboard?"

"No, sir, mister, I can't do that."

"And why not?"

"Because I don't have no number for New York and, anyways, they don't answer the phone on Saturdays."

By this time, Mitch was so angry he shouted at the clerk that his luggage better be there or else. Of course, he had absolutely no idea of what the "or else" could be and he felt completely foolish. As he walked away, totally frustrated, two men approached him. They were dressed like farm workers, with high, muddy boots.

"You won't get any satisfaction here, mister," one of the men said, looking at Mitch sympathetically. "We're still waiting for our prepaid tickets so we can go home to Virginia. Vermonters don't take too kindly to foreigners and they kind of enjoy putting cold water on their hurry-up ways, if you get my meaning. You'd be best off if you just take a wait-and-see attitude. You'll save yourself a lot of shoe leather. We've been working construction here for three months and we've learned to get by."

Mitch nodded his thanks at the two men. He reached out his hand, "Good luck, I hope you get home soon."

Mitch walked off to find a telephone to call Ham. Where was he? Didn't Ham say he would be here to meet him? It was not like Ham to be late, either. Mitch dialed and waited. He let it ring a long time, but no one answered. Fortunately, the car rental agency was only a short walk. He had spotted its sign as the bus pulled into the station. He'd go pick up the car, drive to Ham's place and, hopefully, find his friend at home. And at two A.M. he'd drive back down here and see if the clerk really knew what he was talking about.

MITCH STOPPED SEVERAL times to ask directions. It wasn't that people were unfriendly, but they weren't exactly friendly either. No one seemed to recognize the name of Ham's road and there were no signs. When Mitch mentioned the lack of signs to one person, the man just shrugged and told Mitch about all the signs there used to be but how they had all been stolen. My God, thought Mitch, this is Vermont, not New York. When he finally found Ham's house, it seemed deserted.

He rang the bell for a long time before he heard footsteps. When Ham finally opened the door, it took all of

Mitch's willpower not to let his face reflect his thoughts. Ham looked gaunt, almost emaciated. Mitch remembered his one-time newspaper companion as a jolly, red-faced, roly-poly man who loved to eat—though he was no gourmet—much to the consternation of his sweet, shy Irish wife, Kate. Now he was so thin, his clothes hung on him. And the ruddiness was gone, replaced by taut, chalky skin. Ham looked at Mitch apologetically. "Mitch, forgive me. I was so tired, I just fell asleep and the last thing I remember was wondering if your bus was going to make it on time."

Mitch hugged his friend gently. "It's cancer," Ham whispered. "I haven't told anyone at the office. Only the publisher knows." Mitch couldn't imagine how anyone could miss the signs.

THE NEXT DAY was a glorious Vermont Sunday, a crystal-clear, blue-skied, sun-drenched day. No humidity, and no blistering heat. Mitch had roused himself the night before, driven to the bus station through the deserted streets of Southborough and, much to his amazement, found his two pieces of luggage inside the bus station, neatly tagged, "Hold for pick-up." He slept late and had a leisurely breakfast with Ham.

Mitch would have stayed with Ham all day but he could see that his friend tired easily. So he excused himself, telling Ham he wanted to take advantage of the beautiful day to look for property. At Ham's recommendation, he called an eager young real estate agent named Bob Grant. They spent the entire day going from one end of the county to the other and, finally, the agent brought Mitch to a property commanding an uninterrupted view for thirty miles to a low range of mountains.

It was breathtaking. It seemed to have everything Mitch wanted—a view, seclusion, a wooded area, a meadow and enough acreage to protect the property from neighbors. But there was a catch. Grant was not sure the meadow was part of the property. In fact, he wasn't at all sure where the boundaries were. The survey map that he had was seven years old and confusing. Mitch was so excited by the land that he made a date then and there to meet with Grant and a surveyor late the next day.

Meanwhile, he just stood on the crest of the hill, where he had already decided the house would go, and looked down on the meadow below him. It was ringed by trees, tall trees with thin white bark. To the left was a strawberry farm and he could see in the distance a family of four on their hands and knees picking the fruit. To his right were woods, so thick and compressed that Mitch wondered if it was possible to walk there. He felt a surge of possession and wondered what wonderful secrets he would discover—who had lived here before? Was there a house back there in the woods? Maybe an old barn?

CHUBB ANDERS WAS pointing to the bottom of the dip, where the meadow ran into a copse of trees, mostly poplars, that bordered a tiny brook. "The trees have moved. That's why that fella over there thinks it's his property."

"Moved? The trees moved?" Mitch looked perplexed. "How could they move?"

"New growth, Mr. Stevens." Anders pointed again, more to the right. "See that old maple?" Mitch, who couldn't tell a maple from an elm, looked uncertain. "That big old gnarled tree. That's what the deed says is the northeast corner. It probably stood all alone at one time, but now you can hardly make it out, and there are several other maples down in that hollow, so which is the true corner?"

The two men were standing midway down the slope of the hill on top of a granite ledge, looking north at the meadow that dipped away until it reached the border of trees at the base of the hill. On the other side of the trees, faintly seen, was another meadow that climbed the hill opposite, on top of which stood a house and stables.

Chubb Anders was a tall, well-built man in his early sixties, his face almost as gnarled as the maple tree he had been pointing out, a result of working outdoors nine months of the year as a surveyor. He had picked up his love of longitude and latitude as a navigator on a Navy reconnaisance amphibian in World War II.

Mitch and Anders stood around, waiting for Bob Grant to show up. "You saw the survey he has, didn't you?" Mitch asked.

"Yup. I got it with me. And I went to Town Hall and checked out the listers' reports, too. But you have to see the land to be dead sure."

"What are listers?"

"Assessors." Anders grinned. "They'll decide what you pay in taxes if you buy the land."

"And you're positive about the meadow, that it's part of the property?"

"As certain as you can be in Vermont," Anders replied. "You oughta have another survey done just to be sure—in fact, a good lawyer will make you do it before you take title. You'd have to by law if it were under ten acres.

"See all them hills and the mountains in the distance?" Anders pointed to the west. "Mayors Peak is thataway. When the English were here, the crown—the king—owned all of this at first and would hand out proprietorships, ten-thousand acres here, five-thousand acres there, running over hill and valley or along a river, but not specific like. And if a stream got dammed up and diverted, well there went that boundary." Anders chuckled. "And after the English were gone, after the Revolution, the land got all broken up. The legislature tried to apply a grid pattern to the counties and such, but inside every square mile there was no rhyme or reason to a person's lines." The surveyor swept his arm around in a half circle. "A maple tree—like that one back there—a stream, a big rock. Just about anything served as markers. You should read some of the old deeds. They're damn near impossible to figure out. I remember one I had recently. It said something like 'sixty paces north of stone wall and thirty paces east of water well to a point abutting Smith's Road.' Now, how you figure what a pace is, exactly? That's anybody's guess, and guesswork is what it is, mostly. In the old days, the land would just pass down within a family and everybody'd know where his lines were, or thought they knew. But now we're getting a lot of outsiders coming in buying land like you. Now, no offense, mind you, but the banks require surveys even when the local ordinances don't. Nearly four-fifths of Vermont still hasn't been properly surveyed."

"That must keep you busy, Mr. Anders." Mitch looked up the hill toward the road, but there was still no sign of Grant.

A light smile crossed Anders's face. "Yup, my crew is at it until the snow stops us."

"But if there was a survey done here once, shouldn't I be able to find the boundary lines myself?"

Anders looked at Mitch as if he was a little slow-witted. "Well"—he drew out the word—"that depends, don't it? Did someone knock over the pins? I bet you won't find any along the meadow near where that farmer mows. He's probably pulled them out to keep them from ruining his equipment. Or maybe the trees that were marked with blazes were struck by lightning and are down. We paint some red and we put orange ribbons on branches, too, so you can see them from a distance, but you can't account for the weather."

Mitch checked his watch. He was paying Anders an hourly fee for consultation and hoped the surveyor would walk the property with him to check the lines.

"I haven't got all day either, Mr. Stevens," said Anders, without hostility. "This is the busiest time of the year for us, especially with all the development going on." There was a flurry of construction activity in and around Southborough, the result of a speculator's plan to build a ski resort not far away, near Mayors Peak. Mitch had spent barely one day at the newspaper office but he had already picked up on the development as the major issue of the moment.

"Condominiums and time-sharing." Anders kept on talking. "Those are new words for the vocabulary of folks like me."

"And for me, as well. I—" Mitch broke off his sentence. "Here's Bob now. That car up by the road."

The young realtor strode quickly down the slope and was apologizing before he even reached Mitch and Anders. "I'm sorry. I got tied up on the phone. It's been ringing off the hook. Have you walked the property yet?"

Mitch answered. "No, I didn't want to bother until you confirmed the owner's asking price."

Anders stepped aside, not wanting to seem like he was listening.

"He won't budge, Mitch. He knows prices are high now with all the demand for land near the ski resort. He's set a figure of thirty-six thousand, take or leave it."

"What do you think?"

"Well, you can offer less, of course, but then you risk someone else coming along and offering what he's asking, or maybe just a dollar more than you and you've lost the property. On the other hand, if you meet his price, say you're willing to pay the thirty-six thou, by law he has to accept your bid. He can't back down."

Mitch rubbed his chin. "How soon do I have to decide?"

Grant shrugged. "He put this land up for sale last week. It's been listed on a computer circuit with all the realtors in the area, and I know it's been shown to other people already. Besides, with a ski resort nearby, everybody knows the value of the land is bound to go up."

Mitch knew Grant wasn't giving him a sales pitch. He'd seen a crumpled cigarette package that had been obviously tossed on the ground recently. "I'd like to talk to my wife about it," he said, although he and Val had already decided that if he had to make a quick move without her—if he saw anything *that* special—he would. And this land was that special.

"Up to you, Mitch."

Mitch looked at Anders, who had been watching and hearing the conversation. "Is it worth it, Mr. Anders?"

"It's all in the beholder's eye, Mr. Stevens. I'm the wrong person to ask, in any case. I've seen the values jump up hereabouts to what my folks would have called unseemly proportions. I don't want to offend you none, Mr. Stevens, but I'm not exactly pleased by New Yorkers coming up here and sending our land values sky-rocketing so local folks can't afford to buy homes anymore."

"Well, you're looking at a city boy, Mr. Anders, who's dreamed of a piece of land like this since he was six years old and saw his first cow. I'm afraid that at this point I'd be hard to discourage." Mitch turned to Grant. "Bob, I think I'd like to walk the property first with Mr. Anders before I make a commitment. It's considerably higher than I had envisioned. And I'd like to see if I can reach my wife, too. Why don't I try to get you later this evening, after seven."

"Okay with me. Why don't I take the walk with you? I'd like to be able to know the lines for sure myself, in case you decide against buying."

"Sure," said Mitch. "Let's get started." He motioned to Anders, who nodded.

Anders took out the old survey map and pointed to a blue line that ran the proportional equivalent of nearly three football fields down into the meadow. "We'll start here by the westerly line over by the farm. We won't find any pins, I'm sure, but if we're on course we ought to be able to find the corner."

"As easy as that?" laughed Mitch.

"Maybe. If and when we do the survey for you, should you buy the property, we'll bring out a laser to be as accurate as possible. I'm just going by experience now."

The meadow was so dry the grass cracked under their shoes as they strode downhill, and the slope so steep that Mitch found he had to brace himself from going too fast. When they reached the woodline at the bottom, Anders led the way into the trees, his eyes intent on the ground.

"There's a pipe!" Mitch shouted, excited that he was the first to spot a marker.

Anders bent down to look at the iron cylinder that came about four inches out of the ground. "Nope. It's not pinched. Whoever surveyed this put it here as a guide to sight on. Now, if we can figure out which way the line goes, we can use it as a guide, too." Anders studied the old survey. "Let's go this way."

As the men moved deeper inside the forest, Mitch felt chilled. The sun barely filtered through to provide any warmth. He had dressed for a warm, late-June afternoon. Now he noticed that Anders wore a down jacket, which he had zippered up, and Grant had not only a sports jacket on, but also a topcoat.

"Over here," called Anders. He was pointing down as they came up to him. "It's a pinched pipe. And look over there," he said, pointing to the east, along what was the northern boundary. "See that tree? The one with the blaze." There was a blotch of red paint about five feet up on the trunk and beyond that, an orange ribbon on some bushes. "We've got it now. Let's go."

They stepped over fallen trees, around boulders, over a narrow stream, going from one red splotch or orange ribbon to the next. Turning at the northeast corner, where there was a break in the trees that looked like an old pony-cart trail, the men started to climb the hillside. The going, through dense forest and heavy underbrush, was laborious. They were all breathless from the exertion. The property seemed endless to Mitch, and he had the feeling that this would be the only time he'd ever bother to see this part of it. It was not inviting. And obviously, despite the old trail that ran through it, no one had ever lived here.

Mitch stepped over a big boulder and jumped across the stream. He could see neither Anders nor Grant, and had no idea whether he was ahead of them or behind. He stopped to catch his breath and look around. Despite the coolness, he was now sweating profusely from the climb. He looked ahead to try to spot the next marker. We should be near the top of the property now, he thought, near where the trees come right up to the road.

Mitch saw the orange ribbon off to his left. Taking a deep gulp of air, he headed for it, one step after another, over a fallen branch. Suddenly, he slipped, his foot skidding out from under him and he fell forward. Mitch reached out to brace himself, hitting the ground without hurting himself, tumbling atop a mound covered with forest debris. Old leaves slipped away from the mound as he reached out to push himself up. His hand sunk into the soft earth as he struggled to regain his balance and touched something hard and icy. Instinctively, he pulled away, brushing aside the leaves. Suddenly his mouth went dry and his arms and legs froze. His attention was riveted on the spot where his hand had been. There, facing him, were the sunken, hollow eye sockets of a human skull.

Mitch stared in fascination. He seemed to be caught in place, on all fours, unable to move, for what seemed like minutes, but was only a matter of seconds. Anders and Grant, coming up from behind, were kidding as they came to help him, saying something about kissing the very land he would own. To Mitch their voices seemed distant and unreal. Their banter stopped abruptly when they saw the look on Mitch's face. Their eyes shifted down to where he was staring.

"Oh, my Lord," said Anders.

"Holy God," Grant whispered.

They helped Mitch to his feet, then Anders bent down and began brushing back the leaves from the mound. As he did, they saw the remains of the body. Flesh still clung to parts that had been covered by clothing, though the clothing itself was falling apart.

"Look at that," said Anders, pointing to a dark stain on what was left of a coat. "Looks like a bullet wound to me."

Grant began to gag. He ducked behind a nearby tree and started to throw up.

Mitch was shivering. He stood, his hands thrust in his pockets for warmth, still staring at the body. "How long," he began weakly, then cleared his throat. "How long do you think it's been here?"

"It's a woman," said Anders. "See that? She was wearing heavy winter boots. Must have been lying here all winter."

"What do you think happened?" Mitch asked.

"A hunting accident, I'd wager," said Anders matter-of-factly, pushing himself up from the ground. "We get some every year. No matter how often you tell people to stay out of the woods, or wear bright clothing if you have to be in them, some people just don't pay no mind. A deer hunter probably shot her."

Grant came back, wiping his mouth with a handkerchief. "Sorry about that." He bent halfway down to look at the corpse. "Hey," he said. "I bet that's Vera Tolvey."

"The one that's missing?" Anders screwed up his face. "My God, I bet you're right. We searched all over for her, but nowhere near here."

"Well, the property wasn't on the market then," Grant said. "Who'd have thought she'd be here."

"Who was she?" Mitch asked.

"A real estate agent—for another firm. She's been missing since last fall. Just dropped out of sight."

"The constable organized a search party," Anders explained. "I was in it. I know the lay of most of the land here-abouts."

"But you were looking on the other side of town," Grant said.

"Yup. That's where they thought she'd be. She'd been showing property over that way before she disappeared. Nobody thought to look around here. There didn't seem to be any reason to."

Grant glanced around. "I wonder what the devil she was doing back here in these woods. The land wasn't up for sale."

"And even if it was," Anders said, "I don't see why she'd have come this far in. None of you agents ever bother to take that kind of trouble."

"This one did," Mitch said.

"Maybe she heard that it would be coming on the market and came around to get an idea of what it was like," said Grant. "It's possible. We try to get a jump on the other agents in town when we can."

"Well, whatever the reason," Anders said, "better call the state police and get them up here." He gestured with his head. "That way should be a shortcut to the road. I don't think we have to walk the rest of the line now." He looked around before moving off himself. "Right, there's a pinched pipe. The property line shifts slightly to the east here. I just want to get my bearings so I can tell the police where she's at."

They started off. "Did she have a family?" Mitch asked, reaching out to support himself against a tree as he stepped over a rock.

"No, she was divorced," said Grant. "Strange, though," he added as he took Mitch's extended hand and stepped over the same rock. "She hated hunting. I mean really hated it. She was on some committee that was trying to get the state to outlaw any hunting whatsoever. I just can't for the life of me understand why she would want to come into the woods at that time of year."

"You should see us in the fall," said Anders. The trees were starting to thin out enough to make out the road up ahead. "We wear orange vests and hats and don't dare go near any trees without something bright on."

"That's what's really strange," said Grant. "We all carry a vest in our cars. I don't know a realtor who doesn't. Vera'd have known better than to go traipsing around in a dense forest in a dark-brown coat. Every kid in the state knows better than that."

TWO

SOUTHBOROUGH—The body of Vera S. Tolvey, a local real estate agent who has been missing since mid-November, was discovered yesterday deep in the woods near Mayors Peak.

The police said they believe she was the victim of a hunting accident.

Ms. Tolvey, who worked for Mont Vert Realtors, lived in East Southborough. Her disappearance led to an intensive, week-long search by local authorities and volunteers.

The police said evidence of a bullet wound was found on the partly decomposed body.

There was no indication what Ms. Tolvey was doing in the woods at the time. The 22-acre property was only recently put up for sale.

The body was found by . . .

MITCH PUT THE newspaper aside and regarded Ham Johnson over the top of his glasses. The editor of the *Southborough Courier* was scowling. He tossed several sheets of copy paper to Mitch, who was sitting across the desk from him. Mitch uncrossed his legs and leaned forward to pick up the papers.

"I suppose I shouldn't expect better," Johnson said, "but I am always disappointed. I should know better."

Mitch read quickly, passing each sheet from his right hand to his left as he finished it. "It's better than some of my students do," he said, handing the papers back to Johnson.

"It should be, for God's sake. The guy's been here for over a year now. He's supposed to be a professional." Johnson lifted his glasses up and let them perch above his forehead.

"He handled the Tolvey story without much of a problem," Mitch said, pointing with his thumb to that morning's edition.

"Well for Chrissake he had most of the day to do it after you phoned it in." Johnson scowled again. "I'd hardly call a story about a hunting accident prime material for a Pulitzer.

"The problem is that good reporters don't last long. They get some grounding here and then they move on. I'm constantly dealing with people moving on, or," he added, nodding toward the small copy desk that was in the newsroom outside his office wall, "getting them on the way down."

"It's the nature of the business, Ham," said Mitch, smiling lightly at Johnson's complaints. He knew that Johnson was well aware what the business was all about and just venting a gripe. Newspapermen were chronic complainers. It was part of their nature. "That's how I made my way," Mitch went on. "From a weekly to a daily, et cetera, et cetera. You did, too, if I recall correctly."

Johnson tossed his head and laughed, nearly losing his glasses in the process. "You sonofabitch," he said, catching the glasses before they fell to the floor. "Now you're going to tell me for the umpteenth time about how you took all the photos, too, and delivered the papers on top of that."

Mitch winced. "Have I told you about that more than once?"

"More than once? How often after once is more than once?"

Mitch was glad to see Johnson smiling. Ham kept himself remarkably controlled while working. But in the evenings, he collapsed. Mitch found himself trying to be a nursemaid, constantly badgering Ham to eat more, trying to keep his mind on newspaper business and his spirits on the fighting edge. Kate, Ham's wife, had been dead less than two years and it was too easy for Ham to speak nostalgically of joining her. It frightened Mitch and he did what he could to discourage Ham from giving in to his disease. The evenings he spent nursing Ham exhausted Mitch and his days at the paper were a relief in spite of the constant pressure of deadlines.

A young, eager face appeared in the doorway. "Ernie would like to get a start on the copy for tomorrow if it's okay with you."

"No, it's not okay, Roger. I want a rewrite." Johnson picked up the papers he and Mitch had just read and handed them to the reporter. "I told you, the selectmen announced last fall that they were going to repair that bridge. This is a follow-up. The lead is in the fact that they finally appropriated the funds last night, not that they're going to repair the bridge. And if you don't learn to spell Alphonse Lachite's name right, we're going to have a libel suit and I'll personally hang you by your privates from the school flagpole."

Roger Barrows blushed. He mumbled something and went off, dejected. Mitch looked over his glasses again at Johnson.

"What the hell are you looking at me like that for?" Johnson asked. "You would have said the same thing the same way."

"Yeah, I guess so," said Mitch. He'd been introduced to Barrows on the day of his arrival and was aware that the young man was awed by his newspaper credentials. A drubbing down in public was something every newspaper person had to get used to, but Mitch felt for Barrows. He looked so bewildered and vulnerable. He would have to learn to toughen up, to take criticism in public, learn from it and sluff it off. So many bright young people led charmed academic lives, rarely hearing a word of criticism from professors who give out grades as if they were candy and are frankly afraid of being criticized by their students. And then these young people venture out into the big bad world and wilt at the first word of criticism. In this business, Mitch thought, deadlines and tradition didn't make for niceties and tact. He imagined an editor calling a reporter into his office and, with the door closed, suggesting that his story did not, unfortunately, quite live up to expectations. "It sucks," shouted across a crowded newsroom, was a more typical scenario. How many times had Mitch heard that about one of his stories when he was a cub reporter in New Jersey? And how many times had he said that to a reporter, even a prize-winning one, when he was the editor of the *Trib* in New York? In class he was never brutal, he hoped, but he knew that his students described him as "damn tough."

"What about lunch?" Johnson intruded on Mitch's thoughts. "We can go over to the Seedling. The food's decent. I'd like to go over some more things with you." Johnson, Mitch realized, was getting overly anxious about leaving the newspaper in his hands. "That is," Johnson was saying, "unless you're planning on going house hunting again today."

"Land hunting, not house hunting," Mitch said, getting to his feet and rolling down his sleeves. "Val doesn't want someone else's house. She wants to design her own. Anyway," he continued as he buttoned his cuffs and reached for his jacket, "I've stopped looking since I saw that property Sunday. I put a bid on it."

"The land where the Tolvey woman was found?" Following Mitch's lead, Johnson put on his coat. "Didn't that bother Val at all? I mean, women can get funny about things like that."

"What a chauvinist thing to say, Ham. Just because your wife was superstitious doesn't mean every woman gets rattled. Though I gotta admit that if Val had seen the body she might have been turned off, too. But she didn't, thank goodness"—the image of the decayed corpse flashed through Mitch's mind—"and she's planning to come up this weekend to look at the land. Incidentally, if you're free Sunday, we'd like to take you out for a celebratory dinner. After all, we'll soon be your neighbors. It'll be an early meal. We'll have plenty of time to get here to work on the Monday paper."

"I was planning on attending the afternoon concert at Mont Vert—but, hey, why don't you folks come along? I'm sure I can get a couple of comp tickets. We give them lots of publicity. But can we do brunch beforehand rather than dinner afterwards? *I* get too tired."

Nat & Yanna Brandt

They were on the sidewalk outside the *Courier*'s offices now, walking up Hill Street by the crowded municipal parking lot, where cars, many of them with out-of-state license plates, slowly circled the aisles, waiting for a space to be vacated. A cement mixer, its huge vat rotating, was trying to turn onto Southborough's main street, which was much too narrow to handle the midday traffic congestion, and had gotten snagged in a gridlock.

Hill Street was an amalgam of architectural styles. The town had been founded in the years before the American Revolution, but not one structure in its heart dated from that period. The earliest ones were late nineteenth century, with ornamental cornices and often the date and the name of the proprietor or company carved onto a lintel: Hamilton Pipe Organ, 1879; Worth Building, 1891; De Moulin & Co., 1893. Other buildings, especially those with dress and shoe stores, had been modernized with sheets of glossy aluminum and bright signs. The town was like a dozen other communities Mitch had passed through on the bus trip through New England, except, he noticed with pleasure, it boasted three bookstores. Most towns of similar size that Mitch was familiar with had more bars than bookstores. He guessed the number of bookstores could be attributed to the presence of Southborough College as well as the cosmopolitan "flatlanders" who, attracted by the Mont Vert Music Festival in the summer, had stayed on and purchased homes in the area. Almost half the residents of Vermont, he had heard, were now from out-of-state.

The only jarring note was a decrepit two-story brick building with a tower that housed a clock without hands. "What's with that place?" Mitch asked.

Johnson looked up at the building and snickered. "The old Buller Tower? There's a big to-do over whether to restore it or tear it down."

"It looks like it was a beauty, once," Mitch said. "What's our position on it?"

"The newspaper's? Our publisher sees it as an eyesore and a deterrent to further municipal progress."

"And you?"

Johnson shrugged off the question. "It isn't worth making a big deal over."

"Pity," said Mitch. He craned his neck to look up at the clock face as they walked by. "It has character."

Mitch could understand why well-off doctors, lawyers and other professionals from Boston, New York and New Haven were taken with the area. The Green Mountains offered literally hundreds of secluded little valleys and hillsides, many with spectacular views. Like the plot he wanted to buy—except that now every time he visualized that magnificent piece of land, he also remembered the moment his hands had sunk into the moist leaves and touched something icy. Would he be able to put aside that dark hollow image of a dead woman he'd never known? Mitch knew himself well enough to know that the image was lingering because he wanted it to.

Mitch took in the profusion of what looked like new specialty shops featuring everything from freshly-made pasta to hand-screened T-shirts. He had the distinct impression that the Southborough merchants, the old-timers, had reluctantly accepted the new times. They responded to the influx of outsiders with some trendy packaging but they also clung tenaciously to the New England style, a style built on thrift and understated good taste. As a result, it was common on Main Street to see two stores side by side, sometimes owned by the same merchant, one featuring the latest in funky miniskirts, the other antique quilts and rocking chairs. And set right in the middle of a group of food boutiques displaying every kind of high-priced gourmet treat imaginable, there was that New England standard, the general store, where you could buy anything from bolts of cloth to nails and where no attempt was made to accommodate the modern age.

There was one other ingredient in the Southborough mix that Mitch observed, the 'sixties hippy. His generation. Yet, Mitch didn't really identify with them. They had come in droves twenty years ago, settled on communes, insisted on growing their own organic vegetables and wearing clothes they made themselves. At first they were the outsiders, looked at with mistrust and even fear, for some at least were drug users. But eventually they assimilated. They were now affluent restaurant owners and shopkeepers selling pottery, leather goods, woven wares and other crafts. Several had banded together to open a summer playhouse in a renovated factory back of the railroad tracks, virtually unused except for an occasional freight train or the sleeper that passed through en route to or from Canada. "Art" films were shown there during the rest of the year. They were not all that different from some of Mitch's anti-war protest buddies in New York, many of whom now had short hair and Wall Street jobs.

But whether an old-time resident or latter-day hippie, they shared at least one common sentiment—an underlying animosity toward outsiders, a resentment toward their aggressive impatience, their free way with a dollar and their occasional lack of respect for the way Vermonters do business. Mitch remembered only too well when earlier in the week he had raced out of the office to grab a take-out sandwich. He'd stood in line, impatiently watching the cook making three grilled cheeses in a row, one at a time, and in exasperation shouted out his order. He had been put neatly in his place and told to wait his turn. And, as if to prove a point, the cook had then gotten into a long, friendly conversation with the man ahead of him, who was clearly a regular customer. When he finally got his grilled cheese, he vowed to slow down and to try to adopt a leisurely pace. But he was finding it difficult. His goal, which he realized was important if he was to be useful to the paper in his short time here, was not to be perceived as a "flatlander," the derogatory term coined by the residents for the "summer people." Mitch prided himself on his ability to blend in with the rhythms of a community, rather than stand out. It had taken him less than a month on his first job as a cub reporter on a Connecticut weekly to be acccepted, and to be confided in, by the local townspeople. But that required a skill and a patience Mitch hadn't used in years.

Actually, as Ham Johnson had pointed out, Southborough represented four distinct—and not always harmonious—communities: the townsfolk, whose livelihood was dependent on the downtown area's success; the farmers, distinct in their visored hats and plaid shirts, who came into town only on Saturdays to shop, while their children attended a matinee at the seedy, rundown old Paramount movie house; the 'sixties wave of immigrants to the area who came as outsiders and still maintained a separate lifestyle in spite of their commercial success; and finally, the flatlanders, who had come in growing numbers to spend weekends, build vacation homes and often retire here.

Mitch and Ham headed to the restaurant that catered

mostly to the vegetarian, natural-food crowd. It was across from Town Hall, which was housed in a gingerbread Victorian monstrosity, and down the street from where construction was going on for a contemporary shopping mall, the downtown equivalent of the malls that Mitch saw gracing the highway leading into the community.

"If you're planning on building, you better get yourself a contractor quick-like," said Johnson as the two men stepped off the pavement to get around a ditch by the construction site. "Every and anyone who can swing a hammer is tied up with the ski resort or working on expanding buildings. The developers had to bring in extra gear and laborers from New Hampshire to meet their schedules."

"We hadn't gone that far in our thinking," Mitch said. "Maybe you can recommend one. Do you know of anyone reliable?"

"Well," said Johnson, "there's Clem Vogel. He's highly regarded around here, but he only does one house at a time, so he's hard to pin down if you're going to be in a rush. I'll get you his number when we get back to the office."

"That'll be fine," said Mitch. "Val doesn't want to use an architect, so I hope this Vogel guy is someone you can work with."

"He likes women, so Val won't have any trouble with him. He's got quite a reputation that way. Nothing to worry about, mind you." Johnson looked at Mitch. "Well, maybe in Val's case, you do."

The Seedling was on the second floor of a red-brick building that housed a hardware store below. The menu was predictable—a serve-yourself fresh vegetable soup was always available—as well as omelets, salads and sandwiches. A glass case with shelves of dessert offerings, mostly homemade pies and cakes, faced Ham and Mitch as they entered.

"Hi, Ham." A waitress, her arms hugging several reed baskets full of bread, swept by them. "Take any table you find free," she called back to them. "I'll be right with you."

"Hi, Betty," Johnson said when the waitress returned. "That tofu salad special today," he nodded to a blackboard mounted on an easel by the dessert case. "You recommend it?"

"It's good, but—" she looked around to see if the owner was nearby—"personally I'd stick with the soybean burger."

"Okay by me," Johnson said. "Mitch?" Mitch nodded agreement. "Make it two, Betty.

"Look at that big bugger," said Johnson, turning to the window. A long flatbed truck was rumbling by, braying its horn at a slow driver in a sedan. Steel girders stretched its length and beyond. A red flag waved from the end of one. "We're getting so many construction vehicles that they're breaking up the streets. Well, I guess that's the price of progress and prosperity."

Johnson leaned back in his chair and grimaced. "Time to take a pill, I guess. I hate getting so dependent on pain killers."

"Can I get anything for you?" offered Mitch.

"Naw, it'll go away." He straightened up. "The medication wears off, but I better not take another pill until I get something in my stomach." He picked up a spoon and began turning it over in his hand. "Mitch, ordinarily in the summer, things die down so much that we get hard pressed just to fill up the front page. I mean the concerts at Mont Vert are hardly earthshaking. There's nothing happening with the board of selectmen, court is in recess, no school board news, nothing much. You find yourself relying on the police and volunteer fire department for the excitement, so accidents and fires get played way out of proportion to what they're worth."

"And you blow up photos to twice the size just to fill space."

"How'd you know?" Johnson asked, smiling.

"Figured that's why you took a wire service."

"Yeah. We get UPI B wire for state news, the A for national and foreign. With the advertising hole increasing so much, we need to have copy to fill up the paper."

"Let me guess," said Mitch. "You work features to death."

"Our low point, just before you came, was a front-page one on the municipal garbage hauler," Johnson acknowledged.

"And," Mitch continued, "you cover—in detail—every softball game in the local league."

"Men and women's. You've been reading our files."

"And—" Mitch began.

"Hold it, fella. What do you suggest instead?"

Mitch let the waitress serve their lunches before he answered. "I know what I'd like to do."

"Go ahead."

"That realtor's death—Vera Tolvey. You've got yourself more than a one-day shot at that story."

"How do you figure that, Mitch?" Johnson paused, his fork in midair. "It was routine. Great for page one this morning, but she wasn't the first person killed in a hunting accident here. It was a tragedy, but *c'est la vie*."

"You can keep a story like that going," Mitch insisted. He bit into the soybean burger. It tasted grainy, though not inedible. "You remember that Long Island Railroad death we handled on the *Trib* back when you were on the metro desk? The kid who drove across the track when the gate wasn't working and got slammed into by an express? As I recall, you kept that one alive for a week. You had stories about the kid, ones about how frequently those accidents occur, what the railroad was doing about the situation, descriptions of the different grade crossings. I don't even remember everything you did, but you milked it dry."

"We got a Silurian award for that one," Johnson reminded him.

"Aha, you do remember. Sure, you got the railroad to overhaul its gate system. In fact, I don't know if you've heard about it, but the line is putting most of its tracks off the ground, elevating them, to eliminate the problem in the first place. God knows they wouldn't have done it if it hadn't been for that series."

Johnson was pleased that Mitch had remembered the series as being his idea. "How about a ginger beer?" he offered.

"No, thanks," said Mitch, wiping his lips with a napkin. "Look, Ham, I think we can do the same with this. It lends itself to all sorts of stories—how often the accidents occur, how to prevent them, should hunting be allowed at all. I know, I know—" he waved Johnson's incipient protest away—"it's a touchy subject around here. More's the reason for doing it. You've got yourself a hot little issue here, Ham. Let's go with it."

"Whoa," said Johnson. "You big city types get carried away so easily. We don't have the manpower for that kind of thing. Most of those bylines you see are correspondents out in the boondocks who send in a couple of graphs just to see their own names in print like they were honest-to-goodness stringers. Forget about how good—or bad—our people are, we've got only three real reporters, and they should be taking some vacation time while you're on board."

"I'd like to tackle it myself," said Mitch. He pushed his plate away and waited for Johnson's response.

"Hold it." Johnson put the last of a buttered piece of whole-wheat bread in his mouth. He ate with relish, the pains he had felt seeming to subside as the food settled in his stomach. "I thought I was getting an editor, not a reporter. You're going to have a mess of responsibilities. You'll be on call to the publisher. You have to be around to guide the reporters and the deskmen. You've got to decide the lead story every day and what else goes on page one. You're supposed to write an editorial every day, too—that's something I wanted to talk over with you. And you'll have to take on some social duties, like attending the Kiwanis meetings, and other local functions. You and the publisher are the *Courier*'s representatives."

"You're lecturing me, Hamilton. I know all that." Mitch took the paper napkin from his lap and began to fold it neatly. "I figured I could start now, while you're around. And don't forget, I'm getting an intern in a week. Someone to do my legwork."

Johnson thought for a moment about the idea while Mitch unfolded and refolded his napkin. "Shoot, it is going to be your paper for a while, I guess."

"I didn't want to start something behind your back," said Mitch.

"But you would have, wouldn't you?"

"It's good story, Ham. Can't you smell it? I can see running a box on what the National Rifle Association position is and, abutting it, a box on the position of the local Humane Society or a school parents' association. You can even—"

"Just an hour or two a day, Mitch, okay? I don't want the publisher to think you're not going to sit on his paper and guard it."

"No problem. I can manage the time. Hell, except for the time when Val visits, I'll be able to put in fourteen- or sixteen-hour days. What else have I got to do?"

Johnson stood up. "The best way to get the check here," he explained, "is to make like you're going to leave without paying."

Mitch got up, also. Their waitress, who had been talking to another waitress, came scuttling across the room.

"You aren't keeping something from me that I ought to know?" asked Johnson, waving off Mitch's outstretched hand and taking the check.

"Like what?"

"I don't know. Do you suspect it was something other than an accident?"

"No. It's just that I can't get over the fact that a hunter would shoot someone, and not know it, or know it and not report it."

Ham turned and looked at him. "You told me yourself, the woods were so thick, you could hardly see ahead of you. The hunter could easily have overlooked the body. It's happened before and it'll happen again."

They were walking to the door, Johnson tipping his finger to his forehead to a man sitting alone at a small corner table who had looked up from a copy of *Forbes* magazine and seen them. "Bert Lester," he explained. "The First State Bank. He's the president. Wait a minute. I ought to introduce you to him."

Ham turned and made his way to the corner, Mitch behind him. The man at the table followed them with his eyes. "Bert," Ham said, "I'd like you to meet Mitch

43

Stevens. Mitch, this is Bert Lester."

Mitch and Lester shook hands as Ham explained, "Mitch is going to cover for me for a while. He'll be running the paper."

"Oh, really?" said Lester, suddenly interested. "Glad to meetcha. You from these parts?"

"No, New York," Mitch answered. "This is my first time in Southborough."

"Well, I hope you like our little town. You city fellas sometimes get a bit itchy here."

Mitch laughed politely. Ham tipped his finger to his forehead again. "We best be going, Mitch. See you, Bert."

"A good advertiser, I take it," said Mitch, blinking, as they walked out the building into the bright afternoon sun.

"He's the financier behind all this development," said Johnson. "His bank is."

"So what are you worried about, Ham? You keep asking me about the story as though you couldn't see it for what it is yourself."

"I'm just nervous, Mitch. About everything."

They were standing on the corner, letting the sun warm them. Mitch put his arm on Johnson's shoulder. "I'm not going to wreck your paper, Ham, or your community. Don't worry. My God, you'd think I was about to expose some serial murderer who turns out to be the governor in disguise."

THREE

Ham Johnson grimaced in pain.

"Did you take your pill yet?" Mitch asked.

"Yeah, when we got back from lunch." He rubbed his stomach. "I think I'm going into the hospital in the nick of time."

"Look, why don't you go home?" Mitch said. "I'll stick with the paper and lock it up." Johnson hesitated. "It'll be good practice for me. Come on. It's silly, your hanging around. You get comfortable and I'll catch up with you later this evening when I'm through."

"You're right, Mitch. Okay. I'll pick up some groceries for us on the way home." He reached for his coat. "Rog's story on the selectmen vote should be the lead."

"Two-column head enough?" asked Mitch.

Johnson paused in the midst of putting on his jacket. "Well, I'd go to three if nothing else comes along off the wires. I'd like to get Robin's story on the court battle over the disco above the fold if you can manage it."

"No problem. It's shaping up as a slow day." Johnson

hesitated. "Go home, Ham," Mitch insisted. "Nothing's going to happen."

"You'll call if you need help?"

"Yes, of course I will. Now go, for Chrissake, before I have you arrested for loitering."

"I'll be at the house in less than an hour," Johnson said as he left the office.

Mitch waited until he was out of sight, then sat in Johnson's chair and sorted through the papers that had been dropped on it while they were at lunch. The advance UPI menu of state stories the agency planned to file that afternoon was slim. The same was true for the rundown of national and foreign news items that would be coming in on the A wire. Unless something broke—an unexpected story out of Washington, or an air or train disaster—it was going to be tough to fill up the paper.

Mitch picked up a slip of paper left by the advertising department detailing ad-space requirements for next morning's edition. Just under eighty-two columns' worth, display and classified. Not overwhelming. Later on, someone in the ad department would drop off dummies of the inside pages showing where the major display advertisements would fall. The *Courier* ran six columns to a page. That meant the ads would take up—Mitch jotted down the figure—roughly thirteen and two-third pages. Figure fourteen, Mitch thought, striking out the fraction. The paper operated on a ratio of sixty-five percent advertising to thirty-five percent editorial, or, simply put, one page of editorial matter for every two pages of advertisements. You can't have an odd number of pages, Mitch figured quickly, so that means the paper would have to run to twenty-two pages tomorrow—slightly less than fourteen pages of ads to slightly more than eight pages of editorial. A "news hole" of forty-eight-plus columns. That indeed could be rough on a slow day. It was always more difficult to find news to fill up a paper than to trim back what you had in hand. But a ratio of 63.66 to 34.34 wasn't terrible, considering.

Still, Mitch thought as he reached for another slip of paper, it would be stretching things to fill up those eight pages he was responsible for. Mitch wrote down the routine allotments. Sports would take up two. Then there was a page of comics, and, of course, the editorial page. That left four full pages—twenty-four columns—for local, state, national and foreign news. Much too much on a slow day. Mitch upped the sports section to three pages; it was usually easy to find action photographs to fill up the space. That's better, he thought, sitting back and surveying his scrawls. Three pages left for the rest of the news, text and pictorial. Wait, even less. He had forgotten the daily television and radio listings. They ate up about half a page. Even better, he said to himself.

Mitch checked his watch: 2:30. Ernie Holliday, the early man on the copy desk, would already be busy with the listings, stories the wire service had already filed and fillers, which would be used to plug up any empty spaces. The late man, Abe Keller, wouldn't show up until five, when things really began humming. Mitch could hear the clack of a typewriter in the corner outside his office where the reporters had desks. Roger Barrows had already reworked his story—the revise was in a basket on Mitch's right—and was out checking the police blotter. So whoever was pecking away was either Robin Summer or Lyle Timski. Robin, a slightly frazzled young woman in her mid-twenties, was supposed to be at the courthouse in Newfair, unless she had gotten back early, which wasn't likely. So that meant it was probably Timski. Mitch checked an assignment list that Johnson had made out that morning. Lyle was down for two stories—an interview with the new chef at the Sugar House Inn, and a wee-hours-in-the-morning car accident on the Camp-bellville Road. "Vermonters are continually running into electric poles," Johnson had said when Mitch first saw the assignment sheet that morning. "They get to drinking and then they drive right into a patch of fog without a care in the world. You wouldn't believe the number of power outages we have."

The newsroom occupied all of the second floor of the old wooden building except for a closed-off area that was the publisher's office. His secretary, Jessie Cummings, sat typing at a desk outside it, surrounded by plants. Prominently displayed on the wall behind her was the *Courier*'s logo. Maxine Longe, Johnson's secretary, office manager and general factotum, was at a smaller desk outside Ham's office. The newsroom beyond had no frills whatsoever. Its walls were a dull beige, its ceiling embossed tin, and fluorescent lights hung down from thin metal rods. The only grace note was the clock, an antique Seth Thomas in working order.

Walking through the newsroom, hearing the creak of the wooden floor, stopping briefly to read a notice or cartoon tacked to a wall, Mitch felt elated. The smell of the place—the lingering odor of newspaper ink that rose from the press on the floor below—brought back a rush of memories of other newsrooms. After six years of teaching, of being on the outside, away from the action, Mitch felt a renewed sense of energy and purpose.

Sure enough, it was Timski on the typewriter. Lyle was a fair-haired man pushing thirty—kind of old, Mitch knew, for a reporter on the *Courier*. He was not exactly effete, but there was an air of sensitivity about him that one didn't ordinarily find in journalists. "He'll cover the concerts for you without putting in for comp time," Johnson had said. "He loves to write about them—any plays our local thespians perform, too. And he knows what he's talking about." Mitch wondered what kept Timski in a town like Southborough. As though the man had read his thoughts, Timski looked up from his typewriter and smiled at Mitch, then bent his head and resumed pounding the keys.

The typewriters the reporters worked on were all old Royal manuals, the DC-3s of the newspaper business. Sturdy, reliable, they took a lot of punishment. "We can't afford word processors yet," Johnson had explained. "They go for several thousand each. It just doesn't make sense for us, not yet anyhow. But John—our publisher, John Haye—goes to every demonstration he's invited to and swears he'll get us some when the price goes down."

Mitch crossed over to the small copy desk. There was enough room for six men to sit around it, but it was rarely occupied by more than three—Ernie, Abe Keller and, tonight, when they would be on deadline, Mitch. Ernie did indeed wear a green eyeshade, and stuck smack in the middle of his mouth was stuck a dark, wet, smelly cigar. At his elbow was a jar of honey and a spoon. Mitch had yet to see Ernie eat anything else.

Mitch dropped his breakdown of editorial pages in front of Ernie, who acknowledged his presence by wagging his pencil at him before going back to working on a piece of copy. Mitch looked over his shoulder. It was an agency story out of Washington, embargoed for release at six that night: the FCC had decided to drop its restriction on the ownership of certain cable stations. Mitch wondered if the average reader in Southborough and environs cared a hoot about the FCC, but you had to

49

fill the paper with something. "There are three kinds of stories you can always run in a paper on a slow day," he remembered a near-to-retirement editor once telling him. "You can write about the weather, a child, or a dog. You'll never miss. Everybody will read it. Keep that in mind, son, if you ever get stuck for space." Mitch almost asked Ernie whether they had run a weather story recently, but restrained himself. "Slow day," he said instead.

"Hmmm," responded Ernie from behind his cigar.

"I've got the lead in my box. I'll pass it through in a little while."

"That the one slugged 'Bridge'?"

"Yes, Roger's story. You can think about a two-column head, but don't bother working on it until I firm up the front page."

"Hmmm."

Not unfriendly, really, Mitch realized. Veteran copy editors such as Ernie were literally a dying breed. They refused to learn the mechanics of editing on word processors, which every major newspaper in the country now used. The savings, going from hot type to cold, were enormous. No more Linotype machines, no more typesetters to operate them, no more composing room. No more smell of printer's ink, or atmosphere either. Instead, a spotless room where cotton-gloved makeup men pasted glossy galleys down on cardboard to be photographed. It was too sterile as far as Mitch was concerned, even more so for the likes of an Ernie, who distrusted the new setup. Which is why he—and other dinosaurs like him—ended up on weeklies or small dailies that were still "handmade."

And like those other dinosaurs, Ernie—Mitch well understood—had been around a long time, had met hundreds of reporters and other editors, and had seen them all go their own ways. One more body didn't faze them much. As long as the boss knew what he was doing. Ernie liked routine and, whether war, famine, economic depression or a space shot, he never seemed to ingest the news that was happening. He just pushed his No. 2 pencil along, marked the paragraphs, corrected the grammar and spelling, slapped a head onto a story, and, without missing a beat, tossed the edited copy into an open tray with his left hand and vigorously slapped the excess copy onto a stilleto-sharp spike with his right.

Although Ernie hadn't asked, Mitch felt obliged to inform him that he, Mitch, would be in charge that evening: Johnson had gone home. All that drew was another "Hmmm." Mitch told Ernie to keep an eye out for sports pictures coming over the telefax wire. They were going to need all the ones they could use. "Hmmm," acknowledged Ernie, a shower of ash falling on his vest. He didn't bother to brush it away.

Maxine walked into the newsroom from the staircase to the pressroom on the ground floor. Mitch thought he knew why Johnson had not mentioned her in his letter. In his attempt to woo Mitch to come to his rescue, he had written colorful descriptions of every member of his staff—except Maxine. She was a widow, a self-assured, striking woman who had obviously aroused a few lustful feelings in Ham. She pretended nothing but casual interest—it was always "Mr. Johnson"—but Mitch saw in her eyes a deep concern for Ham's health.

"I hear he's gone home," she said.

"Why don't you phone him in an hour or so and make sure he's comfortable," Mitch suggested.

"Good idea. Are you putting the paper to bed today?"

Mitch confirmed that he was. "Ham had an editorial

in the bank, but just in case he doesn't make it back tomorrow, I'm going to sit down now and try to knock one out. Any suggestions?" he asked, including Ernie in his question.

"Yup," said Ernie in what Mitch realized was for him a veritable oration. "How about saying something about all that God-dangled noise those big rigs make coming through town at night?" Ernie lived in a small, two-room apartment in the old Ethan Allen Hotel on Hill Street, which the trucks had to pass to get to the downtown mall construction site. "I haven't slept in three weeks."

"That's kind of difficult to complain about, Ernie. You don't go to sleep till five in the morning. I don't think we can knock the truckers for making noise after nine."

"Hmmm."

"Well, what strikes you about the town, Mr. Stevens?"

"Please, Maxine, it's Mitch. I don't answer to mister." He sighed and pushed his glasses up on his nose. "Well, I know Ham's been doing the farm assistance program to death—what it means for Southborough and such. I think I'd like to take a crack at the hunting regulations."

"It's not in season," Maxine offered.

"I'm going to peg it on finding Vera Tolvey's body," Mitch said. "And that reminds me, I'll probably be late tomorrow. I'm going to do some sniffing around."

Maxine's eyebrows rose. "About the Tolvey story?"

Mitch detected the doubt in her voice. "Yeah, about the Tolvey story," he said brusquely. "I'm sure you can hold the fort until lunchtime. I'll make an assignment sheet for the reporters before I go home tonight. If something comes up first thing tomorrow, I'll make sure Ernie has someone on hand to send out."

"Mr. Haye wanted to talk with Mr. Johnson first thing tomorrow. If he doesn't come in, you'll have to."

"Ask him if he'll see me now," said Mitch as he walked back to his desk. "I'll be in Ham's office."

Maxine came by a minute later. "Jessie says he'll see you now. I told her Mr. Johnson had gone home for the day."

"Okay, thanks." Mitch put on his jacket and straightened his tie in a small mirror that Johnson kept behind the door before walking over to the publisher's office. Jessie Cummings smiled politely as he approached. Haye's secretary, was, Mitch noticed, a more flamboyant dresser than he would have expected for the publisher of a newspaper, but he dismissed the observation without another thought as he entered the office. It was a large room. Its windows overlooked the railroad tracks and the Connecticut River that they paralleled. Directly across the river was New Hampshire. The office was filled with photographs and citations. The desk, which had been used by the *Courier*'s founder, John Haye's grandfather, was a mammoth oak unit with a tambour front and numerous pigeonholes. Anyone sitting behind it—and different members of the staff had tried it when Haye was away on vacation—was always dwarfed by it. Not so John Haye. He was a big, robust, barrel-chested man. He laughed easily, but his eyes didn't: they were sharp and hard.

"You got everything under control?" the publisher asked as Mitch knocked lightly on the open door and walked in.

"No problem. Ham left everything in good shape. It's a slow day."

"Sit down, Mitch. I want to touch base with you before I head up to Montpelier."

Mitch sat in one of the soft leather chairs positioned along one side of the immense desk. A leather couch was on the other. Above it was a portrait of Haye's grandfather, a grim-looking, moustached man with a paunch. He was posed in front of a furled state flag, and a gold pennant bearing in green the Vermont motto, "Freedom and Unity," was carved in the top of the frame. It was clear to Mitch that Grandfather Haye had been a governor.

"We're expecting the paper to go beyond thirty-two pages once the mall is finished," said Haye. "You know the one I mean?" Mitch nodded. "There'll be a dozen or more new stores opening in it, maybe a Britfair Enterprises farther out, too, if Bert—Bert Lester—"

"I know who he is," Mitch said.

"If Bert has his way, and he's got the Chamber of Commerce backing him, there'll be a Britfair in Southborough that'll draw people from as far away as Wilmington and Saxton's River. I think he's on the mark. We're one of the fastest growing parts of this state . . ."

"You can certainly see that," said Mitch. He was wondering why Haye wanted to see him. The conversation so far had been mundane.

"I'd like to see the paper do its bit," the publisher said, reaching for a brochure in his OUT basket and tossing it toward Mitch.

Uh-oh, thought Mitch. Here it comes.

"That's the people who are developing the mall. They're also in the ski resort that's being built out toward the college. They've got a lot of good ideas, and it all spells prosperity for Southborough."

You can argue that, Mitch said to himself. There are limits to what a town can cope with, as many communities in New York's suburbs had discovered. Could the roads handle more traffic, was the police force big enough, were there enough schools to handle the increase in population, and what did you do about the garbage?

"There's a big to-do tomorrow night at the Pilgrim's Pantry—out on the Bennington Road. You've probably passed it. The Chamber's throwing it. I was going to go with Ham," the publisher continued, "but I think you ought to go since he's under the weather so frequently nowadays. The developer will be there, and so will a vice president from the Britfair marketing division. We want to make a big impression on him, show him we're ready to support Britfair to the hilt."

Mitch fidgeted. This was the side of newspapering he disliked. True, a newspaper was a business. It was the ads that paid the salaries. But Mitch hated any pressure about how he did his job and he sensed that Haye would expect the *Courier* to run some favorable stories about the developer and the Britfair chain, as well. Nothing wrong with that, on the surface, unless it meant ignoring the other side of the story—the less desirable effects on the town. It was the kind of situation that Mitch was all too familiar with in New York. Anybody there who ever had to buy or sell a co-op apartment or condominium had at least one dreadful tale of woe to tell about real-estate deals in Manhattan. But you rarely saw the stately *Times* ever look into that sleazy mess. Not when its pages were chockful of ads from those very same developers and realtors. I'm still too much of an idealist, Mitch realized; you'd have thought I'd have learned by now what the business is all about.

"I'll have to be around to lock up the paper," he said.

Haye pondered Mitch's answer. "You're going to be here just when things are heating up," he finally said. "It's critical you be there—vital for the *Courier*. I'm thinking of investing in a new press, one that can double our volume. In fact, it's more important for you to go than it is for Ham, considering what's going to be happening this summer while you're here." Haye leaned over and picked up a pen. "I'm going to phone him later and ask him to make an effort to get in tomorrow and handle the paper."

"He's really feeling poorly," Mitch ventured, trying to think of a way to stave off Haye's insisting Johnson work the next day. "He wouldn't be of much help if he's not all there."

"So you set it up for him and he'll just shepherd it along until Abe can take over." The publisher's voice was insistent, not quite hiding the anger that was building up. "I want you there, Mitch. The paper needs you there. Seven o'clock. Put it on your calendar."

Haye stood up. "I have to get going now," he said, sliding the desk cover down, and giving a decisive pull on his jacket.

Mitch rose and left, a sour taste in his mouth. Jessie Cummings smiled politely again as he passed her desk, but he failed to acknowledge her. He didn't like being ordered around. He went back to Johnson's office—*his* office now—closed the door behind himself so hard even Ernie looked up, and sat in front of the typewriter.

WHEN IS MORE TOO MUCH?

Edmund Burke, the 18th-century English statesman and philosopher, once pointed out that there is "a limit at which forbearance ceases to be a virtue." A limit, that is, to how much any person should condone. Or, put into the perspective of Southborough, how much a community should condone.

When does progress become a burden? When is enough enough?

Take what is happening to our community today...

Mitch thrust his chair back suddenly. He crossed his arms and sat staring at the editorial he had started, then tore the paper from the typewriter. *I shouldn't take out my resentment this way,* he said to himself. *It's just as bad as toadying up to those damn developers. And I'll only embarrass Ham. I'm a temp here. It's not my job to start a crusade.*

He crumbled the paper and threw it at the wastebasket in the corner.

THE PHONE ON the desk rang. Mitch reached for it. "*Courier*, Stevens."

"Mitch, it's me, Lyle. I'm up at the college. The weirdest thing just happened. One of the professors keeled over while giving a talk on the Mideast. His name is Eagleston. They tried everything to revive him, CPR, you name it. There was even a doctor in the audience so the guy really got fast attention, but nothing worked."

"Sounds like a simple heart attack, but it's certainly worth some space. I hate to sound ghoulish, but it beats another weather story."

"You know, he was a buddy of Ham's and barely forty-five years old. It's kind of scary that it can happen that suddenly. His daughter was there. She got absolutely hysterical, screaming that there was nothing wrong with her father's heart, that he just had a complete physical. They had to give her something to settle her down."

Nat & Yanna Brandt

"Listen, if I had a dollar for every time someone comes out of a doctor's office with a clean bill of health and then keels over, I'd be much richer. Lyle, It's 7:20 now. It'll take you too much time to get back and write the story, so get the details, call me back and I'll take what you have over the phone. But no later than eight, okay?"

"Gotcha."

Mitch looked at the the front-page dummy in front of him. He had just finished marking it up with the stories that would appear on page one, where they would go and what kind of headline each would take. Most newspapers had a shorthand nomenclature for the "heads"—an A head, for example, would be a three-line, single-column headline with an inverted pyramid bank of three lines, followed by a crossline and underneath that another three-line inverted pyramid. A half-A head would be what Mitch had just ordered, only he didn't trust that he had memorized all the *Courier* codes as yet, so he chose to be specific.

Mitch sat at the head of the copy desk, Ernie Holliday and Abe Keller on either side of him. Abe eschewed a green eyeshade, but a cigarette dangled from his mouth. Abe was a thin, balding man who, like Ernie, talked only when necessary. They were two peas in a pod, Mitch realized. Solid, dependable deskmen. They would make up for any mistakes he might make.

"We've got to remake the front page."

Abe didn't bat an eye. "The news summary," was all he said. Mitch had forgotten about it. He tried not to be annoyed at being reminded twice. He boxed out an area in the lower left-hand corner for it.

As Mitch reworked the front page, he allowed room for a two-column head for the professor's death. Was it overkill? Was a simple heart attack really worth that much coverage? Who was this man? How important was he to the community? Mitch hesitated. He wanted to call Ham and ask his advice—after all, he had barely scratched the surface of this town. But was it fair to trouble Ham with every little decision?

Without thinking it through, he reached for the phone. Before he could dial, the direct line from the composing room rang on the other phone. Mitch got up to answer it. "We got a problem here with page three, Mitch."

"I'll be up as soon as I make a quick call." He sat down and dialed Ham's number. There was no point in trying to wing it now. He'd have enough challenges once Ham was in the hospital and totally out of reach. The phone rang a long time before he heard Ham's voice at the other end. Oh God, Mitch thought, I've woken him up.

"Ham, I'm sorry to bother you, but Lyle told me you knew Professor Eagleston, that he was a buddy of yours."

"Mitch, what do you mean, knew?"

"There's no easy way to say this. He's dead. Keeled over at a lecture. Cause of death, probable heart attack." There was a long silence on the other end. "Ham, are you all right? Ham, talk to me. . . ."

"Mitch, I'm sorry, I'm in shock, I guess. The man was so young, Christ, he was five years younger than I am."

"Who was he, Ham? Important enough to warrant a two-column head on the front page on a slow news day?"

"He's big. . . . He was big in local politics. He's been around here since I don't know—before I came, that's for sure. He was also involved in getting the zoning variance for the ski resort through the Board of Selectmen. In a behind-the-scenes way. Politics Southborough-style."

"Is it as sleazy as it sounds?"

"Depends on what side of the fence you're sitting on.

If you're a local farmer, you want the status quo, you don't want change and you certainly don't want to see land gobbled up for ski resorts. But if you're a developer like Harvey Troupe or even an economist like Eagleston, you don't want the town to stand still and watch her neighbors grow and prosper. Money is power here, just like anywhere else and it's the real-estate developers who bring money and grab power. Eagleston knew that and he used it to his advantage."

"I thought Lyle said you were a friend of his. You don't sound like you liked him much."

"A friend, yes, an admirer, no. Friendly disagreement, you might say."

"Well, is he worth a two-column head, or isn't he?"

"Absolutely. He was a controversial local figure."

"And he died a mysterious death, maybe."

Ham sighed, "Mitch, I thought you said it was a heart attack. Is there something you haven't told me?"

"No, not really, but just as you were talking, it occurred to me that I've been here less than a week and two people are dead under rather unusual circumstances."

"Mitch, your imagination is running away with you. Vera Tolvey died months ago—you just happened to find her body now."

When Mitch didn't answer right away, Ham went on, "Oh, by the way, I got a call from Haye."

"I know," said Mitch, frowning. "He pissed me off, Ham. Really pissed me off."

"He's just protecting the paper," Johnson explained. "He's right about your going to that get-together tomorrow night."

"It's inconsiderate of him to ask you to run the ship."

"I'll be all right, Mitch. I feel worse sitting at home

than I would in the office. Bring home the proofs. I want to see what you're doing to my baby."

MICKEY PEABODY WAS hunched over a metal chase, one of eight that ran the length of a long table. He was locking it with a frame key as Mitch came up. "Over here," he said, gesturing with his head to a chase farther down the table. He pointed to a gap in the metal type, which read backwards and upside down. "It's too much space to lead out—it'd look like hell," Peabody said.

"Don't you have any fillers?"

"None this small."

Mitch went to the phone that linked the composing room to the newsroom. He picked it up and waited for Ernie or Abe to answer. "Hmmm?" It was Ernie.

"Ernie, we need a two-incher, with a one-line crossline. Mark it for page three so it doesn't go astray."

"Hmhmmm."

"Anything else?" Mitch asked, turning back to the compositor. He was wondering why Peabody had gotten him upstairs. The request for the filler could have been made over the phone.

Peabody wiped his ink-stained hands on his apron. There were smudges of ink on his forehead and on his arms up to the elbow. "I knew Vera Tolvey," he said.

"And?" Mitch coaxed.

"And she would have known better than to go into the woods like that."

"Do you know why she was there to begin with?" Mitch asked.

"Nope, I can't say I do," Peabody answered. "But you might ask Bert Lester or Harvey Troupe."

"Who's Troupe?"

"The guy who's doing all that building. Vera was getting all kinds of phone calls all night long from both of them."

"She tell you this?" Mitch asked.

"I heard her talking to them," Peabody admitted.

All hours of the night? Mitch had noticed that Peabody wore a wedding ring, so he realized that the compositor and the realtor must have had a clandestine affair going.

Peabody reached for a tray of type and began transferring it into an empty column beside an ad.

"Thanks," said Mitch, realizing he would be treading on sensitive ground if he asked for too many details. He looked up at the huge, round clock on the wall: 7:47. "Will we make it?"

"No problem." Peabody picked up some thin rules and began laying them along the sides of the metal type to delineate the column. "And sorry about getting you up here on a false pretense."

"No problem," said Mitch. "I'll see you in a little while when we lock up page one."

Mitch stopped on the landing heading back downstairs to the newsroom. That hunting accident, he thought. Peabody was obviously trying to hint at something. But what? Murder. If that's what he suspected, why not just say so, or wasn't that the New England way? Let people stumble around for a while on their own, for God's sake, don't point them in the right direction unless they ask directly. And what about Eagleston? Mitch had been half joking with Ham. He had absolutely no basis for suspicion, so why did he feel this prickly sensation on the back of his neck?

FOUR

Mitch leaned on the high counter. A cool breeze swept through the office from an open window. It brought with it the sound of traffic on Route 6. State trooper Jed Livsey was seated at a metal desk, sorting through a stack of reports.

"Here it is," said Livsey, a young, sturdy-looking man with a ready smile. "It was in this pile for filing."

"Can you read it off to me?" asked Mitch.

"You want all the details?"

"Every one," said Mitch, pen in hand and a reporter's notebook open on the counter.

"Vera was—Vera Tolvey," Livsey corrected himself, trying to sound official, "was thirty-six years old. Address: Granite Hill Road, East Southborough—that's out by Putney Road. She lived alone as far as we can tell. Her office—Mont Vert Realtors—gave us the name and address of an aunt in Rutland as next of kin. Mrs. Matilda Slocum, P.O. Box eight-two-nine–C, Patriots Avenue."

Mitch wrote quickly, using his own made-up shorthand to keep up with the trooper. "Got a phone number on her?" he asked.

"It's 524-6339. We phoned her right off. She came down from Rutland but I don't know if she's still in town."

"What was Vera Tolvey's phone number?"

Livsey ran his finger back up the report. "It's 527-6472. And the office," he said, anticipating Mitch's next question, "is 527-7777."

Mitch looked up, waiting for Livsey to go on.

"The medical examiner estimated she died sometime back in the middle of November, but that wouldn't be difficult to guess since it was a hunting accident and that's deer season.

"Let's see. He attributed the death to a bullet to the heart, but you know that had to be a guess, too. There wasn't anything much left of her to determine that, only the old bloodstain on her coat and some shattered ribs."

"So she was shot from the front?"

"Yup," Livsey agreed. "Jeez," he said, suddenly realizing what that meant. "She must have been facing the hunter straight on and didn't know it."

"And he must have been facing her straight on and didn't recognize that she wasn't an animal," said Mitch. "Is something like that really possible?"

"You ever been hunting?" Livsey asked. Mitch shook his head. "Sometimes in the woods—I mean deep forest—it's hard to see any great distance. Colors tend to blend into one another—grays and browns—dull colors. If you're using a bow and arrow you have to get up close to a deer, or wait for one to come to you. With rifles you work from far away, out of sight, sound and smell if you can. Some hunting rifles have a range of a mile. And after a while your eyes get tired of straining to make out a deer from all that background. You see something move and, whammo, you take a quick shot at it."

"I don't understand why Tolvey would go into the woods without wearing something bright," Mitch said.

"No sane person would," agreed Livsey. "You should see us when we have to. We got these blaze-orange vests for highway patrol at night. We put them on before we set off from a road in broad daylight during hunting season. But these things happen, you know."

"Anything else on that report?" Mitch asked.

Livsey turned the paper over. "Nope. That's it. There wasn't much else to say."

"I take it no bullet was found. Anything that might indicate the caliber or type of weapon that was used."

"Nope, and no way to trace its path. There was hardly enough left of her to bury."

"Don't hunters have to be licensed?" Mitch asked. "I mean, you would have a record of who's got a permit and maybe could trace who was in the area that day."

Livsey laughed lightly. "You got to be kidding. You can get a license most anywhere in the state—general stores, gun shops, by mail—you name it. And you can travel a hundred miles from where you got it to do your hunting. Do you know how many people in this state hunt, or come to Vermont to hunt?"

"It wouldn't be impossible, though, would it?"

"Prit near."

"I wonder," said Mitch, "what the hunter thought when he saw what he had shot."

"I know if it was me," Livsey said, "I think it would haunt me all my life."

* * *

Nat & Yanna Brandt

MONT VERT REALTORS was located around the corner from the *Courier*'s office. Mitch decided to drop by it on his way into work. The agency sign—in the shape of a mountain peak—hung above its door. Inside was a row of six desks, one behind the other, and all littered with papers. Only one desk was occupied; it sat against the rear wall, beside the copy machine. On the wall was an immense map of Galelin County. Blue lines on it indicated brooks, streams and the Connecticut River. Pale brown lines represented the contours of the land, hills and mountains. Black lines defined the town boundaries, and red the main highway and major side roads. On another wall were blown-up color photographs of homes and farms for which Mont Vert Realtors had acted as agent. Across the top of the third wall was a sign, in contemporary lettering: MONT VERT SKILAND, and underneath it were pastel architectural drawings of the resort and the different types of condominiums being offered.

"Can I help you?" a large, broad-chested man at the far desk called out gruffly.

Mitch walked to the back. A placard on the desk gave his name as William McC. Handler. Mitch introduced himself as being with the *Courier* and explained that he was doing a feature story on Vera Tolvey's career.

"Here, sit down," Handler offered in an accent that surprised Mitch: It was very New York. The realtor swept some papers to the side of his desk with a huge, hairy hand. "Call me Bill." He offered a cigarette to Mitch, who turned it down with a wave of his hand. Handler put it to his own lips and lit it with an old Army lighter.

"She'd been with us for nearly ten years," Handler said. He inhaled deeply and blew a cloud of smoke toward the ceiling. "Came from Rutland, where she'd worked for an agency. She was a fucking good realtor, could really bring both sides together to make a deal." Handler reeled off the names of the buyers of homes Vera Tolvey had sold, but none were familiar to Mitch. As he talked, he flicked the ashes from his cigarette toward the floor and, getting out of his chair, came around the desk and hoisted himself onto its edge right in front of Mitch. "And the Wynman farm, too," Handler was saying, as Mitch, uncomfortable because the realtor's legs were so close to his, tried to push his chair back, but bumped against the desk behind him. "Now that was one big motherfucker of a sale. That's where the ski resort is going. Must be three hundred goddamn acres. Got a pond, view of Mayors Peak, steep enough for some good runs. We've sold larger units, but the price on this one set a record for us. We took a damn cut in our percentage, too, and still did well."

Mitch wondered whether Handler was as foulmouthed with clients as he was being with him. He couldn't believe anyone would respond favorably to such cursing. Maybe he's putting on an act for my benefit, Mitch thought.

"Do you have any idea why she was up on that property where she was found?" Mitch had decided beforehand not to mention that he had made a bid for the property through another agency.

"It's up for sale."

"But I understood it wasn't then," said Mitch.

"You know that it abuts the back of the Wynman land?"

Mitch's eyebrows raised. "No, I didn't know about it abutting the land. I just thought it was nearby." The pony cart trail where the two meadows connected in the northeast corner, Mitch thought to himself. It must lead to the Wynman land.

"That property would almost be as valuable as the Wynman place itself—sort of guilt by association, you might say," Handler said, chuckling at his pun. He took another drag on his cigarette, then leaned around and stubbed it out in an already overflowing ashtray.

Holy God, Mitch thought to himself, I'm about to purchase it. Do I really want to be right next door to a ski resort? "But what was she doing there then?"

"Well," Handler said, "she could have heard it was coming on the market. Or even took the fucking bull by the horns and decided to broach the idea of selling to the owner on her own. Nothing unusual at all about that."

"Just out of curiosity, Bill—you're not a Vermonter, are you? You're from New York."

The big man's eyes narrowed momentarily, then a huge grin spread across his face, revealing several missing teeth on both sides of his lower jaw. "I'm a damn flatlander, all right. I was a cop down in the Big Apple. I retired after getting shot up in a goddamn supermarket shootout. How'd you . . . ?"

The phone rang. Handler reached around for it. "Hold on," he said to Mitch. "Mont Vert Realtors," he said into the mouthpiece. "How can I help you?"

Mitch got up and waved a hand at Handler. "Thanks for your help," he half-whispered to the realtor, who was nodding his head that he had heard and waved in return.

The map of Galelin County caught his eye. As Handler talked on the phone, Mitch searched for the area where the Wynman farm and the land he had bid on were located. There, he said to himself, in a direct line west of Mayors Peak. He bent closer, trying to make out the squiggle of lines. The hill at the bottom of the meadow was too insignificant to make the map, but the Wynman pond was there. I ought to call Bob Grant and check on how soon he thinks I have to turn in a sealed bid, Mitch said to himself. I hope it can wait until Val sees the land.

Mitch turned to wave good-bye to Handler. He was disconcerted to find that, though still talking on the phone, the realtor was following him with his eyes, as though he had never let him out of sight. But this time Handler did not return the wave.

"Bob, Mitch Stevens here. Listen, do we still have time to wait until my wife sees that land before I turn in a bid?"

"I was just about to phone you, Mitch. It's already too late. You can't get the land. The guy took an offer already. I heard it was even higher than he was asking—which is kinda amazing, but then funny things seem to be happening to the market lately."

"You're kidding—too late? Christ, that went fast." Mitch started to get annoyed. "Why the devil didn't you tell me, Bob? I could've tried to move sooner."

"I'm sorry, Mitch, I had no idea what was going on. I just learned about it myself. The owner sold without an agent involved. He apparently was approached directly by the buyer."

"What's this guy's name again?"

"Silas Wiley."

"Do you know who he's selling to?"

"He wouldn't tell me. He said the buyer asked not to be identified."

"Shit!" Mitch picked up a pencil from his desk and threw it against the wall. "Is it all done—the papers signed and everything—or is there still a chance?"

"They've closed."

"Already?"

"That land around in that area is starting to attract big bucks, Mitch. Remember, I warned you because it's near that ski resort that's going up, you know."

"Yeah, I know." Mitch sighed. "Look, I apologize. I really liked that property and I was certain my wife would, too. It's a shame but it isn't the end of the world. I'm not sure now that I would want to be next to a ski resort. Will you keep your eyes open for something else for us, Bob? She's coming up this weekend."

"I'll go through my listings now. We'll find you something. Vermont's a big state. Don't you worry none."

Mitch hung up the phone. "Shit!"

FIVE

The Pilgrim's Pride, a sprawling, two-story restaurant, built to simulate a log cabin, was situated on the highway to Bennington just outside Southborough's town limits. At lunch hour, it was a meeting place for local merchants and contractors, as the four-wheel-drive wagons and heavy-duty pick-ups in its large parking lot bore witness. Jeeps, Ramblers and Subarus were standard issue. Winters were brutal and snowfall before Halloween not uncommon. There was only one thing worse than winter in Vermont, Johnson had told Mitch when they drove by a fence-enclosed acre of hulking yellow snowplows. "That's when the snow melts. It's called mud season and it's a great time to take a vacation."

At dinnertime, however, the parking lot of the Pilgrim's Pride was congested with cars, vans and recreational vehicles, most of them bearing out-of-state plates. Tired travelers were drawn by the sign reading STEAKS. CHOPS. SALAD BAR. CHILDREN'S MENU. ALL DRINKS. That day's legion of summer vacationers crowded the dining room as Mitch walked in. The buzz of conversation, punctuated by bursts of laughter and the cry of a baby, filled the air. The hostess, a middle-aged woman dressed in a blue gown with a lace bib and bearing an armload of menus, approached him. "Table for one?" she asked, ready to turn and lead him into the dining room.

"I'm looking for John Haye," said Mitch. "I was supposed to meet him at a dinner party here."

"Oh, yes, they're all upstairs in the Molly Stark Room. Over there," the hostess added, pointing to a staircase with her free hand.

As Mitch reached the top step he saw a private dining room off to the right, its double doors open. A bar was set up in the far corner of the room and around it stood a group of men holding drinks and chatting. The wallpaper had a fife-and-drum motif. Only an old painting of a Morgan horse broke its monotony. A long table covered with a white cloth was set for eight places. Baskets of bread and saucers with slabs of butter and chopped ice sat between vases of wildflowers. A busboy in white shirt and black trousers was removing a place setting, while a young waitress in a colonial gown was serving cheddar cheese and crackers from a tray.

Mitch stood at the doorway, hesitating. He'd forgotten what it was like to work on a small-town newspaper: how you had to meet socially with people whose policies or actions you might be reporting or editorializing on; the price you sometimes paid by having to rub elbows with the paper's advertisers. It made for awkwardness, having to make a choice between principle and expedience.

"Mitch. Good to see you." John Haye broke out in a grin. He was standing by the open doors as Mitch entered, at his side a white-haired, smallish man—not more than five-two, Mitch guessed—who exuded the energy of a bantam.

"It looks like you thought I wasn't coming." Mitch smiled over at the busboy, who was now taking away one of the dining chairs.

"Oh, no, Mitch," said Haye reassuringly. "We figured you got held up at the paper. It's Yuri Putzgarov who can't make it. He got called to a last-minute rehearsal at the festival."

"Putzgarov? The second violinist with the Moskova Quartet?" Mitch couldn't imagine why a musician had been asked to a business conference.

"He's a good friend of Southborough. He's planning to build a home not far from the campus on a piece of land he's had for I-don't-know how many years," explained the publisher as he turned to the man beside him. "Say hello to Bert Lester, our bank president," he continued. "Bert, this is Mitch Stevens. Hot off the press from our office."

Mitch forced a smile. "We've met before." He reached out his hand and was greeted by a limp, moist hand that seemed in contradiction to Lester's jovial manner. He remembered being introduced to the bank president at the Seedling, but the man had been seated and his height hadn't been apparent.

"You must be doing a dandy job for Ham," said Lester. "I haven't noticed that the *Courier* has skipped a beat at all."

"Ham's still around, Mr. Lester, so I can't take credit—or responsibility—for anything yet."

"Bert, call me Bert," said Lester. "We're not formal around here. We're all friends."

73

Haye tugged at Mitch's elbow. "Come on, I want you to meet some people. Over at the bar first. What'll you have?"

Before Mitch could answer, the cluster of men at the bar opened up at Haye's approach. "Gentlemen, I'd like you to meet Mitch Stevens," the publisher began. "He's going to be running the paper this summer."

It was easy for Mitch to guess which of the men was Harvey Troupe. The Boston developer was the nattiest dresser—wide lapels on his dark suit jacket, a stickpin in his tie. His hair was black and worn long. He had the smile and two-handed clasp of a salesman. Next to him were two men representing Britfair Enterprises. They were businessmen with penetrating eyes and quick smiles, Guy Jones and H.B.—"Call me Heebee"—Sims: a marketing vice president, and a corporate development specialist. Both wore conservative brown summer suits and rep ties. Jones, the older of the two, was graying at the temples. Sims had a distracting facial tic. Pleasantries were exchanged until Haye touched Mitch's elbow and interrupted. "Let me introduce Mitch to the rest of the gang before we sit down to supper and start talking serious."

The publisher led the way over to two men who were standing by the head of the table, drinks in hand, heads close together. "Mr. Handler I know," said Mitch, offering his hand to the big, strapping real-estate agent he had interviewed that morning. "Nice to see you again."

Handler, the only man in the room smoking, switched the cigarette between two fingers of his left hand, which held his drink, and took Mitch's hand with his right. "Bill. Everybody calls me Bill."

"Do you know our leading selectman, Brad Cummings?" asked the publisher.

"No, I don't. It's a pleasure, Mr. Cum—Brad." Cummings was a man in his mid-forties with a Vandyke beard that, Mitch saw, hid a scar—a Vietnam War memento, he later learned while sitting next to the selectman.

"Listen, everyone," the publisher said loudly, turning around so that all could hear him. "Let's take our drinks to the table and get down to some eating. We have all evening to talk."

Hearing him, the waitress put her tray atop the bar and leaned over the table to light the candles. Haye, meanwhile, was pointing out where each man should sit. Harvey Troupe took the head of the table, on either side of him one of the Britfair officials. Haye positioned himself in the middle next to Jones, and placed Bert Lester across the table next to Sims. Brad Cummings was given the foot of the table, with Mitch and Handler on either side of the selectman. As Mitch slipped his attaché case under the table in front of him, three groups of conversation seemed to start at once. The waitress, meanwhile, closed the double doors to the hallway as the busboy began filling water glasses.

The meal, despite Mitch's apprehension, went along amicably. These men were relaxed, or at least appeared so. The talk was general, ranging from the weather—"A dry summer, good for the tourist trade," from Lester, whose bank held most of the mortgages and loans in the area—to a discussion on city versus state control over schools and taxes— "I'll get into bed with anybody, even the socialists, when it comes to home rule," from Haye, whose newspaper took a decided Republican tone on political issues. The food was straightforward: prime ribs, baked potato, fresh sweet corn, a tossed salad, followed by pie made with local blueberries. A decent

Nat & Yanna Brandt

California red accompanied the main course. Mitch began to unwind, his annoyance at having to attend fading as the meal and talk progressed. He found himself in deep conversation with Cummings about the way the military had handled the war in the Persian Gulf. Mitch was critical of the unrelenting bombing that hit civilian targets. Cummings, though, defended it, saying the air strikes had saved many American lives. As he spoke, he became agitated, rubbing his beard so vigorously that the scar it hid turned red. As hard as Mitch tried to ignore it, he found himself staring at the wound. He totally lost the train of their conversation until he realized Cummings' eyes were fastened on him, obviously waiting for an answer to a question. Mitch was saved by the sound of a spoon against glass as Haye called for attention.

"Folks, folks, can I have your—" He broke off as Troupe and Jones guffawed at a joke. He waited for their laughter to die down. "Guy and Heebee have gone to a lot of trouble to come up from Hartford to be with us this evening, and I know we'd first of all like to thank them for doing so." Both Jones and Sims tipped their heads to acknowledge the gesture of gratitude. "I'm going to ask Harvey to tell them a little bit about SkiLand that they may not have read in the brochure, but first I'd like to put them in the overall picture."

Haye turned to an easel behind him. He flipped over a blank white sheet of paper, revealing a map of Vermont. Two bold, red lines stood out; one, running south to north, Interstate 91, paralleled Vermont's border with New Hampshire; the other, sweeping down from the northwest corner of the state, Interstate 89, crossed I-91 at White River Junction. Haye pointed at a gold star butting the red I-91 line in the southeast corner of the state. "Southborough, right on the interstate from Massachusetts and Connecticut—an arrow straight north, linking up with I-89 into New Hampshire.

"I don't have to tell you gentlemen what those two federal highways have done for Vermont—and for Southborough," Haye continued, pointing at the gold star. "We Vermonters have prided ourselves on being independent for more than two hundred years. Hell, we were a republic for nearly fifteen years before joining the rest of the union in 1791—did you know that? We were the first to adopt universal suffrage, the first to abolish slavery, and even though we were diehard Republicans up until World War II, and even though we're known as the whitest state in the Union, we had ourselves the first Socialist mayor in the whole country, and our last governor was a woman and a Jew, an immigrant."

Haye paused to take a sip of water, then continued: "It's the interstates that've done it. There are no longer more cows than people, and probably fewer native Vermonters than people from other states, people who followed that I-91 here. Look at what IBM did for Burlington. They put eight thousand people to work there, and now there are more than a hundred thirty, hundred thirty-five thousand folks in the area—and they're buying in shopping malls, living in housing subdivisions, raising families. We're still the most rural state in the nation, true. But that spells land, that spells opportunity."

Haye nodded to Troupe. "Harvey, you take over from here."

Troupe coughed into his fist before standing. "We are building the most modern, best-equipped ski resort in all of Vermont—all of New England, I don't mind saying." His broad "A's" reminded Mitch of the way John F. Kennedy spoke. "And I'm proud to say that we're already getting responses—they started before we even broke ground—from as far away as Philadelphia and Washington. My office in Boston is fielding calls from not just people interested in buying condos but merchants, individuals who want to set up shop in this area. We are drawing interest like a magnet—the kind of interest this state hasn't experienced since Sugarbush and Killington were developed.

"Let me put it another way," he went on, turning alternately to Jones and Sims. "We're building condos that will accommodate, we figure, between five- and six-hundred people, at a minimum, not counting children."

"All year round," interjected Lester.

"All year round," Troupe echoed. "SkiLand, as Bert points out, is a year-round resort. Skiing, of course, in the winter, but we're going to have a golf course, tennis courts, swimming pools for adults and kids—you name it. And boutiques to cater to them."

"And that means work for scores of people in the area," Cummings chimed in. "We've already got the lowest unemployment rate in the state, so we expect the town to grow substantially because of new families coming in to run the resort and the stores."

"Land is already at a premium," said Handler, fumbling in his pocket for a pack of cigarettes. "But there is a tidy bit that we've reserved for a major retail operation."

"What we think we have here is a bonanza right smack where every person who comes to Vermont goes through—a gateway to a gold mine." Cummings, his voice booming, seemed carried away by his own rhetoric.

Troupe gave Cummings a look that was clearly intended to shut him up. "We believe," the banker interjected in a quiet, assured manner, "that it will draw industry into the area, too.

"Industry means workers," Troupe went on. "We're talking about wage earners, heads of families who spend their dollars on furniture, clothes, appliances, not farmers minding their nickels and dimes. We're talking about all those well-to-do Yuppies up from Boston or New York to ski and swim. We're talking about those rich older folks who already find Southborough a haven.

"It's a unique opportunity for the businessman, a one-of-a-kind opportunity for Britfair. You're not going to be able to get these demographics anywhere else in the state. And we're here to offer you the chance to get in on it." Troupe started to sit down, but stopped. "I'm talking megabucks, you know, not some penny ante discount trade. Southborough will be the economic heart of Vermont and Britfair can be smack in its center."

Jones and Sims had been sitting quietly, their heads following the course of the pitch as now Troupe, then the others, spoke. Looking down and flicking a piece of lint from his sleeve, Jones said, "We'd like to hear a little bit about that land—Bill, is it . . . ?"

"That's right." Handler leaned forward. He took a long drag on his cigarette and was about to flick the ashes onto the floor but caught himself and reached instead toward an ashtray in the middle of the table, exhaling from the side of his mouth. "About twenty-one, twenty-two acres, just behind SkiLand. A more perfect spot you couldn't imagine—and within ten minutes of downtown Southborough."

Mitch, who had angled his chair and crossed his legs, sat up suddenly. That's the land I was after, he thought.

"And what is this piece of property going to cost Britfair?" Sims asked.

"It's mine," said Troupe, "but I'm not going to hold you up. I won't be taking you over the barrel on the price."

"Because we want you," said Lester. "We know what having a Britfair store will do for Southborough."

"There's already a discount chain on the other side of town," Jones pointed out. "What makes you think that Southborough can afford us, too?"

"Because," the bank president answered, "I can tell you for a fact—we've got their mortgage—that store is going to be abandoned. The chain is pulling back all across the northeast. I was told they're fighting a buyout."

"You still haven't said how much it would cost Britfair," Sims said to Troupe, his facial tic quickening.

The developer looked around the table. "Two-hundred thousand for twenty-plus prime acres."

"Ten thousand an acre?" Jones asked, sounding like he couldn't believe his ears.

I don't blame him, Mitch thought to himself. I offered thirty-six thousand for the whole parcel. How much more could Troupe have been willing to pay? Another five just to sew it up for himself? Talk about profiteering!

"And I'll do the construction for you at a special cost-plus figure," Troupe said. "It's all been perc-tested. I've even had plans drawn up to show you how it would fit in with the ski resort architecturally."

"That's zoned for farm and residential use out there," said Sims, who had already checked with the town clerk the status of various locations that Britfair management thought it might be offered in Southborough. "We can't site a store down there."

"We'll guarantee it," said Cummings. "The Board of

Selectmen gave its approval to SkiLand without a to-do. You don't have to fret none about it. After all, it just means extending the zoning to adjacent property. There's no reason why we can't swing this deal, too."

"How sure of this can you be?" asked Sims. His tic forced his face into a wince. "We read where you had to scale back on that condominium development on East River. You had every environmental nut in Vermont on you for that one."

"That was a goof, I'll admit," said Cummings. "The land there butted up against a winter deer habitat and some prime farmland. But we still got the project through, maybe not all of it, but plenty enough to make a helluva profit. We cut back from two-hundred and two units to eighty-eight and still made money. Jeez, those things sold for a hundred-twenty thousand and up."

"And you're telling me we're not going to rouse up those nuts again? Is that what you want me to believe?" Sims pointed his finger at Cummings. "Look at what's happened upstate. Danville refused to take advantage of the planning law—Act Two-hundred I think you call it. It got uppity about protecting the right to run its own affairs without state intervention. And a number of other towns are following its lead."

"Oh, hell, Heebee," Cummings said, "that's up north, in what we call the Northeast Kingdom. Those counties—Caledonia, Orleans, Essex—they're the hinterlands. Nobody'd want to live up there. Every damn little village thinks it's the last outpost of the War for Independence. They've got their heads in the sand."

"May I, gentlemen?" interrupted Haye. He rose, smartened his jacket and looked down at Jones, then across the table at Sims. "We've done our homework, too. Britfair is locked in a competitive tug-of-war with J.T.

Linney. Stop me if I'm wrong. You've gone into the securities business but found you can't compete with traditional investment services. Your automotive shops can't sell enough tires—no one can anymore. The only thing you've got going for you is your insurance business and your name. And, if I read my *Fortune* magazine rightly, your top management has decided to go back to basics and to use that name as retailers first and foremost."

Both Jones and Sims smiled. "This is a hardball game," Jones said. "We could go to White River Junction."

"Too far north and you know it," said Haye. "People up there can shop by catalogue. We're talking here about an active, mobile, high-spending, growing community through which thousands of tourists drive."

"We're talking," interrupted Lester, "about walk-in trade, the kind that's easiest to sell to."

"Look at what happened to Manchester, across the state from us," Cummings said. "Fancy factory outlets, boutiques, ritzy shops. And Manchester isn't even close to an interstate. The name it has acquired—"

"Is clutter," Jones butted in, finishing the sentence for him. "They zoned themselves into a nightmare. And we don't want a nightmare. Maybe they don't have a huge McDonald's arch on Main Street and maybe they got everybody to put up 'Ye Olde Shoppe' signs, but it's a discount merchandiser traffic jam. We don't need that kind of competition." Jones leaned back in his chair. "We don't need it, and we don't want it."

"Let me send you my architects' plans," said Troupe. "You'll be able to spread out with enough room for a thousand cars if you want and still have room to house a catalogue warehouse. There'd be no competition in the vicinity. We're going to comply with every comma and semicolon in the state's building code and environmental rules. No crowding whatsoever."

"Looka here," Troupe went on. "We're right off the interstate and have connections east and west as well."

"But Vermont," said Sims, "is people poor. There are more men, women and children in Jacksonville, Florida, than in the entire state of Vermont. Christ, your capital, Montpelier, has got only—what?—seventy-five hundred people. And your Vermonter is poor. A farmer with a quarter inch of topsoil and eight hundred feet of granite beneath it."

"Sure, poor," Handler said, "but rich in land." The realtor tapped his cigarette against the side of an ashtray. "The land may be lousy for farming, but it's got some of the greatest views in the world. Hell, the average price of a house in this state is now more than a hundred thousand dollars. Somebody's paying that price. No, not somebody. Everybody. I don't have trouble earning my commission."

"You're looking at the glass the wrong way, Heebee," said Haye. "It's not half-empty. It's half-full. Vermont can grow by leaps and bounds because we've got the acreage here to support the influx. Just take a look at Burlington, up north on Lake Champlain. It grew by a third just because IBM set up a computer factory there. And do you know why IBM chose Burlington? Because its chairman liked to ski. So, hey, why not a factory there, right? SkiLand is going to attract all sorts of interest—and we've got the space for whatever, you name it."

"And how are people going to know we're here?" Jones asked. "Vermont doesn't allow billboards."

"You advertise—and I don't mean only in my newspaper," Haye said. "You let the folks down in Boston know you're here, you tell 'em in Springfield, even in New York City. You spread the word. And we'll help spread it also, my newspaper will, you can count on it.

"We're perched right on the doorsill, gentlemen. And the door's wide open. Come on in."

Jones and Sims exchanged looks. "It's an interesting concept," the marketing vice president said. "We'd like to bring it to the attention of our retail and service divisions." He turned to Troupe. "Let's see those drawings. If Britfair does decide to go ahead, we'll want to move fast so that we can get a return on our investment as soon as possible."

"Anything else we can provide?" Haye asked.

Jones shook his head no. "We got the picture. Heebee and I are staying overnight, so we might just run up to that site tomorrow morning before we turn back to headquarters."

"I'll show it to you," Handler quickly offered.

The men began to get up, pushing their chairs behind them. Jones turned to Haye. "What about that promotion you offered? We're likely to be your biggest advertiser if this gets on its feet. We'd have to count on cooperation."

"Not to worry," the publisher answered. "Mitch down there," he said, "will do whatever is necessary to print any advance stories you want to run this summer. By the time you open, everyone in this state will know where you are."

Mitch didn't like the sound of that promise. Not that newspapers didn't run stories to publicize their advertisers. That was standard operating procedure. Hell, every newspaper except maybe the *Times* ran favorable reviews for any restaurant that advertised in it, even if it meant stretching the truth a bit or overlooking a dirty soup spoon. It was just that he didn't like being committed so openly. It made the *Courier* seem like a whore, Mitch thought, its columns open to anyone with the price of a want ad.

He headed for the doorway, grappling with a growing reluctance to cooperate, as Jones and Sims made their farewells and started down the stairs behind him. Mitch suddenly remembered he had left his attaché case under the dining table. He turned and brushed by the two Britfair men, smiling lightly and mumbling an apology, as he made his way back up the stairs.

Mitch re-entered the Molly Stark Room. Cummings and Handler were huddled with Troupe by the bar in the far corner. Handler and Troupe had their backs to Mitch, but he could see Brad Cummings clearly. He was compulsively rubbing his scar again.

Troupe was talking. "Well, we're off and running. I thought that it went pretty well."

"What the fuck are you talking about, Harvey? Those bastards are too smart for their own good."

"Calm down, Bill. They're just smart businessmen doing their job."

Cummings chimed in, anger in his voice. "That may be, but it's just going to end up costing us more money. I just know it."

Mitch's ears perked up. What was the selectman talking about? Mitch reached under the table for his attaché case and was about to leave when Troupe said, "We can afford it."

Mitch backed up against the wall to listen, feeling conspicuous but too curious to move.

Haye, hearing Troupe's last remark, walked up to the

group, Lester behind him. "You fellows will be able to afford most anything if this goes through," he said lightly.

"You priced that parcel a bit high, didn't you, Troupe?" said Lester. "They aren't stupid. All you have to do is check the real estate ads in the *Courier* to get an idea of what land is going for nowadays."

"Maybe we need a story about how land prices are going up, something that would encourage them to buy quickly," said Troupe. "What about it, John?"

"That might be obvious, Harvey," the publisher said. "Let me think on it."

"I could foreclose on the Smythe place, I suppose, if they don't want those twenty-two acres," said Lester. "It's a lot smaller, so it wouldn't cost them as much."

"Let's not jump ahead," Troupe admonished the banker. "We're tying up money in that land. We don't want to jeopardize it."

"Gentlemen," Haye said, "why don't we figure on meeting next week to discuss our next move, if we have to make a move at all. I'm hoping we'll get a reaction from Britfair before then."

"Well, they certainly sounded like they'd already been thinking about it for a while," Cummings said.

"They're professionals," Troupe pointed out. "They're not going to recommend anything to their people unless they can prove in dollars and cents that it's a smart move. You'll see, they'll want other concessions beyond the zoning."

"Like what?" Cummings asked.

"Maybe broadening the road there to four lanes for easier access. A traffic light, too. I'd bet they'd want a promise that a police officer would be stationed there during peak shopping hours."

"That'll cost the town money," the selectman said.

"You haven't heard it all," said Troupe. "Lights—street lights. For night shopping. Sewer lines, maybe. They'll come up with a shopping list as long as your arm. You'll see," he added as he started for the door. The circle around him began to break up.

Turning, Haye stopped short, surprised to see Mitch still in the room. "I thought you'd left," he said. "How long have you been here?"

"I forgot my case," Mitch began.

Haye gripped him by the elbow and steered him toward the door—a physical gesture that bothered Mitch. "We'll want to do all we can for the Britfair people," Haye said.

"You don't want to sell the paper cheap," Mitch cautioned. "They might expect you to bend a few rules if you do."

"What are you talking about, Mitch? We don't make the news, we just report it."

"I've seen it happen before." Mitch stopped at the head of the stairs. "Supposing there's a fire there and an inspector uncovers some violations. They'll be all over the paper trying to hush that up. You don't want to put yourself in that kind of position editorially. You don't want to owe them anything."

"You telling me my business?" Haye's voice was gruff. He started down the staircase.

"Nope, just reacting as any newspaperman would react," said Mitch, following him.

"This is a big step forward for Southborough."

"And for some of the leading citizens of Southborough. You start to grow by those leaps and bounds you talked about and everybody's taxes will shoot sky high just for paying for the public schools all those families coming here will need. And that's only the first service they'll expect from your Southborough. You know that. Land values will go up and with them property taxes. You'll lose farmers, and their farms will become the sites for condominiums and Levittowns. It's progress, I guess, but toward what?"

"Listen, Stevens," said Haye as he reached the foot of the stairs. He turned to face Mitch, the tone of his voice hard. "You're here to run my paper for a brief six weeks in your entire life. I don't expect or want you to do anything but what you're being paid for. This is not your business, and I didn't ask for your opinion. Got it?"

Mitch looked the publisher in the eye. He wanted to argue, wanted to convince him that he was wrong, wanted to tell him off. Then he thought of Ham Johnson. This is not my concern, it can't be, he realized. I'm an interloper, a temp. "Got it, Mr. Haye," Mitch finally said. "You'll get your money's worth."

And then some, Mitch added to himself as he left Haye and walked out of the restaurant. I wouldn't put anything past them. They've obviously got the town in their pocket. I wonder how much each of them is getting out of this. He bristled at the thought of what Troupe and his cronies might do to the town.

Walking to his car, Mitch remembered the time he had covered the scandal surrounding Horace Whitteley. The scion of an old, respected New York family, Whitteley had used his social prestige to convince the city that its purchase of fifty acres of abandoned railroad tracks and right of way in Harlem would turn a wasteland into a flourishing park, a political ploy that the mayor was especially avid to support. Whitteley courted members of the City Council, gave generously to re-election campaign coffers, and pictured himself—with the help of a public-relations agency—as a champion of the poor people. Whitteley Park—named not for himself, of course, but for a great-great uncle who had once been a state judge—would provide an oasis around which a revitalized Harlem would grow. Whitteley, however, hadn't said anything about how he had quietly bought the property in the name of a dummy corporation, or that he had bribed a municipal appraiser to boost the value of the land. His rationale—and he was being perfectly sincere—was that what was good for business was good for New York.

Mitch started the engine and rolled down his window. He was about to back up when a long, black Jaguar sedan passed him in the rear. Harvey Troupe was at the wheel, banging on the horn, impatiently urging the car ahead to get out of his way. Mitch could see his lips moving. "Come on, come on," he seemed to be saying.

SIX

"Come on back to bed."

"There isn't time, Mitch, you know that."

Val stood in front of the mirror, appraising herself. The morning sunlight, filtered through the venetian blinds, outlined her body through the sheer white nightgown. God, Mitch had missed her. Even though she was just an hour away in Williamstown, her rehearsal schedule was so grueling that this was the first chance she had been able to get away. And, Mitch thought rather guiltily, I had promised to come down to her. Well, so much for promises made in moments of passion. He would definitely be there for her play, he vowed to himself. He would not let anything interfere, not a tyrannical publisher nor a miscellaneous body or two.

"You're still as beautiful as ever," Mitch said, hoisting himself on one elbow to watch her. "And as desirable. Come on back to bed. I want to show you something."

"I know exactly what you want to show me." Val laughed. "There isn't time. Ham'll be back soon, and we're going out for brunch with him before the concert."

Mitch threw back the blanket. "But look what you're missing."

Val studied him, a warm smile lighting her face. "I think I see a silver hair amidst all that finery."

"Where?" said Mitch, looking down at himself.

A car crunched to a stop on the gravel driveway outside the house.

"There's Ham now," Val said. She went over to the window and held down one of the slats to look out. The car door opened. "Yes, it's Ham, with an armful of groceries. Why did he want to buy all those things if we're going out to eat?"

"He's just laying in food for me," said Mitch as he sat up on the edge of the bed. "He's worried I'll starve while he's in the hospital."

They could hear the front door downstairs open and close.

"Mitch! Val! It's me, Ham. Are you decent?"

"Well, I am even though you're not," Val said in a half whisper to Mitch as she put on a silk bathrobe and reached for the doorknob.

"Wait for me. It'll just take a second to get back to normal." He made a face, purposely looking gloomy. "Who knows when that will happen again. Maybe never in my lifetime."

"I wouldn't bet on it," his wife said, opening the door to go downstairs.

"Hey, wait'll I put on my bathrobe."

WITH JOHNSON DRIVING—Mitch at his side and Val in the back seat—they reached Southborough College and fell into line behind several cars waiting to be guided by attendants onto a back meadow parking lot. Looking at the campus, Mitch was reminded of the University of Virginia. The school was comprised of a series of three-story white wooden buildings surrounding a large lawn. At one end stood the domed library, patterned, Mitch realized, after the library at the University of Virginia that Thomas Jefferson had designed and which he had visited many years earlier while covering a conference on urban rehabilitation. The buildings on one side of the quadrangle housed classrooms, those on the facing side student dormitories. At the other end, opposite the library, was a small theater—perfect undoubtedly for student productions, but certainly not big enough to handle the number of people who came in the summer to hear the concerts put on by the Mont Vert Music Festival. They were performed, instead, on the basketball court of the modern, glass-walled school gymnasium that stood behind and off to the right of the library.

As they approached the gymnasium, young musicians, carrying violin cases or lugging cases that held cellos and bass fiddles, scurried down a side path leading to the performers' entrance and backstage. All the women were dressed in long, black skirts and white blouses, the men in dark suits, their collars unbuttoned and jackets flapping open. Many of them, Mitch reflected, were oriental, Japanese and Korean string instrumentalists who had come to the United States to study. As Johnson had explained, the Mont Vert Music Festival was an unusual opportunity for talented but relatively inexperienced musicians to perform with acclaimed international concert artists, older musicians who passed along the traditions of Europe where they, as youngsters, had studied.

Every so often, Mitch observed, one of the older musicians—*alte cockers* as they called themselves in

Yiddish, whether they were Jewish or not—would amble by in the same direction, stopping often to say hello to a concertgoer with either a handshake, a hug or a kiss. Lyle Timski, who was reviewing the concert for the *Courier,* was talking with one of them. His hair was white, worn long but carefully combed, his black business suit neatly pressed, his gestures broad. Mitch couldn't make out whether his accent was Russian or German. Obviously an established performer, used to being held in awe by younger musicians, he nonetheless seemed pleased by the attention Timski was paying him.

Val and Mitch stood together, watching the arrival of the musicians and the concertgoers while Johnson went off to pick up their tickets. People stood busily chatting away or greeting each other, waiting for the bell that would call them to their seats. They turned together as a chorus of hoots came from behind them. One of the older musicians was doing a little jig to a small crowd, holding his violin case high above his head, and singing in a Russian accent, "I could have danced all night. . . ." His audience was well-dressed in an informal way—polo shirts and plaid summer jackets, or linen skirts and open cotton blouses. Judging by their uninhibited boisterousness, Mitch was certain they were New Yorkers. It was a rare Vermonter, he had already learned, that behaved like that in public. They were clapping now in unison as the musician whirled in a circle.

"That's Yuri Putzgarov, second violinist in the Moskova Quartet," said Ham, coming up behind Val and Mitch. "He's in another world up here, the most popular guy for miles around."

"Funny," said Val, "I always think of the second violinist in a quartet as nondescript, always overshadowed by the first violinist."

Nat & Yanna Brandt

"Not necessarily, and certainly not in Putzgarov's case," said Ham. "He wants to play first violin, but obviously he's never been asked. Probably compensates with all that bravado. Here they think he's a god and he struts around like one. That's why he loves coming here. And he does everything to maintain that image."

"Are you saying he's not a good violinist?" Val asked.

"No, he's good—but not great."

The musician, his jacket stretched taut over his paunch, waved good-bye to the visitors and walked towards them. "Ah, Hamala," he said in a Russian accent, thrusting his hand out to meet Johnson's. "So what's new? Or should I say what's news?" As he laughed at his own joke, which Mitch suspected Johnson had probably heard more than once, Putzgarov turned expectantly toward Val, a sudden gleam in his eye. "So," he said, stepping back to appraise her, "such beauty is—how do you newspaper people say?—a front-page banner headline. You must tell me your name, my dear."

Ham made the introductions as Val beamed at Putzgarov's attention.

"Stevens? I know that name," said Putzgarov, frowning. "Of course," his eyes lit up. "We were supposed to meet at that dinner. But, alas, I couldn't make it. Music," he said, holding up the violin case in his left hand, "comes first. No, I apologize," he continued, looking at Val, "you, my dear, would come first if you were mine."

"Putzoo! Putzoo!"

"Oi," said Putzgarov, spotting a tall, middle-aged woman advancing toward them. "Darlings, I must go. The music calls. I see afterwards at the party."

The musician hurried off before the woman reached them. "Oh, I missed him," she said dejectedly. "I'll catch him later."

Val, Mitch and Ham smiled solicitiously at her as the concert bell clanged. The groups of people on the lawn began to funnel toward the entranceway to the gym.

"What are we hearing?" Val asked.

"I don't know," said Ham, elbowing his way by a couple in order to keep up with Val and Mitch. "They usually don't post what they're playing until the night before. It depends on what they have ready."

"I hope there's a Mozart," she said as she squeezed by a post in front of the door. "I adore Mozart."

"What about you, Mitch?" asked Ham.

"I'm new to chamber music—willing to learn, but new. Val's been trying to get me beyond Tchaikovsky. And I've been listening and learning."

As they entered the lobby, some concertgoers were making last-minute visits to the restrooms while others were bunched at a counter to buy chamber music recorded at previous summer concerts. Most, however, were shuffling slowly toward the two adjacent doors that led to the basketball court.

Mitch heard his name being called and looked back to see John Haye waving to him. Mitch gently pulled Val to his side as Haye came up. The publisher introduced his wife, Elizabeth, to Mitch, who in turn introduced Val to the Hayes. The ritual was repeated as Bert Lester and his wife, Mary, following on Haye's heels, came up to enlarge the small circle they had created, forcing others waiting to get inside the concert hall to jostle around them. Jessie and Brad Cummings added to the congestion by joining them. Mary Lester, like Elizabeth Haye, was dressed in an old-fashioned summer print with a narrow belt. Though the colors and design of their dresses were different, the two of them looked indistinguishable, refined but bland, though there was a strange reticence about Haye's wife that puzzled Mitch. Jessie Cummings, on the other hand, was behaving vivaciously, all smiles and hand gestures in a manner that surprised, and amused, Mitch, who was used to seeing her in a less demonstrative mood at the *Courier*.

Introductions made, they all began to head again toward the door to the basketball court-concert hall. As they entered, an usher directed them to their seats, pointing the way. The stage, Mitch saw, was actually a raised platform that had been installed at the far end of the court. Tall wooden baffles were positioned behind it to bounce the music into the audience. The gym's large windows were opened to provide ventilationand with it the trill of birds and the sound of cars on a road behind the campus could be heard. Veteran concertgoers carried padded cushions for the hard metal folding chairs provided for the audience.

Mitch, Val and Ham edged by a couple who were already seated, excusing themselves and reaching for the concert programs that rested on their seats. The mimeographed programs were folded inside a festival brochure that described its history and purpose and included an envelope for a mail-in donation. Mitch's gaze wandered up from the program and became riveted on a scene outside the hall. Through one of the floor-to-roof thermal windows that ran along the oblong sides of the gym he could see Putzgarov. The violinist, his back to the gym, was gesturing wildly at a tall man whose face had turned red with anger. Mitch recognized Harvey Troupe. The developer pointed a finger at Putzgarov, jabbing it at him to emphasize a point, and then stalked away. Putzgarov turned to watch him go and lifted his chin to shout something short and vehement at him.

"Mitch, what's the matter?" said Val, leaning over to

him so Johnson couldn't hear. "You seem out of it all of a sudden."

Mitch didn't answer. He was watching the three couples they had just met taking their seats several rows in front of them. The men—Haye, Lester and Cummings—let their wives sit down next to one another, then took the next three seats, all the while talking heatedly amongst themselves.

"Mitch?"

ONLY A PIANO stood on the stage. Mitch read that the first piece in the concert was actually a series of pieces—Schumann *lieder* for soprano and tenor—and on the back of the program was the translation of the verses. The pianist, a young Korean woman, adjusted her chair and then looked expectantly at the soprano, who nodded slightly. With that, the pianist began the introduction to the first song. The soprano clasped her hands in front of her, waiting for her cue. Beside her, the tenor stared woodenly out at the audience.

Mitch closed his eyes as the soprano lifted her voice in a love song. German *lieder* had never appealed to Mitch. He had always thought his distaste was due to the fact that he didn't know what the words meant. But now, even with the translation in hand, the language flowery and archaic, he found it hard to concentrate. He was still distracted by the scene he had just witnessed. Was there a connection between it and the conversation he had overheard at the Pilgrim's Pride? What's going on? he wondered. Was he being too suspicious? This is how business is done, Mitch had to acknowledge. The buddy system, old school ties, contacts—call it what you will, people made business. And people were responsible for making a town prosper. When a community such as Southborough did find a way to expand, to attract business or industry, some people in town benefited in the long run. Lots of people. Or did they? Was growth always good? Is big better?

Mitch was wrestling with the implications of those questions as the audience around him began to applaud. He opened his eyes to see the soprano smiling widely as she bowed to the audience, her hand linked with that of the tenor, who was also bowing. Behind them, the pianist beamed. The three performers walked off the stage, only to return seconds later as the applause continued.

Val was smiling, too. She leaned over to Mitch. "That was so lovely, wasn't it? She has a beautiful voice—they both do."

After the three performers left the stage a second time and the applause died down, three young men appeared from backstage to move the piano back against the rear wall and position four stands and chairs for the next selection on the program. Val nudged Mitch with her elbow. "It's a Mozart, one of my favorites. You'll love it."

Quartet in G Minor, K.V. 478 (1785), Mitch read, surprised that it only had three movements instead of the usual four—*Allegro, Andante* and *Rondo (Allegro)*. He looked up as the four musicians appeared on stage. A Korean woman in her early twenties, this one holding a violin, led them on. She was followed by a bearded man about her own age carrying a cello, then a blonde woman, who couldn't have been much older, with a viola tucked under her arm. Bringing up the rear, a paternal smile on his face, was Yuri Putzgarov. He was about to show off his three students to the audience, his face seemed to say, and if they played well, it would be because of him.

While the musicians sat down and began tuning their instruments, Putzgarov, standing by his chair—he was the first violin—looked out on the audience, took a handkerchief out of the inside pocket of his jacket and draped it over the chin rest of his violin. He then sat, brought up his instrument, tilted his head into it and began plucking the strings, adjusting them until he had the violin in tune. His young colleagues were still tuning, so he sat looking out at the audience, his violin resting upright on his thigh, raising an eyebrow when he spotted someone he knew—working the crowd, Mitch couldn't help thinking. After a silence indicating they were ready, Putzgarov waited a beat longer than necessary before bringing his bow up to the strings and leaning into the instrument.

Putzgarov sat on the edge of his chair, weaving back and forth with the music and every so often looking up sharply at the cellist. It seemed to Mitch that something was bothering him. Maybe the fellow had played a wrong note. Mitch was aware that the cello seemed to dominate the other instruments. Was he wrong, Mitch wondered, was Putzgarov playing louder now, trying to outdo the cellist? Whatever was going on, Mitch was so distracted that he realized he wasn't really listening. His mind started to wander again, this time to an interview he'd once had with an opera singer when he was a young reporter. He—a basso profundo—had an enormous ego and was constantly preening himself, looking into every mirror they passed as he and Mitch made their way into a posh East Side restaurant for lunch. The singer's eyes constantly darted around, searching the restaurant, looking for other celebrities, even while he was answering Mitch's questions. It was as though Mitch didn't exist, and he never felt sure that he got truthful answers to his questions, benign as they were. Weeks later, after the feature appeared in the Sunday edition, Mitch heard over the radio in his car that the singer had been found tied up and dead in a seedy hotel in the Bowery, a murder victim. He realized then how little you could know about someone in a typical, fast, in-and-out newspaper interview unless you stayed alert to the nuances. You often picked up more insights from what the person you were interviewing did than from what was said. What clues, he wondered, was Putzgarov giving off?

"I just love that quartet. Wasn't it marvelous, Mitch?" Val turned to Ham Johnson, saying the same thing. The two were applauding vigorously and touching heads, talking about the performance. Mitch, however, was following Putzgarov with his eyes, fascinated. The violinist had stepped back to get in line with the other musicians to take their bows. The cellist had moved slightly ahead of him. Putzgarov is being upstaged, Mitch thought to himself, just like Val says actors do to each other. Putzgarov shot a quick glance of annoyance at the bearded young man and stepped to the side so that he stood out alone. He then held out his arm, inviting the others to leave the stage first, and followed last, looking back at the audience. As he did so, the paternal smile returned to his face. He likes the limelight, doesn't he?, Mitch thought to himself.

"Ham says there's time to go to the trustees' party before you have to get back to the newspaper. He says he's up to it if we are," Val said as the three of them stood up and stretched.

"There's still a piece after the intermission," Mitch pointed out as he arched his back. The seats were hard and uncomfortable.

"It's a Haydn trio. Ham says it's a quickie."

Mitch's face lit up in a devilish grin at the word "quickie." Val grinned back at him.

THE TRUSTEES' PARTY, Mitch decided, was a strange amalgam of people—musicians, lawyers, doctors, businessmen—a disparate blend that produced an unsettling feeling beneath the surface conviviality.

The trustees themselves represented a curious mixture—local patrons of the arts who dressed in prim fashion and spoke in low voices, and those from New York and Boston, louder and flashier, all accomplished fund-raisers. In the midst of them was the head of the festival itself, Sigmund Ranke. The aging, balding conductor was walking from one trustee to another, his head tilted slightly, shyly shaking hands and beaming his thanks to them for their comments about the concert. Ranke had built up the Mont Vert Festival from nothing through grit, determination and the sheer power of his personality. From what Ham had told him, Ranke ran the place with an iron hand that antagonized some of the musicians who had strong egos of their own. But the man was genuinely loved and admired, and his name alone attracted grants and donations and sold-out audiences despite the fact that, as only other professional musicians understood, he was no longer capable of any sustained podium duties.

Ham led Val and Mitch through the welter of partygoers surrounding the tables laid out with bottles of liquor, mixes and snacks. The home they were in—the summer residence of one of the New York trustees—was an eighteenth-century farmhouse. Large hooked rugs were scattered on the floors of the living room and parlor, and on the walls were American primitive portraits and landscapes darkened with age. Val was admiring the exposed beams and frail-looking furniture when the flash of a strobe temporarily blinded them. Next to them, Jessie and Brad Cummings and a young musician were posing for a photographer. Behind the Cummingses and also temporarily blinded by the flash was Elizabeth Haye. She appeared to be embarrassed at being in the background of the photograph and began looking this way and that, searching, Mitch guessed, for her husband. Ham and Val, meanwhile, had ducked away as the photographer called out, "Just one more." Mitch began to follow, but too late. The flash again blinded him. When his vision cleared, he could see that the publisher's wife, also caught again in the flash, seemed on the verge of crying.

Mitch tried to catch up with Ham and Val, brushing by snatches of conversation as he elbowed his way through the crowd:

"Well, you know, I only write what I think will ultimately help the performer," a music critic from a New York newspaper, his eyeglasses halfway down his nose, was saying to two women bracketing him. "But no one ever listens to what I have to say. That soprano at the Metropolitan the other night, her lung control . . ."

". . . and Rilkoff, late for a concert as usual, was speeding down the highway, when a traffic policeman stopped him." The musician telling the story was a violinist—Mitch could tell by the large red welt under the left side of his chin, the "rehearsal badge" which the man would have all his life. "He asks to see his registration, so Rilkoff opens the glove compartment and out pops all those speeding tickets he's never paid. So the police officer . . ."

". . . he's terrible, just terrible," a middle-aged woman was saying to a male companion of the same age. "I don't see what the critics see in him. He plays Chopin like a bricklayer and . . ."

". . . the last movement—oh, my God, what beauty." The petite Japanese girl held her hand to her lips. "I cried while I was playing it. And to think, he never . . ."

". . . don't you dare take that tone with me, you sonofabitch."

Mitch turned sharply to the speaker. It was John Haye. The publisher was haranguing Putzgarov. The two men were standing by a side door that led to a kitchen, oblivious to the swirl of people around them. Putzgarov pushed Haye back against the wall. Stunned by the sudden violence, Haye started to say something when he saw that Mitch had seen what had happened. The publisher whispered something angrily to the musician and pushed by him and into the crowd. Putzgarov, in the meantime, had started to fight his way to the front door but several people blocked his path, offering congratulations on the concert and trying to engage him in conversation. He answered, but Mitch could see that he wanted desperately to get away.

"Mitch?" Val handed him a piece of cheese on a cracker. "What is it, Mitch? You're off somewhere else again."

"It's nothing, honey," said Mitch, taking the cracker and leaning over to kiss his wife on the cheek. "I was just thinking that we really ought to head out. Ham and I have to get to the newspaper before it gets too late. The Monday morning edition is waiting for us."

Val, he could tell, was not pleased, but she didn't say anything further. Johnson approached, jiggling three glasses in his hands. "Punch—virgin punch," he said, handing out the glasses. "I hope you don't mind, Val, it's not spiced but Mitch and I—"

Before Johnson could finish the sentence, their attention was diverted by a loud crash. The table where Johnson had gotten the punch lay overturned on the floor, the punchbowl and glasses that had been on it scattered about, mostly in pieces, a large puddle of punch seeping through the cracks of the old floorboards. Those who had been near the table had jumped away. A few women were bending over to search for scratches on their legs; Haye was steadying one of them, his wife Elizabeth, who was dabbing a bloody scratch with a flimsy handkerchief. Putzgarov was elbowing people away from him as he pushed his way to the front door.

"What's going on?" someone near Mitch said.

"It's probably Putzoo having one of his tantrums."

"It's the nature of second violins," the first said matter-of-factly. "They're always ready to kill to be first."

SEVEN

M‍ITCH LOOKED UP, pushing the glasses back on his nose automatically. "Yes, Maxine."

"It's Mr. Johnson on the phone."

"I thought he was being operated on today."

"He said it's been postponed until tomorrow morning because they got an emergency case in."

Mitch reached for the phone. "Ham, you okay?"

"Sure, sure." Johnson sounded aggravated. "I'm stuck in this goddamn bed. They won't let me out even though nothing's going to happen before tomorrow."

"I'll drive up later after the paper is under control," Mitch offered.

"Don't bother," Johnson said. "They won't let me have visitors after seven. They say it's because I'll have to be up so early for the operation. I was just calling to see if you need any questions answered."

Mitch looked at the small pile of copy on his desk. He had already passed along to Ernie and Abe the bulk of the major local stories. "Nothing unusual happening,

Ham. Nothing to worry about at all."

"What about that Tolvey story of yours?" Johnson couldn't help but voice his concern that once he went into the hospital Mitch would spend too much time working on the realtor's death.

"Come on, Ham. You're getting to sound like a worrywart. I'm going to get that intern to help out on that, once she gets here."

"What do you mean? Didn't she show up today?"

"No, I got a call from her parents that her car broke down. She's stuck somewhere south of Springfield. They said she expects to reach Southborough tomorrow."

Johnson mumbled something.

"What did you say?" Mitch asked.

"That was the nurse. I got to go. They want to do something to me."

"Good luck again, Ham. Maxine is going to keep in touch with the hospital for us—and we'll all come by as soon as you're able to have visitors."

"Mitch?"

"Yeah."

"I'm worried."

"Ham, Ham. They do these operations often." Mitch tried to sound comforting, though he knew it was difficult to reassure someone over the phone. "Your doctor made that abundantly clear. If—"

"That's not what I'm worried about, Mitch. It's that business you told me about after the dinner at the Pilgrim's Pride. I can't get it out of my head that something is out of kilter, something that's going to put Southborough on the dirty end of the stick."

"Ham, I'm sure I'm just imagining things. Christ, I'm like that. Ask Val. I see shadows at noontime and look under my bed at night. I mean, those guys—Lester,

Cummings, Haye himself—they're the backbone of this community. You've never had cause before to worry, have you? So don't let me get you started."

"You're bulling me and you know it, Mitch. Look—" There was some more mumbling and a creaking sound. "Jeez, they're bringing in some contraption. I've got to go."

"Please don't worry, Ham," said Mitch. "I'd really be upset if I kept you from getting a good night's sleep."

"Sure. Not to worry. They'll stuff me with dope anyway."

"Take care, Ham. Good luck."

Mitch put the phone back on the hook, turned his chair toward the window overlooking Southborough's main street, and blinked back tears. He was worried about his friend.

IT WAS STILL light out when Mitch left the *Courier's* office and headed home. Ernie and Abe had the newspaper routine so under control that he actually felt in the way once he had completed the layouts. They handled the minor adjustments and cuts to fit stories on a page without having to think twice—as any experienced deskman should have been able to do. But they also knew that, unlike a major metropolitan area, nothing much was likely to happen after five o'clock in Southborough. And if the world did fall apart, they assured Mitch, he was only a phone call away. "Go on home, Mitch. Beat it," Abe said. "We don't need you." To which Ernie added, "Hmmm."

The phone was ringing when Mitch entered Johnson's home. He raced down the hall, hoping it hadn't been ringing for long. "Hello," he said quickly.

"It's me—Abe. That girl you got coming up from New York just walked in."

"Rachel Beldon?"

"Yeah. She doesn't know what to do. What do you want me to tell her?"

Mitch asked Abe to put her on. "This is a surprise, Rachel. I didn't expect you until tomorrow."

Rachel explained that she decided to head on into Southborough as soon as she could get her car fixed. "So here I am, professor, rarin' to go."

"Mitch—call me Mitch. We're not at school here." Why was his tone so sharp? Rachel didn't seem to notice.

Mitch had arranged for Rachel to stay in a spare attic room at a local inn, the Colonial House, that was well known for its food and high prices. But as the room was a floor away from any bathroom facility, the newspaper got a bargain rate.

"Tell Abe—Abe Keller, the guy who put you on the phone—tell Abe to give you directions to the Colonial House. They're expecting you. I'll see you first thing in the morning. I've already got something lined up for you to dig into. No, wait. Come in mid-morning. Take a stroll around Southborough first—get a feel of the place before you show up. I'd be interested in your impressions."

Mitch hung up and went to close the front door. The dusk outside could be felt inside. Mitch went through the house, turning on lights in the hallway and living room before going into the kitchen. He looked into the refrigerator, debating what to have for dinner. If Val were around, he'd have taken the lamb chops out of the freezer, tossed two potatoes into the oven and made a salad. But she wasn't, and he disliked cooking for himself. He reached instead for a frozen pizza.

By the time it was ready, Mitch was already settled in front of the television set in the living room, watching a Red Sox game and feeling guilty about not doing anything more edifying. But, truth to tell, he needed to escape, to do something mindless. He wasn't up to reading a book after spending a good part of the day reading copy. His eyes were tired. He closed them when a beer commercial came on and dozed off.

Ham was running up the middle of High Street, continuing faster until he passed into the distance. Mitch ran after him, shouting, gasping, until, out of breath, he stopped and could only watch Ham fade away. Mitch heard laughter. He turned. A group of men stood on the corner outside the *Courier* office, pointing at him and jeering. Their faces were familiar but he couldn't quite recognize them. He was puzzling over this when a police car, siren shrieking, swooped by, almost hitting him. Mitch jumped out of the way, which made the men laugh more, but when he again turned to them they were gone. He heard catcalls, but everywhere he looked he could not see anyone. Then, abruptly, the sound of the yelling stopped.

Mitch opened his eyes. It was totally dark inside the house. The set was off, the living room lamp out, the hallway light also. Mitch blinked. The dream had left him shaking, his palms wet with perspiration. Something was wrong. He pushed himself out of the armchair and groped his way into the kitchen, which was also dark. He knew there was a flashlight in the kitchen. He remembered seeing it once when Val was putting away something. Mitch went from drawer to drawer, feeling inside them, pricking himself once against the tip of a knife, until he felt the cold aluminum cylinder. He turned it on and then realized he didn't know where the fuse box was. The cellar? Mitch went to the door leading downstairs and flashed the light down the steps, trying to make out a box. When he didn't see one, he stepped gingerly down the stairs, probing with the light into the corners of the basement, which was filled with an odd assortment of old furniture, luggage cases and paint cans. Against the far wall was the fuse box. All the switches were turned on. He pulled the cord of an overhead bulb and then tried the main switch. Nothing. He flipped all the other switches off and on. Still nothing.

Mitch groped back up the stairs and returned to the living room. He looked out of the window. It was pitch black outside. Even stars were hidden by the dense foliage of the trees that surrounded the house. Maybe it's a power outage, he thought. There was no way to tell whether other homes were affected. There were none within eyeshot, and no street lamps to go by either. Holding the flashlight under his armpit, Mitch picked up the phone. The dial tone was loud in the darkness. At least the phone's working, Mitch thought as he dialed information. He asked for the number of the power company. He dialed it and got the regional office in Burlington. The man on duty there gave him the company's emergency number for Southborough, but there was no answer, although he let it ring for a full minute. Annoyed, Mitch asked the operator for the Southborough police station. This time the line rang only once before it was picked up.

"Police, Officer Ray Collins speaking."

Mitch explained that his electricity was out. "Is there anything wrong in my area? I'm near the campus."

"There's an outage over by the Wynman land. The

power company's emergency crew is there now, sir."

That would explain why there was no answer at the local office. "What happened?" Mitch asked. "I didn't hear any storm."

"No, sir, it wasn't a storm. Just some guy hitting a utility pole."

"Serious? Anyone hurt?"

"The guy's dead, I hear. We sent an ambulance out there but I haven't heard from it yet."

"Look, I work for the *Courier*. Can you give me any other details?"

"Sorry, sir, not yet. I told you all I know. But you're not that far away from the accident and there's a police officer on the scene—Tiny, er, George Adams."

Why not go? Mitch thought. He did work for a newspaper and was close by. He'd have himself a little story. And then he smiled to himself at the thought of having his byline again in a newspaper. "Thanks. Would you tell me how to get there from where I'm located?"

"And where would that be, sir?"

MITCH GRABBED THE notepad and pencil by the telephone. He put on a windbreaker and, using the flashlight, left the house and got into his car. The digital clock on the dashboard read 10:22. He hadn't been dozing that long, though it seemed like the middle of the night.

Power outage or not, driving the back roads of Southborough was always the same: you drove with your high beams on. Otherwise it was so dark you couldn't see more than thirty yards ahead. And even with the beams up, there were so many ruts and bends hidden in the shadows that you didn't rush it, unless you wanted to lose an axle. Collins had told him to take a side road that cut in by a red house with white shutters. Ordinarily at this hour, that house might have been lit up and easy to spot, but not tonight. Mitch almost passed it, but a bump in the dirt road made his headlights jump and he saw the house in time to turn. Several bends in the road later he saw the flashing lights of a police car and an ambulance. A power company truck with a cherry picker was nudged up beside a utility pole, a bright spotlight aimed at the top of the line. A police officer was watching a repairman strap on a heavy gear belt.

Mitch pulled off to the side of the road to park about thirty yards away. As he got out of his car he saw two men carrying a stretcher to the rear door of the ambulance. The body on it was covered with a blanket, but as the men hoisted the stretcher into the ambulance, the blanket slipped away. Mitch was aware of seeing a mangled, contorted lump, arms swinging lifeless, before he instinctively turned away, sickened, bile rising to his throat. One of the stretcher bearers was stooping to retrieve the blanket and put it back on the body as Mitch looked back. The man closed the rear door and got into the passenger side of the front of the ambulance. As it pulled away, it revealed the wreck of a car pinned to the utility pole. Its front end was smashed into the front seat. Nuggets of glass littered the ground and crunched underfoot as Mitch approached the car and looked into the side window. Black splotches of blood coated what was left of the windshield and window on the driver's side. There was a heavy odor, a medicinal one, Mitch thought, but before he could identify it, a deep voice behind him said, "Can I help you, mister?"

Tiny Adams, Mitch guessed, was nearly six-foot-six

and seemed that wide in girth, too. The tone of his voice was polite but formal.

Mitch identified himself. "Can you tell me anything about the accident?"

"Looks like the usual—a drunken driver."

"Got any identity?"

"Yeah, wait a minute." Adams pulled a bulging notebook out of his back pocket and stooped by the headlights of his patrol car to read his notes. "I better spell it for you. I can't pronounce it. P-U-T-Z-G-A-R-O-V, first name Y-U-R-I, sixty-two years old according to his license. The address is a New York City one, but the car was carrying Vermont plates." Adams looked up. "Something the matter?"

Mitch had jerked back, stunned. Putzgarov! He had just seen him perform. He had talked to him. He had seen him arguing with . . .

"I said, something the matter?"

Mitch shook himself alert. "No, everything's okay. Can you tell me what happened?"

"Not much else, I'm afraid. He was drunk as hell, to judge by the smell inside the vehicle. He just smashed headlong into that pole up there. It knocked out everybody's lights for miles around."

"No one else in the car?"

"Nope."

"Who spotted the accident?"

"No one saw it. The farmer up the hill there," Adams said, pointing into the darkness, "figured it was another accident when his lights went out, and he came down in his truck looking for it. He says the victim looked dead to begin with, but told us to send an ambulance anyway."

Mitch, who had been scrawling notes on his pad,

stopped suddenly. "Why would he be out here, officer? Did he have a house nearby?"

"Beats me," shrugged Adams. "I don't know the fellow. We'll have to ask around. Do you know the guy?"

"Yes, I know him," said Mitch. "I know who he is—was."

EIGHT

THE NEXT MORNING, Mitch stood outside the *Courier*'s entrance, pacing back and forth on the sidewalk. He was eager to get started, to write the story of Putzgarov's death before he got immersed in the daily routine, and to assign a number of stories he had thought up to go with it. So eager, in fact, that he was the first to show up at the office, only to find that he was locked out. There had never been any reason for him to have a key, so he was forced to wait until someone—he presumed it would be Maxine Longe or one of the advertising reps—let him in. Frustrated, he made a mental note to ask for a key. For what must have been the tenth time he checked his watch. It was 9:02. Where was everybody?

At that moment, around the corner from the newspaper's parking lot, Jessie Cummings appeared in a tight-fitting skirt, walking briskly. She looked startled to see Mitch.

"Have you been waiting long?" she asked, groping in her purse for a key ring. "I'm sorry, I'm usually here before nine, but one of those cement trucks heading for the mall just dragged its feet going through town. I ought to get Brad to have something done about rerouting the traffic through town."

"It's okay," said Mitch, following her into the building. Jessie was turning on light switches as they made their way into the newsroom. "I'm anxious to get going this morning." He stopped by his office door. "Would you please tell Maxine when she gets in that I'd appreciate her locating Timski and Robin and getting them in to see me?"

Jessie asked what had happened. "Putzgarov's dead—the violinist—killed in a car accident," Mitch said, and before she could say anything, he stepped into his office, taking off his jacket. He stopped in front of his desk, rolled up the cuffs of his shirt, loosened his tie, opened the top button, and sat down. He reached with both hands for the typewriter table and pulled it toward him. He then took a piece of copy paper and fed it into the machine, wondering as he did so what Putzgarov was doing on that back road so late at night.

ACCIDENT

stevens

Yuri Putzgarov, one of the leading members of the Mont Vert Music Festival, was killed last night when the car he was driving hit a utility pole on the Story Hill Road.

The accident caused a power outage in the area that lasted for two hours.

Police Officer George Adams reported that Putzgarov was found dead by the crew of the emergency ambulance service that was summoned to the scene.

Adams said that he detected the odor of alcohol in the car when he arrived at the scene about 10:15 p.m. He said an autopsy would be performed on Putzgarov's body within the next day or two.
                              --more--

Mitch pulled out the paper and fed a new sheet into the typewriter:

ACCIDENT-2

stevens

Putzgarov was riding alone in the car, according to Adams. The front end of the vehicle, a 1986 Jeep station wagon, was totally demolished.
   Putzgarov, who performed during the Festival's first weekend of concerts on Sunday afternoon, lived in New York City. He was regarded as

"You wanted to see us, Mitch?"
Mitch looked sideways over his shoulder to find Lyle Timski and Robin Summer in his doorway. He swung around to face them. "Come on in. You heard what happened?"
"You mean about Putzgarov?" Timski asked as he and Summer stepped in front of Mitch's desk. "Yes, Maxine told us just now."
"Good. I was there—at the accident scene. I'm working on a lead story. Lyle, I'd like you to get up a full obit on him. We may have something in the clips, but you'll probably have to make a mess of phone calls. And you better get cracking—I want to run the obit right up there on the front page with my story."
"Right." Timski headed for the door.
"And Lyle," Mitch called after him, "I want a full obit,

warts and all. No press agentry. Watch your adjectives. And don't gloss over anything.

"Robin," Mitch continued, turning his attention to the young woman standing before him, "I'd like you to do a sidebar on the Festival's reaction to Putzgarov's death. Get up there and speak to other musicians. And find out who'll replace him or whether this will mean any change in their plans at all. Got that?"

"Okay," she said excitedly. Her assignments were usually more mundane—church socials, simple court cases, features about 4-H winners. "I'll leave right away."

"Have you seen Rog at all?" Mitch asked.

"He isn't in yet." Robin paused. She didn't want to get a fellow reporter in trouble for being late. "I think he had something to cover first thing this morning."

Mitch didn't recall any morning coverage on the assignment sheet. "Okay," he said, dismissing Robin and wondering what Barrows was up to. "No, wait. Tell Maxine to tell Rog I want to see him."

Robin nodded and left. Mitch returned to the typewriter. He picked up the copy drooping from the machine and read it over. Satisfied, he placed his fingers on the keys:

one of the few remaining violinists who

"Mitch? You wanted to see me?"

Mitch looked at the young reporter, exasperated that he had been interrupted again and so soon. "Where the hell have you been?" he asked sharply.

Barrows was taken aback by Mitch's tone of voice. "My, er, my—"

"Never mind," Mitch cut in abruptly. He realized he had been unduly curt. "We've got a big story going—you heard about Putzgarov's death?"

"Yes, Maxine told me. Who was he?"

Mitch's mouth almost fell open. He paused, wondering whether to lecture the young reporter about reading his own newspaper—Putzgarov's name and photo had appeared with Timski's review of the Sunday concert in the Monday edition. "He was a musician with the Festival and he got himself killed in a car accident last night."

"Aha," said Barrows.

"I've put Lyle and Robin on stories to go with the accident, so you'll have to pick up whatever they had on tap for today. If there's any problem, let me know immediately. Okay?"

Barrows looked positively relieved that he didn't have to handle any of the Putzgarov stories. "No sweat," he assured Mitch. "I'll get right to it."

"Fine." With that, Mitch turned back again to his typewriter. Where the hell was I? he asked himself. I've lost my train of thought.

"Professor—I mean boss, chief, Mitch."

Mitch let out a deep breath before turning to face his student intern. "Hi, Rachel, come in."

Rachel was dressed in skin-tight jeans and T-shirt. It was hard to ignore the fact that she was not wearing a bra. Mitch tried to avert his eyes, but it took some effort to avoid staring at her breasts. He immediately wondered what she looked like undressed. Mitch cursed himself for the thought. Why did this young talented woman feel the need to come on so strong? He was beginning to regret his decision to bring her to Vermont. He really didn't want to have to deal with Rachel's problems or their impact on him. Mitch felt himself getting annoyed at her, and made an effort to remain objective.

"You settled in all right?"

"Yes, thank you. The inn is lovely."

"I didn't expect you so early." The irritation in his voice was hard to ignore despite his attempt to mask it.

"Well, I got up early and did what you wanted me to do—I drove into town and got out and walked around." Rachel smiled. "I saw you pacing up and down the street but you were too far away for me to shout. I think Southborough is—"

"Hold it," Mitch said. "I don't mean to be rude, but we're kind of busy this morning, so we'll have to talk about things later." He reached for the pad in front of him. "I'd like you to get started on some research. I'd been meaning to do it, but I haven't had the chance. Ready?"

"I don't have any paper or a pencil," Rachel said, and smiled again coquettishly.

"You should know better by now than to show up for your first day of work dressed like that and without the tools of your trade." Mitch's voice came out somewhat harsher than he had intended. Rachel's face fell. Mitch tossed her a ballpoint pen and slid some copy paper over to the edge of the desk.

"There was a body found not too long ago, the body of a real-estate agent named Vera Tolvey, who was killed in a hunting accident. Maxine—Maxine Longe, my secretary—can get you the clips on it. I'd like you to work up research that I can use to do a profile of the typical victim of a hunting accident. Call the Fish and Wildlife Department in Waterbury. Find out how many accidents occur every year, how the typical one happens if indeed there is a typical one. If you can, get the name of a victim, or better still, the name of the person who shot someone else by mistake. Maybe we can interview them." Mitch paused, waiting for Rachel, who was writing hastily, to catch up. "I'd also like to know whether a hunter would be aware that he'd shot a human being instead of an animal. And how many times the hunter scoots away without identifying himself afterward.

"Take it from there, Rachel. Any questions that come along or that you can think of now, ask them. Got it?"

"Where do I work?"

"I'm sorry, I forgot to tell you. Maxine has made room for you on a desk in the corner. She'll show you where, and ask her, please, to introduce you around to the staff. I'll catch up with you as soon as I can."

"All right, I'll start right now."

"And one other thing, Rachel." Mitch hesitated. "Look, we're not formal here, but did you bring any other clothes?" Rachel pressed her lips together tightly. "I mean if I have to send you out on a story or something, you really can't go like that. I can't have you representing the newspaper in tight pants and no bra. This is New England, not the East Village."

Rachel looked him full in the face. It was almost a challenge and it made Mitch uncomfortable.

"I certainly didn't mean to be provocative. I dress like this all the time and don't think twice about it. But, of course, Mitch, I understand. I promise to be a good girl and dress more conservatively."

Mitch took a deep breath in an effort to relax. "Fine," he smiled, in control again, "if you run into any snags on the Tolvey business, let me know."

Rachel got up and started to leave. "And Rachel,"

Mitch added, deciding to end the meeting on a positive note, "I'm glad you're here. We can use the help."

After she left, he rose slowly from his chair and stood by the window, staring out but not paying any attention to the scene below. Was working with Rachel going to be such a struggle? How the hell do I handle the sex bit? *Can I handle the sex bit?* Mitch shrugged his head. One thing at a time, he told himself. Back to work. He sat down, swiveling his chair to face the typewriter. Just then the intercom buzzed.

"Yes."

"Mitch, Bob Grant is on the phone for you."

"Okay, Maxine, but no calls after this till I tell you." Mitch pushed down the lighted button on his phone. "Bob, hi. What is it?"

"Mitch, you got a moment to talk over something?"

"If it's important, shoot. Otherwise it'll have to hold."

"I'll make it brief," Grant said. "I heard about that Putzgarov fellow getting killed and—"

"Word travels fast around here."

"What'd you expect in a small town, Mitch? Look, Putzgarov had property not far from where you saw that other land you wanted. He was building on it. On the other side of the ski resort, though. I'm not certain of the acreage, but his death probably means it's available."

"My God, Bob, the man is hardly dead. What kind of person do you take me for?"

"I know. I know what it sounds like, but that's how the real-estate game is played sometimes. Don't tell me the realtors in New York City don't do the same thing."

Not only the realtors, thought Mitch, but also people looking for apartments. They searched the obituary notices. "What makes you think the property might be available?"

"I don't know that it is, but if you want me to pursue it, I'd be only too glad to. I know how disappointed you were by losing that other land."

"Look, Bob, we may be jumping the gun. He was a single man but that doesn't mean he didn't have relatives somewhere. We're just working up an obit on him. But whether he did or not, it's a bit premature, not to say ghoulish, to contact the survivors this very day."

"Mitch, I'm only trying to act in your interest. Word'll get around about his death and even before you have your obit in everybody's mailbox tomorrow, you'll see—there'll be offers."

"I can't imagine how you're going to be able to do it."

"The same way one of your reporters would, Mitch. I bet the Festival office has someone to notify in case of an accident. That's routine on most job forms."

Mitch mulled over the idea. If I give Grant the go-ahead, he thought, I'll feel like a vulture myself. And what about the proximity to the ski resort? On the other hand, I might be cutting off my nose to spite my face. I might be able to get the land at a good price. I suppose there isn't any harm in trying. The man's dead. I can't hurt *his* feelings.

"Bob, if you can do it tactfully, go ahead," Mitch said finally. "See what you can find out. Hey, wait a minute," he suddenly said. "I've never seen his land. I'm not sure that's such a hot idea."

"Let me at least try, Mitch. You're not making a firm commitment yet. You can run up to the property anytime in the next few days. And you'll see for yourself that it's very private. If you position the house right, you'll never even see the ski resort. What d' you say?"

Mitch clenched his eyes. "Well, I guess it's worth a look. Okay, okay." He opened them, the decision made.

Nat & Yanna Brandt

"And thanks for calling me about it. I appreciate it."

Mitch sat unmoving, his fingers poised once again over the keys of the typewriter. Here I am, writing about this poor guy's death and maybe going to benefit as a result of it. What kind of nutty world is this?

WHERE HAD THE day gone? The accident story was finished, copy-edited and already in type. Mitch had already seen the galleys and Ernie was busy working on a headline. Robin and Lyle's stories had just been dropped into his hopper, Rachel was en route to Waterbury ("The guy said he wouldn't give me names over the phone. Don't worry, I'll change into a skirt before I go"), and Maxine had long ago—was it before lunch or after?—stuck her head into his office to announce that the hospital said Ham Johnson's operation had gone off without a hitch. Ham was still in the recovery room and wouldn't be able to be reached until the evening at the earliest, but no complications were expected. "I'll check again in a couple of hours," Maxine had offered. All in all, a productive day.

He should be feeling good about things in general and with himself in particular, Mitch realized, then why did he so suddenly feel so uneasy? What had happened to put him on edge? Mitch reached into his hopper for Robin's story:

FESTIVAL

Summer

Musicians at the Mont Vert Music Festival expressed dismay yesterday over the untimely death of their colleague, Yuri Putzgarov. Many said he would be sorely missed during the season's chamber-music performances.

"This is a blow to us, a terrible loss," Herman Katz, administrator of the Festival, said. "We will make do, of course. The music must go on. But all of us are in a dreadful state of shock now."

Mr. Katz said that it was too early to know whether the Festival would attempt to replace Putzgarov on its roster of "master" musicians. There are a number of other violinists on the roster who might be able to take up the slack, he explained.

The three young musicians who joined Mr. Putzgarov in performing a Mozart quartet in the opening concert last Sunday said they were distraught by the violinist's passing. One, Kim Koo Son, said that she

Not bad, not bad at all, Mitch said to himself. That was good thinking to interview his co-performers. I've underestimated Robin. She's been given some lousy assignments. She deserves better. Mitch crossed out "passing," substituting instead the word "death" and wrote in Robin's byline. He was about to continue with her story when Lyle Timski poked his head in the door.

"Have you got to my copy yet, Mitch?"

"I'm about to, Lyle. Give me a minute. I'm just going over Robin's."

"Listen, there's something I have to tell you," Timski said, pressing.

"It'll have to wait. Ernie and Abe are hungry for more copy. I'll get back to you as soon as I've read your obit."

"Please, it's important," Timski persisted. He was getting upset, Mitch realized, which was not like the usually phlegmatic reporter.

Mitch made an annoyed face but put Robin's copy back into the hopper and took out Lyle's. "Okay," he said, "give me a minute to read your piece and I'll get back to you."

"I've got to talk to you, Mitch."

"All right already," Mitch said, starting to get annoyed. "I said I'd get back to you. I want to read your obit first. Get out of here."

Lyle's copy read well, too. As Mitch perused it, pencil in hand, he wrote in Lyle's byline and made some minor emendations:

PUTZGAROV PBIT

timski

by Lyle Timski

A private concert will be held tonight on the campus of Southborough College in memory of Yuri Putzgarov, second violinist with the Moskova Quartet and a participant in the Mont Vert Music Festival for the past ten years, who died Monday night in a car accident.

Mr. Putzgarov, 62, was known for his vibrant humor and high spirits. He was a popular figure among both concertgoers and younger musicians at the Festival. He recently appeared in a cowboy hat and jeans to play "Happy Birthday" at a party for one of them, an oboist from Texas.

Since his association with the Festival, Mr. Putzgarov has performed in at least five concerts during each summer season here in Southborough. He performed in a Mozart quartet last Sunday afternoon.

Mr. Putzgarov, a native of Kiev, Soviet Union, began studying the violin when he was six years old.

He came from a family of musicians. Both his father and two older brothers were pianists and had careers in Russia both before and after the Russian Revolution.

As a teenager, Mr. Putzgarov went to Berlin, Germany, to continue his studies. There he came under the influence of Otto Leopald, a controversial violin teacher who stressed technique and bowing over what he called "romantic" interpretations of the string literature of the 19th century.

Mr. Putzgarov's connection with Leopald was a fateful one. Many critics later faulted him for his emphasis on technique. "Sparks flew when he played," one reviewer wrote after a performance in New York's Town Hall, "but one wished some more attention had been paid to what Brahms had to say. The empathy was sadly missing."

It was this emphasis on technique that some music observers said was responsible for the fact that Mr. Putzgarov never had a distinguished solo career. He formed his own quartet, the Putzgarov Quartet, in the 1960s, but its concerts were limited to recital halls that he had rented and were not financially successful.

He abandoned the Putzgarov Quartet to join the Moskova Quartet in 1966, taking the role of second violinist. With it, he traveled each year throughout Europe and the United States. He also recorded with the Moskova Quartet.

Mr. Putzgarov immigrated to the United States in 1938 and made his home in New York City. He was briefly married to the ballet dancer Alicia Tolina in the 1940s. The couple had no children.

Mr. Putzgarov is survived by a niece, Mrs. Herbert Yablonski of Rye, N.Y.

No arrangements for a funeral service will be completed, according to Festival officials, until Mrs. Yablonski is contacted and an autopsy is performed in accordance with state police procedures.

#

Mitch pressed the intercom buzzer. "Have Lyle come in, will you."

Timski appeared almost immediately. He must have been waiting outside the door.

"Nice work, Lyle. It's topnotch."

"I can stretch it if you want, Mitch, but I'd only be laying the critical part on kind of thick."

"No, this is the right length for us." Mitch leaned back in his chair. "So what's up?"

"I hope you don't mind, Mitch, but I saw the galleys to your story on Ernie's desk and I took a look at them." Timski hesitated.

"And?"

"Well, that part about the alcohol . . ." Timski looked back over his shoulder. "Do you mind if I shut your door?"

What's all this? Mitch wondered to himself. "Go ahead."

Timski did so. He put both hands on Mitch's desk and leaned over toward him. "I can't believe he was drinking."

"Oh? Why?"

"Putzgarov is—was—a member of Alcoholics Anonymous."

"Who told you that?"

"Can we consider this confidential, Mitch?"

"Go on, Lyle. The door is closed. This is private."

"I'm in A.A. I have been for a couple of years now. They're really a very supportive group here in Southborough. Putzgarov's been with it ever since I can remember. Summers, I mean. He has a group in New York he goes to regularly in the winters."

Perhaps, Mitch thought to himself, that explains why Timski has chosen to stay in Southborough rather than move on to another job in a strange town. "If I understand correctly, Lyle," he said, "alcoholism is an addiction and lots of people backslide."

"I can't believe that about Putzgarov. He blamed drinking for the failure of his marriage, and despite his high spirits, he was really a very lonely man. He craved the attention. But he was still a dedicated AA advocate. He was sober for the past ten years. Why would he suddenly relapse now after all that? He'd never have touched a drop."

Mitch pursed his lips. "You're sure?"

"Dead certain—I'm sorry, that's a terrible way to put it."

"That memorial concert," said Mitch, "can you get us in?"

"Wednesday nights are usually reserved for groups that didn't get to perform on the weekends or to try out a new piece," Timski explained. "They're held in the dining room and are usually strictly for Festival participants. I've been asked now and then because they know I'm interested in music. Let me see if I can wangle us an invitation."

"Fine, see what you can do," said Mitch. "Well, they'll be doing an autopsy on Putzgarov. It'll be interesting to see what they come up with."

"But don't you see, Mitch?" Timski insisted. "If I'm right, if they don't find any alcohol in his blood, something's out of whack."

"I know," said Mitch, nodding slowly. "I've been thinking the same thing." And, he added to himself, I just can't shake the feeling that something sinister is at work here. Was he being melodramatic? How many times had Val told him, trust your instincts, don't ignore them? And his instincts said loud and clear: Putzgarov was murdered. But why?

NINE

Mitch had just finished a late dinner at home and was about to follow a routine from his days on the *Trib*. The next hour would be devoted to going over the day's paper with a sharp critical eye. How could he improve this small-town newspaper, shake it out of its comfortable complacency and bring in something distinctive, something that would set it apart from hundreds of papers exactly like it? Whoa, Mitch leaned back and smiled to himself, your ego is showing. You're only a temp, act like one, don't do anything to jeopardize Ham and his newspaper.

A thought surfaced and Mitch pushed it away. But it came creeping back. Mitch wanted to put his mark on this newspaper, he wanted to be more than a man passing through. He had been away from the firing line for six years and until this very moment, he had refused to admit to himself how profoundly he missed it.

His thoughts were abruptly interrupted by the sounds of a car. The driveway with its gravel surface made it almost impossible for anyone to sneak up on the house, but Mitch was so caught up in his thoughts that he didn't hear anything until a car door slammed shut and a few seconds later, the front doorbell rang.

Mitch went to the door and was caught completely off guard. He wasn't sure exactly who or what he expected, but he was certainly surprised to see Rachel standing at his doorstep.

"Rachel? What in the world are you doing here at this hour? Is something wrong?"

"Mitch, I'm sorry to come by so late but I was so excited about what I found out, I just couldn't wait until tomorrow morning." She smiled ingenuously.

Mitch was still standing at the door, debating with himself whether to ask her in. Rachel, noting his hesitation, pressed on.

"May I come in just for a moment? It won't take long. I promise you, it's worth it." She walked into the house, passing within an inch of Mitch, who was forced to step out of her way. At the last instant, her body brushed against him. Mitch's throat went dry.

He was angry with himself—and furious with Rachel. "Come into the kitchen and I'll give you some milk and cookies."

Rachel ignored his condescending tone. She laughed. "I'm not a child, Professor. What I would like is a glass of wine."

Reluctantly, Mitch turned and led the way into the kitchen. He opened the refrigerator and took out an open bottle of white wine. Rachel had sat down and crossed her legs, pulling the short skirt high above her knees. Mitch didn't see her movements until he turned to pour the wine in a glass. He stopped short, suddenly feeling vulnerable, alone at night in Ham's house with a young woman whose intentions were quite clear, or so it appeared. My God, Mitch thought, you do have ego problems. What makes you think she has any interest in you at all? You're old enough to be her father.

"Well, Rachel, what's so important it couldn't wait until tomorrow?"

Rachel leaned forward. "About a month ago, there was a big hunting scandal, just across the river in New Hampshire. It seems that with all the building, condos and the like that have been going up, a major development was put up right in the middle of what used to be prime hunting ground. In fact, one of the houses, at the outer edge of the development, was no more than twenty feet away from a thickly forested area.

"To make a long story short, a woman was shot and killed by a hunter right in back of her house. She wasn't even near the trees."

"Well, Rachel, that's certainly good material for our hunting backgrounder, but I don't see why that warrants a middle of the night visit, do you?"

"Wait a minute, Mitch, I haven't finished. That's only half the story. The other half, the most important point, is that the man who shot her wasn't indicted. Never mind tried and acquitted. He wasn't even indicted! Can you believe it, he murdered this woman in her front yard, and he gets off scot-free?

"You see what I mean, Mitch, the feelings about hunting run so deep in these communities that they take precedence over human life. They ended up blaming the victim because she was wearing dark clothes at the time. They said she should have known better and worn a bright vest outside during hunting season. It was dusk and the guy was shooting from nearly a mile away. I didn't even know that guns could fire that far, did you? I was told a lightweight .22 could—can you believe it! Anyway, what was the hunter to do? everyone said. Jeez, Mitch, it's just like rape victims in New York who get blamed for 'allowing' themselves to be attacked."

"Rachel, I can understand why you're upset, but this case only illustrates how hard we have to dig for all the facts before we take any position. What is the hunter's point of view about all this? Did the woman know the rules and ignore them? Is there another side?"

Rachel stared at him for a moment, stunned. "How can there be another side? A woman is dead and a man killed her carelessly. What defense can there be?"

"A good newspaper person can't afford to take sides, particularly before all the facts are in. Don't be so quick to make judgments." Mitch was well aware that in playing the devil's advocate, he was also throwing cold water on whatever prurient intentions Rachel may have had.

"Would you like to hear the other facts I've come up with?"

"It's late, Rachel, I'm sure they can wait until tomorrow." Mitch got up and walked to the door but Rachel didn't follow him. She stared at him provocatively. "I'm not really tired yet, Mitch. Can't we have another drink?"

Mitch was in no mood to be polite. "Look, Rachel, next time you have the desire to pay an unannounced visit, call first. We're all entitled to our privacy, and I wish you would respect mine."

Rachel brushed by him and walked to the front door. "I'm sorry I inconvenienced you, Mitch."

Mitch closed the door behind her, locked it and breathed a deep sigh.

* * *

DESPITE THE ALTITUDE, or maybe because of it, a summer day in Vermont without a cloud in the clear blue sky can be very hot. The sun blazes, and if there is no breeze, the day can become almost as sultry as one amidst the skyscrapers of New York. Driving past the municipal park in the morning of what was to be just such a day, Mitch could see a line of young children, towels and bathing suits tucked under their arms, waiting for the outdoor pool to open. They jostled each other, pushing and shoving and yelling. Later, as they played in the water, their screams would echo for miles around.

Curious, and feeling guilty about it, Mitch was up early again, driving to view Putzgarov's land before going to work. Most of the traffic on the road was headed in the opposite direction, toward the downtown area, as merchants and clerks rushed to their stores to prepare for Dollar Day on Saturday. The *Courier* had already run an advance story on the annual event. Every store in town would be participating. High Street was already being festooned with banners, one of which was draped across the middle, announcing the special sales day to motorists and pedestrians alike. As Maxine explained to Mitch, Southborough would be jammed with shoppers from New Hampshire and as far away as Wilmington and Putney. The event used to be called Penny Day, but, he shrugged, that of course was before inflation.

Mitch drew up a mental list of some clothing items he might shop for on Dollar Day as he turned into a back road and headed for the property. Passing the land where he had stumbled on Vera Tolvey's body, Mitch slowed suddenly. It was in those woods—now dense with summer foliage—that the body had lain for nearly six months. How would Val have felt about building a house right where he had found the body? How would he have felt? Would the image have always haunted him? Come to think of it, he said to himself, there's something macabre about my going to look at a piece of property whose owner has just died. Mitch stepped on the gas pedal and pulled away.

Not too far away and on the same side of the road, but farther along than he had ever traveled before, was a NO TRESPASSING sign with Putzgarov's name on it. The property's frontage on the road, Grant had told Mitch, ran for almost a hundred yards. Near where it should have ended, a double row of wooden stakes with orange ribbons on them ran from the road into Putzgarov's land. The two rows were about sixty feet apart, a strange narrow strip that didn't seem to make sense. Mitch pulled over, careful not to park too close to the ditch on the side of the road. Leaving the car without bothering to lock it, he followed the line of stakes as it ran into the property, bordering a line of fir trees.

It was still cool under the tall firs. As hot as the days might get in summer, nights in the mountains were always pleasant and sometimes downright chilly. Mitch trudged along until he came to an open field that was covered with small boulders and straggly, hard-to-get-rid-of juniper. Walking to the center of it, Mitch could see—off to his right—Mayors Peak. That meant the land he had hoped to purchase was to the south, beyond a thick belt of trees, and the ski resort to the east, beyond another clump of trees where the stakes ran. The property seemed secluded, nothing human in sight, but was it too close to the development? Mitch wondered. Would be it be noisy? Would there be a lot of traffic in the area? Where, in fact, was the access road to the resort? He suddenly realized he had a whole new set of questions to ponder if he was seriously going to consider this site as a possibility. The view was fine—the opposite, Mitch realized, of being in an oasis in the desert. Here the barren ground was in the center, the land surrounding it green with life. A house would go here nicely, of course, with a driveway shaded by trees reaching back to the road.

I suppose, he said to himself, it can't hurt to pursue this with Bob Grant. See if he can locate the niece, find out what she'd ask for the land if she didn't want it for herself. Hell, he rationalized, it's not ghoulish; it's business. I'll phone Bob today, he decided, as he started back toward his car.

RACHEL WAS WAITING for him as Mitch entered the newsroom. She was conservatively dressed in a blouse and cotton skirt. She had obviously taken his rebuke literally. Mitch greeted her and motioned for her to follow him into his office. He had had a long talk with himself after she left last night and realized that he had to stop letting this young woman unsettle him.

"You look like you're ready to burst," he said as he hung up his jacket and sat down, rolling up his sleeves. "Grab a chair and fill me in."

"First of all," Rachel began even before she was seated, "even though there are thousands of hunting permits issued each year by the state, there are actually very few accidents. In fact, you can't get a license unless you take a safety course. It's mandatory.

"And then there's more than just the deer season," she continued, speaking rapidly, the words fairly gushing from her. "I mean, deer aren't the only animals hunted. There's small game, too—grouse, rabbits, raccoons, wild turkeys. But with all that going, with all that shooting, the average number of accidents each year is about twelve. That's what it was last year and the year before, and both years only one of those dozen accidents was a fatality.

"Now get this, boss. It doesn't matter how old you are, anyone can get a hunting license. They told me it's guaranteed by the state constitution. All you got to do is pass that safety course. It's an eleven-hour course and they teach everything—even how to survive if you're caught in a forest after dark. Wait a minute, I think I have the brochure here they gave me about what they call 'defensive' turkey shooting."

As Rachel groped in her backpack, Mitch asked, "So Vera Tolvey is this year's fatality in Vermont?"

"Oh, I never thought to ask," Rachel said, looking up. Her embarrassment about not thinking to ask the question made her pause. "I wonder if she counts as last year's or this year's. I mean she was shot last fall but wasn't found until this spring. I could call up and find out," she offered.

"Later," Mitch said. "Go on, what else?"

"I can't seem to find that brochure. It's in here somewhere. Well, anyway," she said, abandoning her search and speaking rapidly again, "I've got all sorts of statistics for you going back to 1970. Half of the fatalities that have occurred over the years happen during deer season, but of all the accidents, nearly two out of every five are self-inflicted—a hunter stumbles and shoots himself, that sort of thing. Otherwise the victim either is mistaken for an animal or—"

"Whoa, hold it! You can put all that down on paper for me later, Rachel. What about someone to interview?"

She sighed. "The man up there who runs the Fish and

Wildlife Department had second thoughts about disclosing anything confidential. But wouldn't the *Courier* have carried the names of anyone injured in a hunting accident, or the name of a hunter who shot someone?"

"Depends," said Mitch. "If it was a local accident, I'm sure we did. If it wasn't, I don't imagine we did unless it involved a fatality. To be honest, I'm not sure, but you can check the files later."

"Well, anyway, the guy—Cal Doolins—told me that they usually find out who did the shooting. Most of the time, the person turns himself in. He said they get a guilt complex about it. But there are times when someone denies it, even when they're pretty sure that he's the only one who could have done it. I have to pursue this more with the Bureau of Criminal Investigation of the State Police. Doolins said they handled all the cases."

"Did he say anything about whether a hunter would know if he'd shot a person instead of an animal?"

"He sure did. He said a hunter would naturally look for the animal he'd downed. Otherwise, why shoot? He said he couldn't imagine that whoever shot Vera Tolvey didn't know he'd done it."

Mitch pursed his lips. "You're doing fine, Rachel," he said finally. "Keep on it. See what the State Police have to say. Check the files for a hunter or victim we can interview."

"I have an idea."

Mitch looked up. "Yes, what is it?"

"Well, you know the case I told you about last night? How about I interview the hunter who killed that woman? I know it's in New Hampshire, not Vermont, and the circumstances are different, but he could certainly give us the hunter's point of view you were talking about last night."

"That's a good idea, Rachel, but I still want you to keep looking for a Vermont hunter or someone who's been wounded by one that we can interview."

"Can I try writing the story myself?" Rachel asked.

Mitch hesitated. This was his story; Rachel was just the legman. On the other hand, he certainly had enough lately to keep him busy. "Okay, Rachel," he said, "it's yours. But before you put anything down on paper, talk to me first. And let's keep it simple. Like in class, nothing the ordinary reader won't understand. You can do it," he added, smiling.

Rachel left hastily, eager to continue her research. Mitch was about to go through his mail when Maxine entered the office. "Lyle asked me to tell you," she said, "that it's all set about going to that memorial concert tonight. He's out on a story, but if he misses you, he'll meet you there."

Mitch acknowledged the message with a nod. "Maxine, while you're here, could you drum up a map for me of the area around where that ski resort is going. Wouldn't we have something like that on hand?"

"We should. I'll check the morgue."

As she left the office, Mitch picked up the phone and dialed Bob Grant's office. The young real-estate agent had just walked in, he was told.

"Mitch, I was about to call you."

"Bob, I was up to the property you talked about this—"

"Forget it, Mitch," Grant said wearily. "I'm sorry I ever mentioned it to you."

"Why? What's happened?" Mitch asked as Maxine entered his office and put a folder on his desk. The edge of a map poked from it.

"It's sold. Can you believe it? It's sold already."

"Come on, Bob, you gotta be kidding. Putzgarov only died two days ago."

"His niece—someone got to her already. She hasn't signed anything, but she made it very clear that she'd given her word and wouldn't go back on it."

"Who?" Mitch asked. "Do you know who?"

"She was contacted by Bill Handler. He's a—"

"I know him, Bob. Who was he acting for?"

"She didn't bother to write down the name, Mitch. She said she figured she'd see it on the papers Handler sent her and what did it matter anyway?"

"Damn!" said Mitch. "What the hell is going on around here?"

"It's the ski resort. She said Handler told her that the buyer had something to do with the ski resort."

"God, you'd have thought they had enough land for the resort as it is," Mitch said. "And what I saw of the land, well it's all right to build a house there, but to do anything more you'd have to clear off a helluva lot of trees and boulders. That seems like a terrible expense."

"What can I tell you?" Bob said. "I'm sorry I got you into this one."

Mitch said good-bye to Grant and hung up. He drummed his fingers agitatedly on the desk, then noticed the folder Maxine had left. He opened it and took out the map. It was a property map dated 1986, indicating ownership of parcels in the area as well as roads and rights of way. He traced his finger along the road to locate the land that he'd originally been interested in. Abutting it was the land where the ski resort was going, and behind it, off the road that he had driven that morning and only a mile or so from a turnoff leading to Story Hill Road, where Putzgarov died, was the musician's property.

Mitch tried to figure out where Vera Tolvey's body had been found in relation to the surrounding properties. Doing so, he suddenly realized that the ski resort would have no access to the main road. The only way to it was through the tiny pony cart trail behind the property he'd lost to Troupe. But that was too narrow for car traffic and so far down at the base of the hill that it would be too costly to bulldoze and pave a proper road. No, the shortest way into the ski resort area was through Putzgarov's property. You could run a road along the woodline right into the resort without too much trouble; in fact, that was the only way that made sense. Of course, you'd need a right-of-way from Putzgarov. But wait a minute, Mitch said to himself, Putzgarov was part of the development group, wasn't he? And those two rows of stakes that I followed along the woodline that morning—mightn't they be the markers for the road? I wouldn't be surprised if the buyer was Troupe. He probably wants to assure himself access to the ski resort. Well, he picked up a nice plot to go with it. And he certainly moved quickly. I guess he had to protect his resort investment.

I wonder, he reflected, as he folded the map and put it back in the folder, whether there's a conspiracy to keep me and Val out of Vermont.

MITCH DROVE DIRECTLY to the Southborough College campus after turning over the newspaper to Ernie and Abe. He had eaten a sandwich at his desk while going over a remake of the front-page layout. He was bone tired after a full day of work—which he had finally realized he wasn't used to after a teacher's less rigorous hours. He had planned on visiting Ham, but Maxine told him the doctors were firm: no visitors other than immediate family for at least the next few days. Although Maxine had explained that Johnson didn't have any family, just friends, the nurse remained adamant. Rules were rules. Fortunately, Ham was doing much better than expected.

Timski was waiting for him by the administration office, waving his arm to make sure Mitch saw him. "I guess they decided to keep to the Wednesday night tradition. The concert's in the dining hall over this way," he said, leading Mitch up a short path to an ungainly-looking white clapboard building with a wooden canopy over its front steps.

"You're lucky, though," he continued as they mounted the steps into a small foyer off which was a room with a wall of open letter boxes. "I had supper with some of the musicians here earlier. They're a rowdy bunch. They threw things across the room at each other for fun. They told me *that* was traditional, too."

Inside the dining area, the tables had been folded and stacked against a wall. The chairs, folding ones like the chairs at the weekend concert, had been lined up in rows to face a slightly raised section of the room at the end. On it, two young men were arranging five music stands and chairs—the first piece would obviously be a quintet. The audience was meager—and noisy, especially a group Mitch took to be the children of some of the musicians. When Mitch commented on the sparse attendance, Timski explained, "The concerts always start a little late. Let me introduce you to a few people."

The reporter led the way back to a corner where a tall, wavy-haired man in his mid-forties was talking and gesturing to a pretty young woman with hair all the way down to her waist. "Forget it, my dear," he was saying, "a Tourte bow would be too costly, way out of line. If I were you, I'd—" He stopped as Timski came up. Timski apologized for interrupting and introduced Mitch.

"And Mitch, this is André Boudreaux. Like you, he's from New York, where he's an instrument maker and dealer, a famous one at that."

Boudreaux feigned humility, raising his hands as though to ward off the compliment. "You do me too much honor," he said, then told the young woman, "I'll speak to you after the concert about what you're looking for." As the young woman moved off, Boudreaux followed her with his eyes. "The young," he said, "want everything all at once. Can you imagine, she was asking me about a Tourte bow? Ridiculous."

Why ridiculous?" asked Mitch.

"A Tourte bow is—how would you say it?—it's like owning a Renoir or a Picasso. They're *très cher*. Unless that girl is a Rothchild, she cannot *begin* to afford it."

"Well, I know Strads are expensive," Mitch said, "but I didn't realize a bow was anything but a bow."

"Stradivarius, Amati, Guarnerius—they're all expensive," said Boudreaux, raising his eyebrows. "And a Tourte bow on top of that! They're worth thousands of dollars, *thousands*. You really have to be a Rothschild or," he raised his shoulders, "a successful musician, to afford one."

"You mean like a Heifetz?"

"Or a Putzgarov," said Boudreaux. He said it matter-of-factly, realizing only after he spoke that his words might sound less than respectful of the dead musician. "Yuri—bless his soul—was about to have his dream come true."

"How's that?" Mitch asked, his curiosity whetted as soon as Putzgarov's name was mentioned.

"Every year, every time he comes into my shop," Boudreaux said, his hands moving expressively, "you know, to have his bow rehaired or his violin repaired, he tells me, 'Andre, *mon ami,* a Stradavarius, someday I must have a Stradavarius.' And he was having one."

"What do you mean?" Mitch persisted.

"He was about to purchase a Strad from me," the instrument dealer said. "A beautiful Strad—lovely neck, a resonant tone. I was representing a private patron who was selling it for some sort of tax reason. Yuri was going to give me the deposit this week—that's one of the reasons that I am up here at the Mont Vert."

"I don't mean to pry," Mitch said, "but how much does a Strad go for nowadays?"

"I can't tell you the price that Yuri was going to pay, that wouldn't be right," Boudreaux said. "But our friend Lyle here knows what they are worth."

"If it's in tiptop condition, Mitch, and the provenance is clear and unquestioned," Timski said, "you're talking about as much as three quarters of a million dollars, maybe even more."

This time it was Mitch's turn to raise his eyebrows. "Wow! That's quite a hunk of money."

"He probably was going to pay it off over a period of time," Timski explained, looking at Boudreaux, who nodded in agreement. "But still, he'd have to put down a substantial deposit."

The bell sounded. They all turned to see people scrambling for seats. "We better grab our places before it's too late," Timski said.

Mitch shook hands with Boudreaux and followed Timski down the far side of an aisle until they found two of seats together. As they sat, Mitch couldn't help wondering where Putzgarov—second violin in an only moderately successful quartet—could get the kind of money needed to buy a Stradavarius.

His thoughts were interrupted as applause filled the dining hall. Five informally dressed young musicians were walking onto the stage from a side door. They took their places at the music stands, sat down and began tuning their instruments. When they were ready, the first violin, a short, thin, tense young man stood up. "This piece—this concert," he corrected himself, "is dedicated to our dear teacher and fellow musician, Yuri Putzgarov. He shall always be in our thoughts. We should like to ask you to stand for a moment of silence in his memory."

There was a thunderous scraping of chairs as everybody rose, heads bowed, in silence. Putzgarov, Putzgarov, Mitch wondered, when did you become a Rothschild?

TEN

D<small>OLLAR</small> D<small>AY</small>. Clowns and jugglers stood in the gutter—parking on High Street was prohibited—entertaining youngsters as their parents pored over boxes of clothing and sundry items or pulled shirts and blouses off racks that lined the sidewalk in front of Southborough's stores. Navigating through the crowds and stalls was a tiresome chore, especially as the day wore on and the hot sun became more oppressive. Car traffic on High Street leading to and from the municipal parking lot was at a virtual standstill, reminding Mitch of the worst of New York City's rush-hour jams. Everyone seemed to be carrying packages and shopping bags; teenage girls eagerly displayed their bargain fashions, while their male counterparts struck poses for each other showing off new baseball hats or T-shirts emblazoned with the names of professional ball teams.

Two days had passed since the memorial concert for Putzgarov, two days in which Mitch had felt harried by the press of time. It had taken him four hours to make the round trip on Thursday to Ham Johnson's bedside at the hospital in Hanover. He had gone up the next day, too, first thing in the morning, after seeing how poorly Ham had looked. He had been so physically worn by the operation that he hadn't even bothered to ask Mitch about the *Courier*—and that, in itself, had worried Mitch, prompting him to return. By Friday, some of Ham's anxiety had been reawakened: Had Mitch made out the vacation schedule yet? (Mitch had, indeed, forgotten.) Had he remembered to tell Mitch to have the annual Grange clambake covered? (No, he hadn't.) Did Maxine file the state insurance forms yet? (Mitch would ask.) Johnson's questions had made Mitch feel positively relieved. Knowing that Maxine, Ernie and Abe were planning to visit Ham over the weekend, Mitch had decided to spend Saturday morning shopping before driving to Williamstown to see Val in a play that night.

Mitch had to nudge by a group of shoppers hovering over a display rack of hand-woven winter sweaters ("$25 each, 2 for $45") to get into Ben's General Store. As he waited at the open door for a couple to exit, Mitch casually glanced down the block. Walking out of the First State Bank were Bert Lester and Brad Cummings. What was the bank doing open on a Saturday? Looking grim, Cummings waited as Lester locked the door. When Lester turned to join Cummings, Mitch saw that the bank president, too, looked grim. He began wondering why when he felt a shove behind him. A teenager was trying to wiggle by him to get into the store. Mitch gave the youngster an annoyed stare and entered the shop.

The scene inside was less hectic, though cases with sales signs on them each drew a beehive of people. Ben himself, a slight man wearing bifocals, stood beside a cashier, surveying the scene, a benign look on his face.

Even before Mitch could ask for help, Ben offered, "Somethin' I can helpya with, mister?"

Mitch asked where boots were sold. Instead of pointing out the section devoted to footwear, Ben, bored with his tour of duty by the register, came around the counter. "Come on, I'll show ya."

Leading the way, Ben squeezed by a farmer and his wife who were contemplating the purchase of a new checkered shirt. Mitch followed as Ben made for a pair of wooden stairs that led to the basement. "We keep the heavy-duty stuff down this way," Ben said as they creaked their way down the steps.

Every bit of basement wall was covered with overalls, rubber rainwear, goosedown jackets and vests. An assortment of hats and caps hung from nails. Woolen blankets were stacked atop one counter, next to a pile of knapsacks. Off to the side, on sloping shelves, were boots and shoes meant for hard work—heavy, square-toed, lace-up items that were made to withstand abusive wear. Above them, draped over a hanger, was a fluorescent orange vest and cap.

"Is that for hunting?" asked Mitch, pointing to the vest.

"Yup," said Ben. "We call that color hunter orange. Is that what you're looking for? I thought you wanted boots."

"No, just interested. Let's see what you have for a rainy day that I can wear in the summer without getting too sweaty."

Ben started to pull down a pair of fawn-colored low boots with rubber soles, but Mitch's attention was still focused on the orange vest. Seeing it reminded him of what Bob Grant had said: All real-estate agents carried such vests their cars in case they had to walk into the woods on a property. If that were so, Mitch thought as Ben passed him one of the boots for consideration, where was Vera Tolvey's vest? She certainly hadn't been wearing one.

"What'd you say?" asked Ben.

"Just talking to myself," said Mitch, unaware he had said anything aloud. "You sell many of those?" he asked, pointing to the vest.

"To everyone and his brother."

"The *Courier* ran a story about hunting safety yesterday."

"Yup. Good story," replied Ben.

Rachel Beldon's story was cram-packed with everything the young intern had been able to find. Everything, that is, but an interview with either a victim or a hunter who had shot someone. The one hunter they could identify—the one from New Hampshire—absolutely refused to be interviewed. It rankled Mitch that they had been unable to track another hunter down. Rachel, however, was beside herself with joy: Her byline, her very first. Mitch put her story on the front page and then jumped it to the bottom of page ten, the editorial page:

HUNTING IN VERMONT: WHAT HAPPENS WHEN THE VICTIM IS NOT AN ANIMAL

by Rachel Beldon

Each year someone dies. Each year almost a dozen people are injured. And each year the State Fish and Game Department urges hunters to be careful.

"Actually hunting accidents have been reduced since the Legislature in Montpelier enacted the safety law which went into effect in 1975," says Cal Doolins, director of the bureau.

That law requires that every hunter be certified as having passed an 11-hour safety course given by trained instructors. Such a course is given in Southborough by the local chapter of the National Hunters Federation.

Despite the training, which stresses that hunters be sure of their target before firing, accidents listed as "Victim mistaken for game" occur with regularity throughout the hunting season.

Similarly, despite instructions about how to carry a rifle or shotgun, and despite warnings about moving about in a forest with a loaded firearm, there are always accidents listed as "Hunter stumbled and fell."

"No matter how much we try," said Doolins, "you've got to realize that there're going to be accidents. We can't control a hunter once he's passed the course, got his certificate and picks up his permit. Then it's up to him to use his head."

Outside of the mandated safety course, Vermont has no restrictions on who can acquire a hunting permit. As the state training guide for instructors says:

"Because Vermont does not have a minimum-age requirement for purchase of a hunting license, there is no way we can restrict a person from entering into a program. If the instructor feels that the person is too young to handle a firearm or is unable to read and to take a written examination, he should tell that person at the beginning of the program that he will not be certified."

A companion guide for instructors notes that "a variety of learning problems" may be encountered by an instructor. Such problems include "slow learners, non-readers, foreign citizens with poor English, hearing or seeing disabilities and physical disability."

"These students," the guide continues, "are entitled to hunt as much as anyone else and we owe it to them to do what we can to serve them. . . . Students are not to be failed because the instructor could not adapt to their disabilities. It is the State's responsibility to ensure that proper instruction is offered."

"You've got to realize," said a bureau employee who asked not to be identified, "that Vermonters believe that hunting is a right and privilege that dates back to the time when you had to feed your family without the benefit of grocery stores and supermarkets. It was a matter of survival then. And that tradition is embedded in the state constitution.

"Personally," he continued, "I think the state goes overboard in defending that right."

Mitch's accompanying editorial had picked up on that theme:

WHAT'S CONSTITUTIONAL ABOUT MURDER?

Vera Tolvey's tragic death in a hunting accident was, of course, a shock to everyone in the community. We shook our heads and said, "It shouldn't have happened." And there we lay the regrettable incident to rest.

Should we leave it at that? Isn't there a lesson to be learned? Does Vera Tolvey's death mean nothing?

Next year, if the statistics compiled by the State Fish and Game Department continue to hold up, someone else will die—at least one person—and many others will be wounded. Whom are we kidding? We have licensed murderers and we are encouraging mayhem.

Those Vermonters who believe a sacred right is involved should not dismiss what is also a sacred duty: the responsibility to protect human life. There are alternatives to the current law that would ensure. . . .

Writing editorials was a fine way to blow off steam, and a unique opportunity for a newspaperman like Mitch to get his opinions off his chest—he'd never had that opportunity as a reporter or editor—but he couldn't help but wonder whether editorials had any real effect. Did they really change people's minds, influence policy, as they did before instant public-opinion polls captured the attention of public officials and politicians? Did anyone even bother to read them?

Ben was looking at him, curious. "You want to try it on?"

Mitch looked down at the boot in his hand, shaken from his reveries. "It's a little heavy for summer. Do you have something lightweight?"

Ben began to search the shelves.

"I was wondering," Mitch said as Ben proffered another boot to him, "whether you picked up some sales as a result of that hunting article."

Ben looked thoughtful for a moment. "Nope, can't say as we sold any vests at all yesterday or today. Whoever needs one mostly has one."

"Did you ever sell one to Vera Tolvey?"

"That real-estate lady that got herself kilt? Hell, I

don't keep track of that sort of thing. Want this pair, mister?"

Mitch made a mental note to have Rachel check with the police on whether they had ever found an orange vest in Vera Tolvey's car, or her home. In spite of Rachel's research, in spite of what had happened in New Hampshire, he was increasingly plagued with the gnawing thought that Vera Tolvey's death was murder.

WILLIAMSTOWN IN WINTER is a lazy campus town, the site of Williams College and a fine art museum, but not much else other than a typical New England village green. In summer, though, the scene literally changes. As the campus hibernates, the town comes alive with summer visitors and theatergoers. Motels and inns in the area fill up, restaurants require reservations, and a steady stream of traffic flows around the intersection of Routes 2 and 7, bringing out-of-staters from north, south, east and west. The Playhouse is home for one of the country's most famous summer-stock companies, one that young dramatic students are willing to work for as set painters and gofers from dawn to dusk without pay. Shakespeare, revivals, a musical, sometimes an original work—the schedule each year is designed to give a handful of professional acting "names" a chance to play a variety of roles. Those fortunate few who work with them—even the interns who labor on the scenery—can afterward proudly put on their resumés that they have participated there.

For Val, one of the "name" actors, Williamstown provided a welcome return to the stage after working on two films. "It's not the same, Mitch, not by a long shot. Don't get me wrong, movies have their place."

"They certainly pay well," Mitch noted.

"And for a good reason," she said. "You sit around for hours, waiting for a set-up, and then, all of sudden, you walk in front of a camera and have to assume a part, an emotion, a reaction out of thin air without any continuity. That's tough work, meboy."

"And pays well," he repeated.

Val threw a pillow at him. "You're in one of your moods, Mitch. One of your financial moods. I can tell."

"No, not at all, honey. You were saying?"

"I was saying," said Val, patting her hair dry with a towel, "that acting on a stage is—well, to me anyway—it's a breath of fresh air. I come alive. For all the money that I can make on a film, I'd still choose the stage."

"Now let me get this straight," said Mitch in a teasing mood, "you would rather get all sweated up under glaring kleig lights, bite your fingernails over the possibility of forgetting your lines, and face the wrath of a live audience than be a Hollywood starlet?"

Val aimed another pillow at him. "I'm hardly a starlet at my age and you know it." Mitch reached for her as she passed by the bed to go into the bathroom. "Nothing doing, Mr. Stevens. I have to perform tonight."

"How about an undress rehearsal?"

"Your juices are flowing tonight, aren't they?"

"Val, sweetheart, it's very lonely up in Southborough. At least here you are surrounded by friends and fellow actors. I don't have much going for me in Southborough, especially now that Ham is in the hospital."

"He'll be out soon, Mitch."

"Sure, and then he might be stuck at home with a nurse until he's fully recuperated. That'll be like living in a nursing home with him."

Val sat on the edge of the bed and reached for Mitch's hand. "Something's troubling you. What is it?"

"I don't feel comfortable in Southborough, but I'm not at all sure I can explain why," he said, sitting up on the bed. "There's something going on that makes me uneasy."

"Tell me about it," she urged.

"There are too many coincidences," he began. "First Vera Tolvey's death—"

"An accident, Mitch."

"An accident on property that one of the guys behind the ski resort then buys. Then that professor who helped them keels over. And now that violinist Putzgarov. He was in with the bunch behind the development and it was through his land that the resort was going to have a right of way. Three people dead and all connected with that ski resort—that's an awful lot of coincidence."

"Mitch, you're in a small town. There are bound to be things that are coincidental. Everybody knows everybody. You know your neighbors. There are connections just because it is a small town. They're flukes."

Mitch rubbed his cheeks with his hands. "I'm not satisfied with that for an answer," he said.

Val sat back, studying her husband. "Mitch, why not leave well enough alone?" Val laughed. "Now why did I say that? You never have and you never will. If I haven't accepted that by now, I'm in deep trouble."

Mitch took her hand and held it tightly. "There are some things I just have to find out."

"So go ahead and find out," Val said, pushing his feet off the bed. "Get it out of your system. Just don't get into any trouble. I don't want to have to worry about you every time you leave home."

"Val, honey, most of the time my life is so quiet and staid you could build a library around me."

"More like a boudoir. Right now, drag your can off my

bed. I want to rest my eyes for a few minutes before going to the theater."

"There's room for two, Val," Mitch said, squirming to the other side of the bed.

"There will be later tonight, but not now. Scat."

"All right for you, Valerie Stevens," Mitch said as he pushed himself off the bed. "And when you enter as Lady Macbeth in Act I and hear someone in the audience hissing, you'll know who it is."

"RACHEL. IT'S ME, Mitch. I'm sorry to bother you on a Saturday night." It was intermission at the theatre and Mitch felt restless and on edge. Finally, cursing himself for being unable to forget the paper for even one night, he decided to call Rachel.

"That's okay, boss. You caught me on my way out to grab a bite to eat. I don't mind your calling, Mitch."

"I'm in Williamstown," he added. He leaned against the wall of the pay phone, watching as the crowd in the lobby grew. "Was Tiny Adams any help?"

"Well, he checked the police file for me but he said there was no indication of any vest in her car at all, nothing unusual in fact."

"Did he have any idea when the Putzgarov autopsy is scheduled for?"

"He thinks it's Monday."

The violinist's body had been sent to Burlington to the Chief Medical Examiner's office, and they were backed up.

"So there's nothing new?" Mitch asked, hoping there was.

"Well," Rachel said, "yes. There's going to be an emergency meeting of the Board of Selectmen Monday night. Abe heard about it while he was buying a toaster at the appliance store. I bumped into him on the street afterwards."

"Did he have any idea what it was about?"

"No, he just said he heard Brad Cummings talking about it on the phone to someone. No wait, he did hear Cummings mention the name Britfair."

"I thought you had to give the public notice of a meeting."

"Abe said they could run an ad in our Monday morning edition that would cover the situation technically if it's really an emergency. And the radio station would pick up on it, wouldn't it?"

Mitch thanked Rachel and hung up. An emergency meeting of the Board? To approve the re-zoning of the tract that Cummings, Troupe, Lester, Haye and Handler were trying to get Britfair interested in? An emergency meeting was a handy device to push through such a motion. Unscheduled, short notice, too quick for any opposition to organize and prepare for. I'd like to cover it myself, Mitch thought, but that would be unethical, considering that I was part of that dinner meeting with the Britfair people. No, I'll put Robin on it—but I'll go, too, out of curiosity.

Mitch checked his ticket and followed the throng returning to their seats. He hadn't seen *Macbeth* since his student days. It was a veritable bloodbath of a tragedy. How many murders were in it . . . ?

ELEVEN

THE SUN WAS starting to set as Mitch walked up the wooden steps of the Town Hall. A few high, billowy clouds were turning from pink to purple. The streetlights along High Street began to come on, though it was not yet dark enough for them to have much effect.

Mitch expected he would be one of the few on hand for the emergency meeting of the Board of Selectmen. He turned at the sound of a foot scraping a board, surprised to see a middle-aged man in overalls helping an old woman up the steps. And inside the lobby stood groups of other people: some obviously had come straight from work, others were more casually dressed. He was surprised that the Assembly Room was already half filled with people even though the meeting had been scheduled on such short notice. The town's grapevine was obviously very efficient. Several barrel-chested men in checkered shirts and baseball caps with company logos stood talking by their chairs, while their wives sat chatting animatedly. Every so often they would wave amiably as another man in a similar shirt and cap entered the room with his wife. Near the front was a group that Mitch recognized—mostly shopkeepers and tradespeople from Main Street. The two groups stayed pretty much to themselves—the salt cellar and the pepper grinder from Ham Johnson's lesson on Southborough politics. Where then, he wondered, was the cruet of olive oil—the "money" interests? Come to think of it, Mitch mused, you can make a decent salad dressing out of salt, pepper and olive oil, but you have to have some vinegar, too. Where was the vinegar—the gentrified hippie element? Wouldn't they be interested in such ecology issues such as zoning and land use?

Mitch turned his head when one of the old, dark brown wooden folding chairs scratched the floor with a high sound that pierced through the jumble of voices. The cause of the noise, he saw, was a serious-looking young brunette dressed in a beige suit and white blouse who was carrying a large portfolio of papers. She began searching through the papers as soon as she was seated, causing Mitch to wonder briefly who she was and what the papers contained. Then a tableaux behind her caught his attention. Coming out of a side door were three men dressed in business suits whom he recognized instantly. As each entered the Assembly Room, even at this distance, Mitch could discern the visible reaction. They were obviously as surprised as Mitch was to see the number of people who had turned out. The three men—John Haye, Bert Lester and Harvey Troupe—began talking excitedly amongst themselves. Troupe, the tallest of the trio, constantly looked over the shoulders of the others, assessing the crowd. Lester fidgeted nervously until finally Haye touched his arm in an effort to calm him down. Mitch watched them arguing. Troupe's face was reddening in anger. Lester had thrown up his hands in despair. Only Haye seemed to remain in control of himself. He leaned toward the others, seeming to talk soothingly. Troupe was shaking his head now, accepting something Haye had said, albeit reluctantly. Lester nodded approval, too. A few more words were exchanged and then they broke up, Haye walking down the outer aisle and taking a seat in the ninth row, Lester taking one on the other side in the eighth row, and Troupe walking down the center aisle and taking a chair in the front row. Apparently, Mitch guessed, they did not want to appear associated with one another. Each nodded to the persons seated nearby as he sat down but otherwise seemed wrapped in his own thoughts.

Mitch checked his watch. It was already a few minutes after eight o'clock, and latecomers began to crowd the doorway to get in. The Assembly Room, he now had time to notice, was a large, high-ceilinged chamber with enough space to accommodate as many as three hundred chairs, and a narrow dais on which a long table rested. A wainscot of dark wood circuited its walls, which were painted a light green. The ceiling of embossed tin, dating back to when the building had been built a century earlier, was also painted green. The only adornments in the otherwise sparse room were two flags, a Vermont one and the Stars and Stripes, which stood in opposite corners behind the table on the dais, and several faded oil paintings of former selectmen, all of whom sported a beard of one sort or another. They made Mitch think of Brad Cummings and his Vandyke.

Mitch spotted Robin Summer off to the side in the front row, talking to Lyle Timski. He walked over to them. "What're you doing here, Lyle?" he asked.

"I wouldn't miss this for a million dollars," said Timski,

looking up at Mitch. "This is old-time democracy at work. Won't you join us?" he asked, patting the chair next to him.

"No thanks," said Mitch, "I think I'll hang back in the rear. This is Robin's story. You can do me a favor, though, Lyle."

"Go ahead," the reporter said.

"Sit with me once the meeting gets started. You can identify some of the people if I don't know who they are."

"No problem," Timski said cheerily. "It'll be like calling a mass wrestling match."

Mitch wandered back to the rear. More people were entering the room now, searching for friends or empty seats. The hum of voices rose in volume until suddenly a chorus of shushes spread throughout the audience as the selectmen came onto the dais from a back door.

Brad Cummings took the center seat on the dais and started banging a gavel. His face flushed, he half rose out of his chair, calling out in a loud, booming voice, "Please, everybody, take your seats, get yourselves settled so that we can get going. We don't want to keep you folks here any longer than necessary."

There was one last round of disruption as another group of latecomers sat down. Timski searched the audience until he spotted Mitch and sat down beside him.

Cummings waited impatiently until the noise died down. There he goes, Mitch thought, scratching his scar again. Cummings stood. "We've called this emergency meeting because the town is faced with having to make a sudden and very important decision. I am pleased that, despite the short notice, so many of you have been able to make it here tonight."

Cummings paused, looked around the room, stroked

his beard. There was a murmur of voices from the audience. "Hold on, now," Cummings said. "I'm going to ask Harvey Troupe to explain what this is all about. Let's give him a chance. Harvey, as you know, is the developer behind the ski resort going up out Mayors Peak way. We are very fortunate that he was able to make it here to explain the urgency of the situation. Harvey?"

Troupe stood up in the front row, cool, calm, in control again. "Thank you, Brad, and the rest of your board," he began, looking at them. He took a deep breath and turned to face the audience. "You people, I know, realize what the ski resort is going to do for Southborough in terms of jobs and revenue. I won't belabor the point because we all know what the benefits are going to be—and you've been very supportive of me and my colleagues in this."

"Well, now," Troupe went on, "Southborough has another unique opportunity, one that will really make it the center of commerce and business in southern Vermont. Britfair Enterprises—one of the nation's most respected firms—has decided it would like to locate a major outlet and warehouse right here in Southborough."

A round of rushed whispers greeted Troupe's words. The developer continued, ignoring the noise, talking quickly and forcefully on what the location of the Britfair store in Southborough would do for the community. "And when all is said and done," he declared, "those two elements together, the ski resort and the Britfair outlet, will make Southborough a boom town.

"Now, why I am here tonight is that the land where Britfair wants to put its store is just across from SkiLand. That land is zoned for residential or farm use. If Southborough is to reap this harvest of prosperity, that land has to be re-zoned for commercial purposes—that, and a piece just next to it that has an access way to the resort."

"So what the devil is the rush?" shouted a man in overalls and a checkered shirt from a back row.

("Who's that?" Mitch asked Timski.

The reporter shrugged. "I've never seen him before.")

"The rush, sir," said Troupe, "is that Britfair made one condition to its move here: that we decide immediately on the re-zoning issue so that the company has time to construct its outlet and warehouse before next winter. Speed is essential to them. I have been told that if Southborough doesn't make up its mind about re-zoning soon, Britfair will go elsewhere, at a backup location they have already chosen."

"Now hold it right there, mister," said another man in overalls and checkered shirt. He stood up, not bothering to take off his cap. ("That's Ben Ward," Timski whispered. "He's head of the local Grange.") "We gave that resort of yours our okay a year ago. I don't know if anyone else remembers, but all those parcels up there were once part of the Wynman property way back. Then that there hippie community took over in the sixties and ran it as a commercial farm until that dreadful fire killed the fella who owned it. We never did find out who set that fire."

Sounds of "Come on, Ben, let's get on with it," came from the crowd.

"Okay, folks, I jest thought it might be good for us all to be reminded of the history of that land.

"When you came to us about SkiLand, Mr. Troupe, it didn't seem we really had much choice, since the hippies had really been running a business for years. And I guess we all thought the community could use the tax boon. You promised us then that the ski resort would stick to a rural look and retain the character of our area. And that was the end of your development plans for the land. What happened to that promise?"

Before Troupe could answer, an elderly woman rose two rows ahead of the farmer. "I remember, Ben, I remember," she said. "And I remember what my husband Will said, too. What's going to happen to those of us who live up thataway? Can you imagine the traffic? I'm scared enough now of driving that area when a gravel truck comes barreling down the road."

"Let me explain," Troupe said, trying to sound patient, but his voice, Mitch felt, had a hard edge. "The road there will be widened—at least that's my understanding," he said, turning slightly to the Board of Selectmen. "Every precaution will be taken to ensure that congestion will be held to a minimum. The Board—so I'm informed—is already considering approaching the state highway department for advice on that. Rest assured," he said, "that the idea is to benefit everyone in Southborough."

Bert Lester stood up. "If I may, Mr. Troupe," the diminutive banker said. The developer nodded and sat down. "Mrs. Thorpe, I understand your concern, just as I understood Will's concern back then. But let me put it in terms that perhaps some of you who've had mortgages with my bank will appreciate." Lester laughed softly. " 'Appreciate'—that's the key word. Your property, your neighbor's property, the land all around for miles, property that some folks have been paying taxes on for years without even thinking it could be productive, all that land is going to appreciate considerably if Britfair locates up that way. Mark my word on that. Let me be candid about it: If not you, then certainly your heirs will appreciate that."

"If I may say something." John Haye rose from the

opposite aisle. "I am concerned—as you all know my ancestors have been for more than a century—with making Southborough a vital, thriving community. Not just for the landowners who might be affected by this kind of circumstance—though more power to them if they can enjoy that kind of benefit. But I'm really concerned with what it means for all of us at large." Haye turned to the Board. "I see the settlement of Britfair in Southborough as a stabilizing influence for the entire area and I urge you to approve the variance with all possible urgency. We don't want to become another Windsor. We don't . . ."

("What's he talking about?" Mitch asked Timski.

"Up the Connecticut River from here. Windsor, Vermont. It's one of the few towns in the state to lose residents in the seventies because two companies moved out. They each employed a thousand workers. Hell, Windsor went down to about four thousand souls. It practically died.")

". . . and so as far as I'm concerned," Haye concluded, "the answer is diversity. A ski resort—yes. But what if it doesn't snow much some winter? You remember the winter of eighty-five–eighty-six. We all talked about what a mild winter that was, and thanked the Lord. But we're not going to thank the Lord if it puts a kibosh on Southborough's success. We need diversity, and a Britfair does that for us. It complements the ski resort."

The young woman with the portfolio jumped up. "Mr. Selectmen, I'm from the state chapter of the National Environmental Protection Organization. NEPO represents concerned citizens throughout Vermont. I'd like, if I may, to read to you from a newspaper article that appeared recently in a national newspaper with the headline, 'Fears Rise Over Vermont Land Deals.'"

Cummings banged his gavel. "I don't know, miss, if we have time to have an entire article read to us. Perhaps you'd like to leave it with us to read afterwards."

"No," she insisted, "I can't do that, but let me read the first few paragraphs," and before Cummings could protest again, she began:

" 'Environmentalists are warning that land speculation in Vermont could have serious social and environmental consequences for the state if it is allowed to continue unchecked.

" 'And, they say, the potential threat is exacerbated by gaps in state regulations that allow developers to buy large areas of undeveloped land and divide them up for sale as building lots without state review.

" 'What we're facing, according to a leader of a conservation advocacy group, is loss of wildlife habitat, the destruction of large parcels of farmland and a drain on town services. If . . .' "

"Thank you, miss," said Cummings, gaveling again. "We get the drift of the message. And let me say," he added, looking out at the audience, "that we plan to take all those factors into account."

"But—" the woman protested. Before she could say anything further, Cummings pointed with his gavel toward an outstretched arm in the middle of the audience. "Clyde, you want to say something?"

("I don't remember his last name," Timski whispered, "but he's from the Grange, too. Ben must have put out the word to all the farmers in the neighborhood.")

"Brad, you and the other selectmen know this is going to mean more expenses for the town, too. It's not all going to be gravy."

Cummings didn't respond. He pointed again with his gavel to another raised hand. It was another farmer. He stood up slowly. "What I don't understand is how even the ski place passed the perc test. All those sites there and now you want to put a Britfair in that area . . ."

("What's a perc test?" Mitch whispered.

("The perc—perculator test—is a way of testing land for proper drainage. For waste. It's required for a building permit on any parcel of land under ten acres, and any land at all used for commercial development. Vermont's the granite state, you know. There's lots of land right smack on top of solid rock ledges with nowhere for runoff to go. It affects the drinking water.")

"Luke," Cummings was saying, "the perc tests are not the Board's business. The ski resort property passed those tests as far as we know. It must've, or Mr. Troupe couldn't be building on it."

Harvey Troupe stood up again. "Mr. Cummings, if I may." He turned toward where the farmer sat. "Sir, we are following every state—and town—regulation to the letter. We have to and we want to. We would be fools to do anything that would jeopardize our investment."

"I'd like to ask a question."

("I recognize him," Mitch said to Timski. "He runs the drug store on High Street.")

"Go ahead, Wilbur."

"That gentleman over there brought it up. What is all this going to mean to Southborough? I don't mean the benefits, I mean the costs. What will we—the town—have to do?"

"Well, Wilbur, we can't pinpoint everything at this time," said Cummings. "Mr. Troupe mentioned widening the road, but we don't have a checklist as yet. However, whatever we do we reckon will be more than offset by tax revenues."

"That can't be true." A middle-aged woman in a plain

blue dress was on her feet. "Brad Cummings, you know that can't be the case . . ."

("Dottie Cahill," said Timski. "She's head of the Parents Association. A formidable lady.")

". . . and how many new schools will the town have to build to house all the children that all these new families are going to bring with them? And how much is the staff for those schools going to cost the town? We're not talking about widening a road here or there. That's peanuts, a one-time expenditure. We're talking about maintaining an expanded school system."

There was an audible rumble of agreement throughout the audience as she went on: "Look at what's happened to one of our neighbors in this state—and you all know what town I mean. They've got empty schoolhouses now—beautiful, large, modern, up-to-date empty buildings. We don't need that either."

("Can I address the meeting?" Mitch asked.

("Why not?" said Timski. "Troupe's an outsider.")

Mitch stood up. "Mr. Chairman—Mr. Cummings. I'd like to ask a question."

There was a rustle of movement as everyone turned in their seats. Taken aback by Mitch's appearance at the town meeting, Cummings looked from side to side, waiting for one of his colleagues on the Board to say something, not knowing what to answer himself. When, at last, an older man in steel-rimmed glasses shrugged his shoulders, Cummings said, "Go ahead, Mr. Stevens."

"You've identified Mr. Troupe as the developer of the ski resort. Am I correct in thinking Mr. Troupe would also be the builder of the Britfair outlet?"

"Yes, that's our understanding," said Cummings. He searched the audience, hoping to find another hand raised, but Mitch was still standing, and still talking.

"Does Mr. Troupe have partners in this venture?"

"I'm sure he must, Mr. Stevens," said the selectman. "It's quite a large venture."

"Is the Board aware of who those partners are?"

"I'm not sure it's the Board's business," said Cummings. He started to scratch his beard nervously. "All the legal work and permits are being made in the name of Mr. Troupe's company."

"Mr. Cummings, a point of order." It was John Haye. The publisher stood up, facing the Board. "The question we are here to consider in this emergency meeting is a simple one, but we don't have all night. Nor is it necessary to belabor the issue with irrelevancies. Britfair is merely asking for a zoning variance. We don't have to know how much they're willing to spend on putting up their outlet. It is not our business to know what Mr. Troupe's profit on that might be. Nor is it our business to know who his backers are as long as he or his company is taking responsibility for all the legal and statutory requirements." He turned around to face Mitch. "Certainly there will be profit. For Britfair, we hope. For Mr. Troupe, of course. But we all hope to profit. We want Southborough to profit. That is not the question." The publisher turned back to the Board. "Gentlemen, I urge you to vote—and vote immediately—to accept Britfair's offer to establish themselves in this community by granting them the zoning variance they require."

"Mr. Selectman, Mr. Selectman." A bespectacled man was trying to get Cummings's attention, but so too were at least four other persons, all of whom had jumped up from their seats and were waving their hands:

"Who's getting rich off of this?"

"What about the school situation?"

"How come no one from Britfair is here?"

"I say," bellowed Haye, "I say that we approve the variance."

"No! No! No!"

Cummings was dismayed by the shouts that rang out across the audience. He banged his gavel, but this only prompted more people to jump to their feet. Waving their fingers at the Board, they shouted:

"We want more time."

"Don't bulldoze us."

"You can't do this to us."

Frightened by the outburst, Cummings leaned over the table, talking heatedly to the other members of the Board. They were shaking their heads. With a look of despair, Cummings began gaveling the audience back to order. "Please, please. Some quiet please!" One by one, the protestors reluctantly sat down. Cummings waited for the last, then said, "The Board has decided not to be rushed on this matter." He allowed a flurry of cheers to die down before continuing. "We'll have a committee look into this matter. Mr. Troupe," he said, looking over to the developer. "You'll just have to ask the Britfair people to wait another week or so. I trust that you will also tell them that Southborough is interested in having them in town but we must satisfy ourselves first that we are doing the right thing. I believe," Cummings said, turning to each side, acknowledging the other members of the Board, "that I've accurately represented what the Board feels about this matter at this time." Heads nodded in agreement. "In that case, this meeting is hereby concluded." He didn't even bother to gavel it closed. Instead, Cummings dropped the gavel on the table, sat down and slumped in his chair.

"Wow!" said Timski. "You opened a can of worms."

But Mitch didn't appear to have heard the reporter.

Instead he was watching John Haye stride purposefully through the exiting crowd, bearing down on him. "You, I want to talk to you," the publisher said menacingly, grabbing Mitch by the arm.

Mitch pulled away. Timski, aware that he was in the midst of an embarrassing scene, backed off, out of eyesight but not earshot. "It's a free country, Mr. Haye," said Mitch.

"The hell it is! You've got no right butting into this business."

"I represent our readers," said Mitch, "many of whom were not given enough notice of this meeting to make it."

"Bullshit! What the hell are you up to, Stevens?" the publisher asked. "You've no business here. You're not a resident here. This isn't any business of yours. If we lose this opportunity because of some cynical, worn-out newspaperman from New York City, I'll make sure that no publisher in the country will ever put you on its payroll." Haye raised his fist in front of Mitch's face. "Goddamn it! I'd fire you right here and now if I could. You better stay out of my way, Stevens, way out of my way." And with that, the publisher moved away, pushing people aside as he headed for the side door where Troupe and Lester were standing, waiting for him.

"Wow!" said Timski, edging back to Mitch, not sure what else he should say.

"Lyle, I'm not the first editor that didn't see eye to eye with his publisher. It may not be par for the course, but it happens."

"I always thought we were all on the same team," the reporter said.

"Our constituencies are different," said Mitch. "The publisher represents the business interests of a town, the people who advertise, who make the paper pay. The editor represents—or at least he should represent—the readers. And sometimes, even in a small town like Southborough, those interests can clash. My constituents are really the people who aren't here tonight."

"But I thought—pardon me, Mitch, I don't mean to be critical," said Timski, measuring his words, "but I thought a newspaperman was supposed to be an observer, not a participant."

"We had our observer here tonight," said Mitch, gesturing with his head toward the front row where Robin Summer had sat. "It's her job to tell the story of this meeting fairly. I asked the questions that have to be asked on a deal like this. Someone had to ask them. I was the vinegar."

"The what? I'm not certain I understand what you're getting at," Timski said.

"Lyle, something's going on in this town that I don't like. Something not legit. It's something hidden—even dangerous." Mitch stopped abruptly. He wasn't sure it would be wise to take Timski into his confidence. "Come on, let's get out of here."

They were almost the last to leave Town Hall. As they walked down the steps to nearly deserted High Street, clearly lit now by the streetlamps, Mitch thought he saw out of the corner of his eye some movement from an alleyway across the street. A figure—or was it two?—had moved back into the shadows. A vagrant in downtown Southborough? He said goodnight to Timski and began to walk to his car two blocks away. The main parking lot behind Town Hall had been full when he arrived, so he had had to leave his car in an out-of-the-way lot. Crossing a street, Mitch instinctively looked back. Out of the alleyway, into the bright spot beneath a streetlight, strode a tall man in a business suit, heading in the other direction. Mitch was too far away to make out his face. Harvey Troupe?

Mitch turned into the deep shadows of the side street leading to the lot. Only one of the streetlights was working. The storefronts here—an auto mechanic's shop, a hairdressing salon and an appliance service center— were dark. There were only two cars left in the lot. As he approached his, Mitch heard the motor of the other car start up and flinched as its headlights blazed into his eyes. He stood squinting into them as the car slowly approached. The car crept forward, coming directly at him. For a second, Mitch thought the car was not going to stop. Just as he was about to jump out of the way, the car halted abruptly. Mitch fumbled with the key to his car, got it into the lock and opened the door. He was breathing quickly as he slid into the front seat and turned to lock the door. As he pressed down the button, a sleeved hand rapped sharply on the window.

"Mr. Stevens?" A young woman looked down at Mitch. She was dressed in a black coat, and her face was hidden by a scarf.

"Yes," Mitch answered weakly. The woman didn't sound threatening, but his heart was pounding.

"I followed you back from the meeting. I didn't want anyone to see us together. May I get into the car and talk?"

Mitch managed a light smile. "Sure, all right, but I don't know you, do I? What's this about?"

"I'm sorry I've been rude," the woman said. She stepped around the front of the car and opened the passenger door as Mitch leaned over to unlock it. As she slid into the seat, she lifted the scarf from her head. "My name is Marion Eagleston. I wanted to talk to you about my father's death."

Mitch shifted in his seat to study her. Her silhouette was outlined in what little light there was. She was thin, almost wiry, and her hair was tied in a tight bun at the nape of her neck. Her movements were small, almost bird-like, and she talked so softly Mitch had to lean forward to hear her.

"My father was murdered, Mr. Stevens, I'm sure of it, but I can't prove it."

"Why come to me, Miss Eagleston? Why not go to the police?"

"I have been to the police, Mr. Stevens, but they aren't very sympathetic. At first they paid some attention, but after the doctor's report came in, they just lost interest."

"Whoa, why don't you start from the beginning and tell me what you suspect and why?"

"My father was involved in getting that Britfair company here. He was really excited by the prospect—talked about how it would change the area and prevent unemployment, bring in new people and new ideas. He was working behind the scenes to help it happen. He was an economist, you know—a professor of economics. His specialty, his area of expertise, was the revival of New England mill towns. I don't know what changed his mind, but he found out something, I don't know what. And he was nervous about it. He wouldn't tell me anything, just kept on saying what a huge mistake he had made and how much it had cost him."

Mitch started to ask a question but the young woman went on, her head bowed. "He had diabetes. He took his medication regularly, and he was careful about what he ate. He knew better. I just can't believe he went into insulin shock and his heart failed. There was nothing wrong with his heart, nothing at all. . . ." Her voice trailed off and she began to cry softly.

"Why did you come to me?" Mitch asked gently. "Why do you think I can help you?"

She turned to face him, and for a moment he saw her face clearly. She was without make-up, a pretty face with sharp distinct features. "I read your editorial about Vera Tolvey's death, and I heard you speak out at the meeting tonight. I can sense it. You know something is going on, too. The *Courier* has always been a bland paper, never for challenging the status quo. But since you've been here, there's been a change. You're shaking things up."

No wonder the publisher is irritated with me, Mitch thought. He's probably getting his ears chewed off. "I have no axe to grind, Miss Eagleston. I'm just making sure the newspaper does the job it's supposed to do."

"Then help me prove my father was murdered. Please, you're really my only hope."

"Have you gone through his papers? Maybe there's something there."

"I'll try, but frankly I've been avoiding touching his things. It's really hard for me."

"Well, that's as good a place as any to start. You'll have to do it sooner or later, and, God knows, you might come across something. In the meantime, I'll see if I can get the police report on your father's death. Maybe there's something there the police overlooked. But, please, don't count on any miracles. I'm not a detective and I have my hands full with my job. I really can't promise you anything." Mitch was sympathetic, but he wasn't ready to communicate his own suspicions to the young woman.

"I understand, Mr. Stevens. I just can't seem to get what happened out of my mind."

Mitch sat quietly for several minutes after Marion Eagleston left. His hands rested on the wheel. He stared ahead, wondering about what she had said, trying to fit it in with the other events. Finally, he rubbed his eyes and took a deep breath. As he turned on the ignition and flicked on his car lights he thought he saw a metallic glint near a clump of trees off in the distance. Another car? Had someone been watching them?

TWELVE

"Can I help you with something, Jessie?"

John Haye's secretary looked up, startled. She was hunched over Mitch's desk, the top drawer of which was open. "Oh, you gave me a fright," she gasped, her hands rushing to her breast.

"Is there anything you need?" said Mitch, surprised to see Jessie rummaging through his effects.

"I, er—I was, er—I came to—Mr. Haye wanted me to . . ." she stuttered. "I, er—my heart is still pounding so."

"What is it, Jessie?" Mitch said, taking off his jacket and hanging it up. "What are you doing in here? Where is Maxine?"

"Mr. Haye wanted me to see if Mr. Johnson had left a brochure on word processors in his desk," she said, regaining her composure. "Maxine went to the ladies' so I was just, er, searching for it until she came back."

"I think Ham had a file on that. Maxine can dig it out for you." Mitch walked around the desk to his chair.

Jessie circled it at the same time, so that she now stood near the door.

"I'll check with her," she offered and left hurriedly.

The drawer Jessie had been searching through was still open. Mitch looked into it as he sat down. His address book lay on top of some papers, but it was backside up, not the way he usually left it. He pulled open the side drawers one by one. Jessie must have searched through them, too; all the contents seemed slightly out of place. Mitch was annoyed. Not that he kept anything personal in the drawers, but he felt like his privacy had been invaded. And come to think of it, what was she searching for? Was she spying on him? He shut the last drawer loudly just as he heard the familiar sound of Maxine's high heels outside his office. The telephone was ringing.

"Maxine, would you get Rachel for me, please. Maxine?"

"I've got Bob Grant on the line for you."

Mitch reached for the phone. "Bob? Hi. What is it?"

The young realtor was bursting with enthusiasm. He had a new property for Mitch to look at. "It's an unusual piece of land, but has a spectacular view. It's only about four acres, but absolutely private."

Rachel appeared in the doorframe. Mitch gestured with his head for her to take a chair. He held up a finger; he'd be with her in a minute. "What's unusual about it, Bob?" he said into the telephone.

"Well, it's wedged between two other properties, shaped like a long, thin arrow. But it sits up on a high ledge with nothing to obstruct the view for miles around. It's got its own access off a town road. And like I said, it's perfectly private. Your nearest neighbors are hidden by forest. And," he added, "the price isn't as steep as the other land."

"How come?"

"Well, it's less acreage, of course. But there's also the question of whether it'll pass a perc test."

"You mean, it may not have drainage?"

"That's the first thing I ask someone trying to sell a piece of land like that," Grant said. "I've gotten permission to run a test if you want to spring for it."

"How much will it cost?"

"About three hundred dollars."

"I think maybe I ought to take a look before I spring for that," Mitch said. "And I'd want to talk to Val about it."

"It's worth it, Mitch, honestly. And I can get the site engineer up there this afternoon. He's been pulled off another job. Otherwise, his schedule is full up until next month."

Mitch chewed his lip thoughtfully. "Okay, go ahead," he said after a brief pause. "And I'll try to get there myself this afternoon for a look. Where did you say it was?" Mitch wrote down directions. "Fine, I've got it. I'll get back to you later today or first thing tomorrow."

Mitch replaced the phone and smiled lightly at the intern. She was wearing, he noted with satisfaction, a denim skirt and short-sleeved white blouse. She had even taken the trouble to subdue her hair; it was tied back in a ponytail. "You're looking smart, Rachel. Southborough must agree with you."

"Thanks, chief," she said. Her continuing to call him "boss" or "chief" sounded patronizing and annoyed him, but Mitch thought it would be petty to protest. He grimaced so slightly that she failed to notice his displeasure.

"I've got some more digging for you to do," Mitch said.

"Shoot," said Rachel, pulling a pad and pencil from her shoulder bag.

"First of all, I'd like to know what happened with that autopsy on Putzgarov."

"I already checked on that with the police this morning," she said. "I was just coming in to tell you when Maxine said you wanted to see me. They said there wasn't a trace of alcohol in his bloodstream."

"What? You're kidding."

"Not a trace, they said. He hadn't even had a harmless beer or a glass of wine."

Mitch thought over the implications of the finding. "What do the police think happened then?" he asked finally.

"They're putting it down as an accident. He just ran into a tree on a dark night, they said. It can happen."

"Rachel, who's the officer on the case?"

"Tiny Adams. He was at the scene."

"Yes, I know." Mitch wrote himself a reminder to telephone Adams.

"What else?" she asked.

"I've been thinking about starting a weekly series of profiles of the town's leading citizens, a filler item for these slow summer months. You know, a movers and shakers kind of thing." Mitch hitched his glasses back on his nose with a finger. "We'll need to compile background files on them pretty quickly so they can get written up."

"Can I try writing one?" Rachel asked.

"Sure, no problem," said Mitch, smiling. "But first I need a rundown on a whole mess of them. That comes first."

"Are you thinking of anyone in particular?"

"Well, let's see," he said, curling his lower lip in

thought. "We ought to have a selectman. Do Brad Cummings. He's the head honcho on the Board. And Bert Lester, I suppose. He's the president of the town's biggest bank. And I guess we ought to have someone who represents the real-estate agents, they've gotten to be so important. How about Bill Handler?"

"How about Bob Grant instead?" Rachel offered.

"No, he's too young," Mitch quickly answered. He nodded at the telephone. "And not quite experienced enough. Let's stick with Handler. He's been in the middle of some major development deals lately." Mitch paused. "What do you think of our doing Mr. Haye?"

"Our publisher?" Rachel shrugged. "You think that might seem like patting our own back?"

"Yeah, though he fits the category of mover and shaker. I don't like the idea of tooting our own horn. On the other hand . . ." He left the thought unspoken.

Rachel half closed her eyes in thought. "Heck, chief, his family's been one of the biggest names in this town for umpteen years. It seems to me we'd be remiss if we didn't do him."

"Well, I guess you're right," Mitch agreed with some reluctance. "Put him on the list, but we won't kick off the series with him. That wouldn't sit right at all."

"Anyone else?" asked the intern. "Hey, how about a woman? We'd look so one-sided if we don't have one."

"Who do you suggest?"

"I hear Dorothy Cahill's name all the time. She's certainly well known in town."

"Fine, Rachel, put her down, too." Mitch stretched his arms. "That should do for a start. Get cracking on them right away. I'd like to have your notes on my desk by the end of the week."

"No sweat, boss," said Rachel, getting up and heading

for the door. "I'll start with the morgue and then call around some."

"Warts and all, Rachel," said Mitch. "I don't want the pieces to be end up sounding like a press agent's release." She was halfway out the door when he added, "Oh, yes, and find out from your police buddies what's in the medical report on that professor who dropped dead at the luncheon." Before Rachel had a chance to get in a question, Mitch went on: "And send Lyle in to me, will you?"

Mitch leaned back in his chair after Rachel left, his hands folded behind his head. He was sure now that Putzgarov's death was not an accident. And that only served to confirm his increasing sense—that there was a connection between his death, the deaths of Vera Tolvey and Telford Eagleston and the business with the ski resort development. At this point, he knew too little even to speculate on what that connection might be. For one thing, he really had to know more about the individuals involved. Hence, his idea for the profiles. As far as anyone would know, Rachel's proddings would look like routine background research for an innocuous summer feature series. He had, he knew, manipulated her into rationalizing the addition of John Haye to the list. He felt a tinge of guilt, which he dismissed quickly. Only one other name needed to be added, but he didn't want to trust a novice like Rachel with the assignment.

"Mitch?" Robin Summer stood in the doorway.

"What are you up to, Robin?"

"Working on the zoning meeting."

"Did Ernie tell you that it's our lead?"

"I figured as much. Is it all right to let it run? I have an awful lot of good quotes."

"No problem. Take as much space as you need. We'll

find room for it. It's the hottest topic in town outside of the weather."

Robin tucked in her shoulders as Lyle Timski poked his head around her. "Hey, no pushing!"

"Sorry. You asked to see me?" said Timski.

"Come on in, Lyle. Sit down a sec. Robin, that's it for now—thanks." Mitch pushed his chair back toward the wall behind him, folding one leg over the other. "I've got something I'd like you to do, Lyle. I'm planning this series, a weekly feature, and I'd like you to . . ."

"OFFICER ADAMS? Hi, this is Mitchell Stevens. I'm with the *Courier*. I was at the scene of that accident involving—"

"Yeah, I remember. Whatcha want?"

"I hear the autopsy showed Putzgarov was clean."

"Clean?"

"That he hadn't been drinking."

"Yeah. It surprised the hell out of me. I could have sworn that smell was whisky. The car really stank of it."

"If he wasn't drinking, what do you think caused the accident?"

"I don't know. To be honest, we didn't even bother to think about it because it seemed so obvious it was a drinking incident."

"What about the car?"

"What about it? It's a wreck—not totaled, but you sure can't move it. If no one claims it, we'll have it towed to the town dump."

"Have you checked it out yet?"

"For what?"

"The steering, faulty brakes—anything that could account for the accident."

"We hadn't... we didn't... we... What are you getting at, Mr. Stevens?"

"I'm just looking for an explanation. I'd like to be able to have the paper say that the police have looked into every possibility. You have to realize, Officer Adams, that Putzgarov was a well-known musician, not only in this country but abroad, too. Once it gets out that the autopsy didn't show anything, people are going to wonder—naturally enough—about what did happen. UPI in New York—United Press International—has already requested us to do a follow-up it can file around the country. I don't think it would sit well if the police didn't eliminate some of the obvious."

"Obvious?"

"Well, that's what I immediately thought of when I heard about the autopsy. The brakes. The steering. God knows what else it might have been. A broken axle? The headlights went out suddenly? I don't know, I'm not a mechanic. But you folks ought to want to know."

"I get your point, Mr. Stevens. We want to be thorough on this one, don't we? I'll get right on it."

"Swell, Officer Adams. And will you let me know what you find out when you do find something?"

"Sure. It'll be a matter of public record. And thanks."

MITCH TOSSED ROBIN Summer's story on the emergency selectmen's meeting into the hopper at Ernie's side. "Give her a byline, will you?"

"Hmmm."

"I told her to let it run so don't be surprised by the length of the piece."

"Hmmm."

"There's nothing else in my basket, so I'm heading out

for a little while. I'll be back in time to dummy the paper."

"Hmmm."

THE PROPERTY BOB Grant wanted Mitch to see was outside the northern end of Southborough, almost astride the town line. It was, as Grant had said, a curious piece of property, tucked between two wide stands of trees up a dirt road that angled upward sharply toward an open plateau. As Mitch drove onto the wide ledge, he saw—and heard—a mud-splattered backhoe clanging along the far side. Getting out of his car, Mitch waved at the driver, who then pulled a series of levers, turning off the raucous engine.

"Howdy," the man said as he approached, extending his hand.

Mitch introduced himself. "How's it going?"

"Stan Lay," the man said. "Nice to meet ya. You got ya'self a nice view here."

"I haven't bought it yet. That's why you're here. I didn't want to do anything until I was sure I could build."

Lay made a face. "You're doing a wise thing."

"How so?" Mitch asked.

"You know anything about soil or perc tests?"

Mitch shook his head. "Not a thing."

"Well," Lay said, taking a well-used handkerchief from a back pocket and running it under his nose, "the state got it into its head to require the tests back in the seventies. For any property less than ten acres. The idea is to make sure you have drainage for your waste—from your toilet and kitchen—primarily so your potable water isn't contaminated." Lay pointed toward the backhoe. "I've been digging a big hole over there—to test the soil composition and see how things stack up with the water levels around these parts.

"I'll be digging another hole over there," he said, pointing to the other side of the ledge, "a deep hole. And I'll put a certain amount of water in it and see how long it takes to be absorbed—that'd be the percolation rate. What I come up with determines whether you can have a septic system or not."

"And if I can't?"

"You don't want to think about alternatives, Mr. Stevens. A septic system means a tank and leach field. That's routine for any house. The alternative is a mound system and that's expensive as all get out. You need your own pump for that. It's really not an alternative unless you're putting up a school or a big factory or somethin'. You don't see many of them in Vermont."

"So you need to pass a perc test to build?"

"Well, some folks who build their own homes put in a septic systems without one. It's not legal but it's been done. Personally, anyway, I think the law is too fussy about the whole thing. Hell, people have been living up here for two, three hundred years without any epidemics or anything. But it's the way I make my living."

Mitch looked down at the hard rock on which they were standing. "Any idea yet what you're hitting here?"

Lay glanced over his shoulder. "It's bothersome, Mr. Stevens, but not a lost cause," he said, lowering his voice.

"What do you mean?" asked Mitch, getting suspicious.

Lay again glanced over his shoulder. "Well, it appears to me that you're sitting atop an outcrop here. You can actually see the bedrock in scattered places." Lay pointed to a smooth gray section of stone ten yards away where a few tiny green shoots had found cracks in which to grow. "You're supposed to have several feet of topsoil and the leach field has to—"

"Are you saying this property isn't going to pass the test?"

"Well, I'd be guessing at this point, Mr. Stevens." Lay took out his handkerchief again and wiped his nose. "If worse comes to worse, you can always ask for an exception. We call it a 4–03–A3. I could probably expedite it for you."

Expedite? Uh-oh, Mitch thought to himself. "You mean you can help me get this land approved for building?"

"If that's what you wish, Mr. Stevens. I'm awful busy, but I give priority to clients who pay up front—in cash."

"I see." Mitch looked off into the distance, toward the mountains across the Connecticut River in New Hampshire. "Let me think on it," he said. "I'll get back to you."

"I'm home most nights by sundown," Lay said, turning back toward the backhoe.

Sonofabitch, Mitch said to himself as he got behind the wheel of his car and pulled the driver's door shut. He's trying to hold me up. Is that how they do business here? I thought Vermonters were above that. I must be naive.

Mitch backed the car up and returned down the access road. Driving back into town proper, he passed a drive-in theater. Just beyond it, some ten yards back on a vacant lot, was a discreet sign, blue letters against a white background: FUTURE HOME OF SKILAND, IN THE HEART OF VERMONT'S HEART. Next came a string of gasoline stations and a motel. Mitch could imagine the strip of commercial stores spreading in either direction once the resort got started.

Mitch hit the steering wheel with his fist. SkiLand!

What had that farmer at the zoning meeting said about the perc tests up there? How did SkiLand pass a perc test?

MITCH PUT HIS feet up on the desk. He picked up the galley proofs of Robin Summer's story on the zoning meeting:

> by Robin Summer
>
> In a matter marked by acrimonious debate, the Board of Selectmen decided Monday night to shelve temporarily a request for a zoning variation for an outlet-warehouse planned for Southborough by Britfair Enterprises.
> Chief Selectman Bradford Cummings said . . .

He skipped the rest of the first galley, holding the next out at arm's length, scanning it, when suddenly his eye was caught by his own name.

> Mitchell Stevens, acting editor of the *Courier*, raised a question about Mr. Troupe's partners in the venture that . . .

He picked up a pencil and leaned over the galley:

> A question was raised about Mr. Troupe's partners in the venture that . . .

That's better, Mitch thought. I've got to keep myself out of the picture as much as possible. I've already made a name for myself with the wrong people. Haye, for one, would react like a bull if he saw my name in print here.

I can hear him now, saying that it looks like I spoke for the newspaper. Well, he's right about my keeping a low profile. I don't want to become a target for his—or anyone else's—hostility.

Mitch picked up the phone. "Maxine, ask Robin in, please."

He was still glancing over the galleys of her story when she came in. Robin sat down without being asked, a yellow legal pad nestled on her lap, a pencil loosely clasped in her fist.

"Nice going on your story. It's thorough."

"Thanks, Mitch. I appreciate your saying that—and I really appreciate the assignment. It's making life interesting."

"You've earned it, Robin." Mitch leaned toward her. "Listen, there's something I'd like you to check on tomorrow down at the Town Hall." Robin picked up the pad, poising the pencil, ready to write. "Find out who the engineer was on the perc testing up at the SkiLand property. If you can get xeroxes of the papers, get 'em."

"That should be relatively easy, Mitch."

"I know, but try to do it without arousing any suspicion. I want this kept under wraps."

"The Town Clerk's a nosy guy," she said. "He's bound to ask why. I can't tell him it's none of his business. That would only tickle his curiosity."

Mitch poked his glasses back up on his nose. "Tell him—if he asks—tell him your editor asked you to check it out. You don't know why, but you think I'm interested in some kind of feature story on what perc engineers run into working in an area like this. Keep it vague. Play dumb. Make me the fall guy. If he gives you any trouble, tell him to give me a buzz."

Robin nodded. "That should do it. He's used to seeing

my name on feature stories like that." She put down her pencil. "Mitch? Can I ask what this is all about?"

"Not yet. And Robin, let's keep this to ourselves around the office, too."

MITCH WAS SOUND asleep when the phone rang. It took him a minute to come to and answer the phone. It was Ham and he sounded agitated.

"Ham, is anything wrong? Are you all right?"

"Never mind me, you son of a bitch. What in hell do you think you're doing, ruining my paper?"

"Ham, calm down. I know you must be better because your language is certainly back to normal. Just calm down and tell me what this is all about."

"Don't play games with me, Mitch, I can see what you're up to. You want to rattle my town, dig up a lot of dirt, leave your mark, get attention for yourself and steal my newspaper away from me."

Mitch was shocked. This was so unlike Ham, the gentlest and kindest of men. The disease was obviously causing all kinds of emotional side effects.

"Ham, please, calm down, I don't need your job. I have a perfectly good job I'm happy with. I'm just doing the job the same way we always used to do it. Remember?"

"This isn't the big city. This is a small town. Everybody knows everybody. You can do damage here, hurt people in a way you can't in a big city."

"Ham, you know that isn't true. The only difference is here you know the people you hurt. Listen, Ham, did the publisher call you about me?"

"So what if he did. He's worried that you stirred up things so much at the meeting, Britfair may be in danger. And it means a lot to this town, more than you can possibly understand." Ham's voice began to rise again. "You think you're such a smart-ass. Well, you don't know everything."

Mitch tried hard to keep his anger in check. After all, his friend was very ill and he did not want to upset him further. "Ham, please, I have to do an honest job. Would you really want me to do otherwise? I promise you one thing, though, if anything really bad comes out, I'll let you know about it before I publish it."

"Mitch." There was alarm in Ham's voice. "What do you mean, something bad? Is there something you're hiding from me? For God's sake, tell me *now*."

Mitch did not like lying to his friend. "No, Ham, no, nothing, I was just trying to calm you down, that's all."

"Mitch, please, don't go off half-cocked. Please, remember, you're only here for a few months. I'm feeling stronger. I may even be back earlier than I thought."

"Yes, Ham, sure, I certainly hope so."

Mitch hung up the phone. He suddenly felt unsure. Was Ham right? Was he grandstanding?

THIRTEEN

Looking back on it on his way home, Mitch couldn't remember a single day in his career that had been so jam-packed with developments. Fraught, perhaps, was a better word. It was as though a half dozen streams converged at one spot into a river. And the river was flowing inexorably toward—what?

Driving past the white, steepled South Village Unitarian Church, Mitch spotted Lyle Timski and an older woman walking toward a side door to the church. He was about to honk at him, but thought better of it. The woman looked familiar. Mitch had seen her somewhere before; he even had the feeling they had been introduced to each other. He couldn't recall the reason. Damn, he said to himself, this is going to bug me all night. And then a second thought occurred to him: I didn't know Lyle was so religious that he attended evening prayer meetings.

Mitch turned into the side road that led to Ham Johnson's house. As he did, a flare of sun made him blink as the car topped a short rise. Just as suddenly, trees overhead blocked the sun again.

Robin Summer's report had been on his desk the first thing in the morning. Tiny Adams's "courtesy" call had come mid-morning. Timski had made an interim verbal report just before lunch—and had asked for more time to track down a lead. (That woman with him, Mitch thought, wore a print dress the time I met her.) There had been another awkward confrontation with John Haye in the early afternoon. Then Val's phone call—had he been able to convince her not to worry? And, to top it all, by the end of the day, Rachel had turned in her notes for the profiles and a brief report on Telford Eagleston. "Would you believe?" Mitch said aloud. And meanwhile, there had been the newspaper to get out.

Topping another hill, a sun flare again caused Mitch to blink. He looked away, checking his rear-view mirror. He could make out, dimly, through the dust kicked up on the dirt road by his car, another vehicle behind him, about fifty yards back. A car? A pickup truck? It was hard to tell. He couldn't even tell its color. Its front end was camouflaged by dust. He hadn't noticed it before. The vehicle hung back, trying, Mitch supposed, to stay as much as possible out of the "wake" of his car. A clean car didn't last long along these back roads.

Mitch stopped beside the mailbox on the road outside the lane to Johnson's home. Leaving the car engine idling, he checked the box. There were a few letters for Ham inside. Turning to get into his car, letters in hand, Mitch noticed that the vehicle following his had pulled off to the side of the road, still some fifty yards back. Was there a mailbox back there, too? Mitch couldn't recall. He turned the car slowly into the driveway.

Mitch,

The perc tests on the SkiLand property were done back in October last year. I couldn't think up a way to explain photocopying all those forms without creating suspicion, but I leafed through them—nonchalantly, I hope—and didn't see anything out of the ordinary on the surface. I didn't get an accurate count either, but there must be at least two hundred. The subdivisions run less than an acre each. The civil engineer who certified the tests was a local one: Stanley C. Lay.

I don't think I got the Town Clerk's curiosity going, though God knows they gossip about everything in this town. You can't hardly go to the bathroom without everyone knowing it. I exaggerate, but I wouldn't swear that my queries will go unheralded.

I've attached the parts of the Environmental Protection Rules which Maxine told me you wanted. Anything else?

Robin

CHAPTER 3. SUBDIVISIONS

3-02. Definitions
  A. "Building development" and "development" means the construction or installation of any structure or building, the useful occupancy of which requires the installation of plumbing or of a sewage disposal system. . . .
*3.02D - 3.04A
  D. "Subdivision" means:
      1) the dividing of a parcel of land by sale, gift, lease, mortgage foreclosure, court-ordered partition or filing of a plot plan on the town records where the act of division creates one or more parcels of

land of less than 10 acres in area, but excluding leases subject to the provisions of Chapter 153 of Title 10 relating to mobile homes. Subdivision shall be deemed to have occurred on the conveyance of the first lot or the filing of a plot plan on the town records, whichever shall first occur. . . .

Chapter 4. Public Buildings

4-03. Permit Required
   A. Approved Plans Required; Exceptions
     3) Home occupations, Self-employment. In addition to *2-02 (N), when reviewing a home occupation or project where the only employee(s) will be the owner and/or owner's immediate family, and the public does not have general access to the facility, the Division may determine that the potential for adverse effect under the criteria of these rules is sufficiently remote that the requirements of the rules should be waived. In such cases, the Division may issue a permit with conditions prohibiting expansion of the project until a revised permit is issued for the expansion. . . .

"Mr. Stevens?"

"Officer Adams?"

"I thought maybe you'd be interested in what we've come up with about what we were talking about the other day."

"Yuri Putzgarov's car?"

"Yeah. The car. We got the guys at the town garage to look it over."

"And?"

"The front end was a mess, but up on a lift they could see that something was wrong with the steering mechanism. A lug was missing. They said it was highly unusual for a lug like that to jar loose in a collision, so it must have come off before the accident."

"I see. Is that suspicious on the surface? I mean, couldn't the lug have worked free on its own?"

"It either worked free or was taken off. I'd like to think the former, but the head mechanic there—Homer Redgren—you know him?"

"No."

"Homer learned his trade with the Marines in Korea. He knows all about engines. Homer says—he can't swear to it, mind you—but he says it looks like a rod has been tampered with. There were hatch marks around it like someone had taken a wrench to it."

"Where does that leave you, Officer Adams?"

"The Chief wants to keep this on the q.t. for now. He asked me to ask you not to print anything until we've corroborated this positively. We've asked the state police in on the case. Whadaya say? Can you keep it out of the paper for now?"

"Well, there's nothing on the record yet, is there?"

"You're a sharp one, Mr. Stevens. The Chief'll appreciate this."

"You'll keep me informed?"

"That's part of the deal."

* * *

Lyle Timski frowned. "I really need more time on this, Mitch, to do it justice."

"What did you have in mind?"

"It's like a house built of matchsticks—no, a better analogy would be a game of dominoes. Every time Harvey Troupe starts up a new project, he borrows from an old one. He's in hock up to his ears. If one goes sour, boom, there goes the whole shebang."

"Listen, Lyle, I don't want to dismiss what you've found out so far, but the way Troupe is operating is nothing new."

Mitch pushed the glasses back on his nose. Thinking back on their conversation now, he pictured Timski going into the church—with that woman he couldn't quite place. Who was she?

"I made a small investment in an apartment house in Houston once many years ago—on the advice of a friend in the Real Estate section—and it fell apart just as you said when the fellow running the operation had a heart attack. He broke us all in the act."

"What Troupe is doing—if we can prove it—is illegal," the reporter insisted. "You don't take from one corporation and lend it to another under these circumstances."

"That sounds like a case for the Securities Exchange Commission."

Timski tossed his pencil on the desk in annoyance. "The trouble is," he said, "that things like that never come out until it's too late—until the house falls down."

"Lyle, if you can come up with anything to substantiate what you're saying, I'd be the first to publish it." Mitch smiled slightly. "In fact, I'd do it with pleasure. But we have to have more to go on."

"That's why I want to go to Boston," Timski persisted. "The prospectuses of all his deals had to be filed. There are records up there that I could trace."

Mitch admired Timski's zeal, but the request was impractical. "Don't get me wrong, Lyle. You have your hands on a good story, but you'd be away from the office for what? A week, two weeks? I wish I could. But we don't have that kind of staff here, we're into vacation season already, and nobody's had any time off yet.

"Look," Mitch continued, "you work up one of those feature profiles for me. Get in the idea of Troupe going from one development to the next. Mention how it's always amazed other developers that he's been able to come up with the money to underwrite his ventures when the banks are being tightfisted. That's true enough. You can hint at what is going on without coming out and saying it point-blank. And better still, phone Troupe himself. Tell him you're working on this feature. Get him to comment on how he swings deals."

"You think he'll talk to me?"

"Hell, Lyle, as far as he's concerned, the *Courier* is a small-town rag that's in his back pocket because of John Haye. We're just doing a series on the local VIPs and he's one of them now. Tell him we want to send a photographer to take his picture for the story." Mitch paused. He couldn't say it to Timski, but he was willing to bet that Troupe might even think that the feature was Haye's idea to begin with. "You know, Lyle, it's possible to make him sound like a wheeler-dealer in a way that he'll think is complimentary. Guys like that are easily flattered."

"I think I'm going to need help writing this one," the reporter said.

"Just ask. I'm always available. Now get out of here and get him on the phone," he added amicably.

* * *

THE DOOR SWUNG open and John Haye's stout figure filled the entry. He shoved the door to Mitch's office closed and stood in front of his desk, looking down at Mitch with disdain.

"Didn't Jessie tell you I wanted to see you? What are you up to now, Stevens?"

Mitch looked up from the copy he was reading. For a brief instant, the face of the woman Timski had been walking with flashed into his mind, then vanished. He turned his full attention then on Haye and said, as civilly as he could, "why don't you sit down and tell me what you're talking about?"

"I'll stand, thank you. What's this feature on Harvey Troupe that Timski's doing? What's that all about?"

Mitch explained the idea for the profile series. "Dottie Cahill's on the list. So are you, come to think of it. It's a typical summer filler kind of thing."

The publisher seemed mollified for a moment. "Oh, I thought you were focusing in on Troupe for some reason. He phoned to tell me Timski wanted an interview."

"Is he leery about giving Lyle one?"

"Why should he be?" asked Haye defensively. "He's just one of those people who like to keep their private affairs private."

"I thought it sounded like good publicity to me," said Mitch. "He's going to want people in town on his side for that Britfair zoning proposal."

"Yes, I suppose you're right." The publisher started to turn to leave but caught himself midway. "I'm sorry I burst in like that. I've gotten trigger happy ever since the zoning meeting."

"We just see things differently on that one," said Mitch. He ought to have stopped there, he realized later, but he couldn't help himself. Despite the apology,

Haye's rudeness on entering his office irritated him. "What's good for business isn't always what's best for the public," Mitch added. "Did you ever see what the developers made of the area around the Gettysburg battlefield, or what happens when a suburb becomes just one sprawling shopping mall after another?"

"You've got a lot of nerve making a remark like that," said Haye, suddenly furious. "This paper is going to be behind the Britfair venture one hundred percent. It's my paper and I say so."

"If it's your paper, why don't you take over running it? You can have this desk anytime you want." Mitch stood up, shaking with anger. "I'm not going to be your dummy. That wasn't part of the bargain when I was hired. Here," he said, pushing the copy toward Haye, "you edit it."

The publisher's face grew red. He opened his mouth to say something, but restrained himself. Instead, he went to the door, pulled it open and plunged out of the office.

"Mitch, you should have bit your tongue."

"I know, I know. I just couldn't help it, Val. He touched a raw nerve. And I can't forgive him for getting Ham all worked up."

"Well, thank God it's just for another month or so." A blur of static garbled her next words. "Did you hear that? There must be an electrical storm coming up."

"We've been having wonderfully dry weather here. Hot and dry, but at least it hasn't been humid. And it cools down at night."

Val's next words were garbled again. "Wow, it must be getting close. You really feel the thunder and lightning up in the mountains, don't you?"

"Did I tell you about that new property Bob Grant had me look at?" Mitch went on to describe the land and his conversation with Stan Lay. "I'm tempted to follow up on what Lay suggested, just to see how much he wants."

"And where would that get us?" his wife asked.

Mitch explained his suspicions about the SkiLand perc tests.

"I knew it, I knew it. I knew you were sniffing around and getting yourself all worked up about something. Mitch, I don't want to have to worry about what you're up to there. I can't concentrate on my work if I do."

"Oh, come on, Val," he said, "it's just newspaper work. Routine, strictly routine. Listen, before I forget, have you heard from Ken lately?"

"You're changing the subject, Mitch. That always gets me more worried."

"No, honestly, Val, there's nothing to be afraid of."

"You said that the last time—I haven't forgotten. Your damn instincts get you in the damnedest situations."

"Val, sweetheart, darling, you've been up here in Southborough. It's farmland, bucolic, old-fashioned—the last place in the world you'd expect—" A loud crackle of static drowned out the end of his sentence. "Val, can you hear me?"

"Barely."

"Look, I'll call again tonight, later on, after dinner. Okay?"

Val's answer was lost in another burst of static. The line went dead.

MITCH WAS STANDING beside Ernie, looking over his shoulder at a yellow sheet of UPI copy, when Rachel walked up to the copy desk with a thick file folder. "Mitch?"

"Not now, Rachel," he said, distracted. He saw the folder she was carrying. "Why don't you just leave that on my desk. I'll get to it later."

"Okay. It's not complete but I'll put a note on it so you'll know what it's all about."

Mitch turned back to Ernie as the intern walked away. "Looks like a typo to me, Ernie," he said. "Why don't you query UPI? They'll be grateful if you caught an error. I never saw the name Fuchs spelled like that."

"Hmmm."

Abe waved him over with his pencil. "What do you want to do with this dredging story?"

"What's the problem?"

"Well, it looks like we're going to be hard up for space tonight and the dredging's going to take place way up the Connecticut from here. Rog has written nearly a column on it."

"Trim it back to six inches—further if you think we can get away with less."

Mitch headed back into his office. Rachel was just coming out of it. She made a little curtsy as he passed her. On his desk was the thick folder she had been carrying earlier, with a note attached to it:

Boss,

Rather than spend a lot of time copying the files, I've pulled clips that would be pertinent to a profile and attached them to a little summary I've been able to come up with for each of the guys/gal on the list. I'd like to do the Cahill one.

RB

Mitch made himself comfortable behind his desk, pressing back against the back of the chair and crossing his legs. He reached for the folder, opened it and took out the first batch of papers:

Robert Slate Lester—

Known as Bert. Born Feb. 13, 1939 in Portland, Maine. Moved here when 8 with family. Went to University of Vermont, graduating in 1960. Served in Vietnam, 2d lt. Army Signal Corps, hq job. On return, joined Southborough Savings & Loan, which an uncle, Bernard Lester, founded. Took over as president on uncle's death in 1979. Bank recharted as First State Bank following year. Married a local girl, Maryann LaBelle, 1966. Three children, two still in high school, one about to start Boston U. Baptist. Hobbies: assistant coach, Little League; fishing, target shooting. Has served on School Board (1975–81), headed United Fund drive, 1983. Was president of Kiwanis following year. Tried to initiate a Development Board but Selectmen in 1985 rejected idea. His bank is leading lender in area. 1984, Standard & Poor downgraded bank to a BB because of its heavy reliance on mortgage financing (as opposed to business loans). Lester reacted to that (see first clip attached) by pledging his bank to get more involved in business underwriting. Underwrote Putney Mall and is a supporter of SkiLand project. Condos are being advertised with rates based on his bank's offer.

RB

Mitch picked up the next batch:

John Nance Haye—
Born Southborough, May 1, 1929. Attended Andover, Yale. Joined family newspaper, founded by grandfa-

ther, on graduation in 1951. Began on editorial side
but switched after year to business, serving first as an
ad rep, then sales manager, comptroller, vice president. Became publisher and president in 1969. Married to former Elizabeth Bent, daughter of a Vermont
congressman, 1954. One child, girl, died in infancy.
Has two adopted daughters, both now married and
living out of state. Congregationalist. Hobbies: Hunting. Has served on every town committee you can
think of, usually as chairman (see clips for full rundown). Served in state legislature (1970–82) and later
was governor's special consultant on Tourism and
Development. A Republican, he travels frequently
around state on missions for party (see clip dated
4/4/84 from *NY Times* re fund-raising for Reagan). Is
considered a possible candidate for GOP nomination
for governor. Wouldn't that be something!

                                                             RB

The file on the publisher was so heavy that Mitch had to use both hands to move it off to the side. He reached for the next set:

Bradford Cummings—
Born Southborough June 1, 1937, oldest of nine (!)
children. After local schools, went for two years to
University of Vermont, but quit to enter family
business, appliance store. He now runs it with a
brother and brother-in-law. Became active in "politics" early on. Was president of senior class,
Southborough High, 1955. (Has also served as president of both local and state Kiwanis, 1978 and 1979,
respectively, and head of Methodist Council of Vermont, 1981). Did not marry until 1970 after return
from Vietnam, where he was a Ranger (has a Bronze

Nat & Yanna Brandt

Medal and Purple Heart). Wife is former Jessica
Clayton of Dummerston (Our Jessie, who, her high
school yearbook says, "is bound to succeed"). Three
children, all boys, all in local schools. Hobbies: Politicking (See clips—he likes to be at every town function and have his pix taken). Was first elected a
Selectman in 1972 and has served on Board ever
since. According to next-door store owner, appliance
store was on verge of going out of business last year.
That's when Jessie joined us, by the way. She'd been
a hausfrau up until then.

RB

A single sheet was next on the pile still in the folder. Mitch picked it up:

William McCoy Handler—

This is toughest profile to pin down. Handler was, of all things, a NYC cop (!) who moved here in 1978. Not clear why. He is about 48—too young to retire? He has apparently never agreed to any sort of interview before. And wouldn't answer any of my questions when I phoned him. He said he didn't want anything written up about him, thank you anyway. There's really no file on him, other than brief mention of him as agent on certain real-estate deals, e.g. some mention of him along with Vera Tolvey re SkiLand. He joined Mont Vert Realtors in '78 and now heads its operation in Southborough. Keeps pretty much to himself, though he's a member of Kiwanis and is known as a friend of Lester, Haye and Cummings. If he won't agree to an interview, maybe he should be scratched from the list???

RB

Mitch glanced at the last batch of papers in the folder. It was material on Dorothy Cahill. He didn't bother to pick it up.

It wasn't surprising that Handler, Lester, Haye and Cummings were all buddies. That much was clear at the dinner with the Britfair representatives at the Pilgrim's Pride. They were all in on SkiLand and the Britfair property deal together. Lester's bank obviously needs the injection of capital that the two developments would spur. Haye undoubtedly sees both as enhancing his image as a prime mover in Vermont's financial future. Cummings must need the business connections to keep his store afloat—isn't he supplying all the stoves, refrigerators, microwaves and air conditioners for SkiLand? Handler? The commission on the sales.

On the surface, the motives are not unusual, Mitch thought. But it's always a matter of degree, isn't it? And people who feel threatened lose all sense of perspective. I can see where Putzgarov fit into all this now. Whenever he thought of the violinist lately, the image of that mystery woman he had seen with Timski flashed in his mind, just as it had briefly when Haye had burst into his office. Who was she? And what was her connection with Putzgarov?

Mitch could guess why Putzgarov had been murdered. They needed his land for access. Maybe he wanted too much in return, was holding back for a bigger share. Okay, let's say that's so. But why Vera Tolvey? Why that professor? Mitch suddenly remembered that there should have been a copy of the police report on Eagleston's death. But as he looked through the notes, he couldn't find it.

There has to be some connection. What I need, Mitch

reflected, is proof that what they are doing is out of the ordinary in the first place, something they don't want uncovered. I need a connection, some link between them and SkiLand and the Britfair site. Damn! That woman's face again. It keeps interrupting my thinking. If it keeps nagging me, I won't be able to sleep.

IT BEGAN WITH a crackling noise. Like the static on the phone line with Val. Only it didn't go away. And it grew in intensity.

Mitch sat upright in bed. "Oh, my God!" He could smell smoke, feel the heat. The house was on fire. He bolted for the door. He ran down the narrow hall to the staircase, flipping on the light switch as he passed it. Dark billows of smoke were rushing upward. It would be madness to try to make his way through them.

He ran back to the bedroom. It faced the rear of the house. He opened the window as far as he could and leaned out. A gutter pipe ran from the roof to a run-off slab of cement below. He could reach if he didn't lose his balance.

He sat on the windowsill, his legs dangling in space. Slowly, he knelt and turned. He struggled to stand, facing into the bedroom, his feet now on the windowsill, his hands holding for dear life onto the frame itself. He let go with his right arm and reached out to the gutter. He was inches away. Grimacing, he stretched his arm as far as he could, reaching for the drain pipe, feeling his toes starting to slip from the sill. Suddenly, he had it. With a lunge, he lurched toward the pipe, reaching out with his left hand for a solid grip, trying to hug the clapboard wall at the same time. He had the pipe in both hands now, but his body was dragging him down. He started to slide, trying to slow his descent with his hands. His palms began to burn from the friction. He half-fell, half-slithered. His feet touched ground at last and he fell backward. As he did so, he looked back up at the bedroom window. A flicker of flame was shooting out of it.

FOURTEEN

Even before turning the bend in the road just before Ham's place he could smell the acrid odor. It floated in the trees and permeated the early-morning air. Mitch shuddered involuntarily.

He was steering carefully with the tips of his fingers which protruded from the bandages covering both hands. A hospital intern had lent him some clothes—the trousers, T-shirt, old sweatsocks and torn sneakers he was wearing—and admonished him to keep the bandages on for at least another day. His raw palms were covered with salve. The rented car—a replacement for the one burned when the fire spread from the house to the adjoining garage—handled smoothly. It was a bigger model sedan than his own had been, but the power steering made it easy for Mitch to maintain control.

Parked just off the dirt road in Johnson's driveway was a bright red stationwagon, its roof sporting a flashing light, its sides covered with the emblem of the marshal of the Southborough Volunteer Fire Company. Mitch left his car pulled to the side of the dirt road and walked by the marshal's car. He stopped abruptly when he saw what remained of Johnson's home—the cement foundation and some of the brick chimney. He gasped.

"Who's that?"

The rough voice startled Mitch. He turned. Coming out of the trees was a tall, somber-looking man in his fifties dressed in jeans, a denim shirt and heavy boots. He eyed Mitch suspiciously.

Mitch told him who he was.

"My name's Ray Boyd," he said. "I'm the fire marshal." He offered his hand to shake, but took it back quickly when he noticed that Mitch's hands were bandaged. "I was just taking a look around back."

"It's a shock seeing it in broad daylight," said Mitch. "There's nothing left. It was too dark to see anything last night."

Talking about it, Mitch caught a sudden flash of images—fire licking through the clapboard walls, window glass bursting from the intense heat, his running in bare feet down the driveway and into the dark dirt road, not knowing which way to turn, stumbling along the ruts in the dirt road, out of breath, sweating, his heart thumping in his chest.

"It took the boys a half hour to get to the house." Boyd reached into the passenger window of the station wagon and took a long, heavy crowbar. "By then it was all over. All they could do was hose down what was left. That's what happens when we don't get a call right away. We keep the pump engine filled, but until we come . . ." He left the sentence unfinished as he started to walk toward the remains of the house, sloshing with his boots through the puddles of water that still remained. "Come on, I want to show you somethin'."

Mitch followed, trying to avoid the deeper puddles

because of the sneakers. The acrid odor was even more pronounced as he approached the remains, and it immediately began to penetrate his clothes.

A few charred studs still stood, though at such precarious angles that they looked like they would fall over if touched. When Boyd did just that with the crowbar, the stud fell lazily into the ashes of what had been the rest of the house. "It was a deep fire," he said.

Blackened pieces of metal stood up at awkward angles everywhere—the debris from bedsprings, table legs, kitchen chairs and stools. Nothing, however, was recognizable. Mitch couldn't even guess where the living room had been. Only the scorched stove covered by a tall mound of detritus indicated where the kitchen once was located.

Boyd had moved around to the side of the house. He was poking about with the crowbar. "Over here. Can you come over here?"

Mitch stepped between pieces of wreckage that had spewed out onto the lawn to reach the fire marshal, who was pointing with the crowbar at the base of the foundation.

"See that blackened area? Looks like a halo."

Mitch nodded.

"The way I see it, the fire started there. There's no reason for it otherwise—unless you kept a pile of rubbish or some wood piled there."

Mitch told Boyd that as far as he recollected, there hadn't been anything left there.

"Well, then," said Boyd, "it's a mystery. There aren't any wires or such into the house at this point, no chimney, nothing. Just a blank wall. But look at the amount of ash here," he continued, poking again. "There must have been something sitting against the wall, something highly inflammable. Are you sure you didn't leave some newspapers or kindling here?"

Mitch shook his head slowly.

"You were lucky, Stevens," the fire marshal said. He had turned and was headed back toward his stationwagon. "I'm going to have to notify the police about this. It looks to me like arson."

Mitch looked down at his hands. They were trembling.

MITCH SAT BESIDE the hospital bed, biting his lip. "I'm sorry, Ham. It all happened so fast, I couldn't do anything about it. The house . . . there is no house any more. I feel terrible about it."

Ham Johnson's color drained from his face. "Damn it to hell. Everything's gone?"

Mitch nodded, averting Johnson's eyes.

"Holy Jesus." Johnson, still pale and weak from his operation, looked weary and dejected. "Everything I had was in there."

"I'm sorry, Ham," said Mitch. "I'll do whatever I can to get you into a new place. Whatever the insurance won't pay for, I will."

"Oh, hell, it isn't that. I'm not broke." Johnson reached out his arm to touch Mitch, but the intravenous tube pulled tight, making him grimace. "The furniture was crap, my clothes and things old. That doesn't bother me." He stared out the window. "It's the photos of Kate. They were the only ones I had of her. I . . ." Johnson clenched his teeth, trying to hold off the tears that were welling in his eyes.

"I understand, Ham. I don't know what to say." Mitch studied his bandaged hands. "I went over in my mind everything I did when I got home last night and I'm positive I didn't leave on the stove or anything like that." For some reason, Mitch felt extraordinarily guilty. He just couldn't bring himself to tell Ham the truth.

"Hell," Johnson said, starting to pull himself together, "it's only a house. The important thing is that you got out all right." He tried again to reach out to Mitch, but the tube tightened once more. "I forget I'm not mobile," he said, trying to muster a smile.

"I don't know what to say," Mitch continued. "I guess I'm just glad to be alive." And not murdered, he said to himself.

"Me, too. I'm glad I'm still kicking," said Johnson. "The doctor says they think they got everything bad out of my system and that it's just a matter of time and probably therapy of some sort." With his free hand, Johnson reached over to the night table beside his bed and picked up a glass of water with a straw in it. He sipped through the straw briefly, then returned it to the table. "Don't worry it, Mitch. The insurance will cover it. The only thing I regret is losing the photos I had of Kate. But, hell, I have the memories."

Mitch started to say something more, but Johnson cut him off. "Let's drop it, okay? I can't worry about something like this from a hospital bed. The important thing is that we're both okay." He turned to the door. A nurse had poked her head into the room and then disappeared. "I sometimes wonder if they lose track of patients here or what. They're always looking in on me like they've lost something."

"Do you want me to get Bob Grant going on finding you a place to live?" Mitch asked.

"Sure, why not. Tell him furnished. I won't get out of here for a while, but we might as well start the ball rolling. Nothing fancy, though, Mitch. I just need a room, a john and some kind of kitchen. And the closer to the office the better. Hey, what about you? What are you going to do?"

"I'm going to stay at the Colonial House—where our intern is. Maxine was able to work out a decent rate for me. That's all I need. I won't be here that much longer."

Ham stared at him. "Mitch, forget what I said the other night. You know I know you're not after my job. I must have had a few too many pills. You know I didn't mean it."

Mitch shifted uncomfortably. "Forget it, Ham." Even if I can't, he thought.

"Does Val know about that?" asked Johnson, gesturing with his head at Mitch's bandaged hands.

"No. I phoned her first thing this morning to tell her what happened, but I didn't see the point of mentioning it. Why worry her? So I'd appreciate it if *you* didn't mention it if she calls to see how you are. I'll be able to take off the bandages tomorrow morning. They just put them on me to cover the ointment on my hands. I'll be all right."

"I wonder how the devil the fire started," Johnson said. "That house isn't that old; it was put up after all sorts of electric wiring and heating codes went into effect. It's not like it was a rat trap. You could've been killed."

MITCH PAUSED, his bandaged hand on the doorknob to his office. "Maxine, no disturbances, no interruptions, please." She nodded, puzzled. "And leave extension one open for me. Make your calls on another line." She nodded again, still looking puzzled.

Mitch turned the doorknob slowly. His palm felt raw still. He pushed against the door.

"Oh!" The papers Jessie was holding fell to the floor.

Mitch closed the door behind him. He stood, leaning against the back of the door. "What is it now, Jessie?"

"Mr. Stevens, please. I was just carrying out Mr. Haye's orders."

"Which were?" Mitch sat down in the visitor's chair, glaring at her.

"He wanted, er—he said . . ." She began to stutter again, flustered by being caught once more. "Oh, please, why don't you ask him." She raced to the door, opened it and ran out.

Mitch sat, staring blankly, trying to control the rage building up inside him. Unconsciously, he started to unwind the bandage of his right hand. Then he took off the bandage on the left hand, too. He got up and took off the ill-fitting light summer jacket he had just purchased at the haberdashery on High Street, moving gently so as not to rub the cloth against his hands. He draped it over the back of his chair, and then took his address book from the top drawer of his desk. He sat down at the desk and carefully rolled up the sleeves of the blue shirt he had bought to go with the jacket and the pair of navy pants he was wearing. He stretched down for the papers Jessie had dropped. They were Rachel's notes for the profile series. He put them back in the top drawer. Reaching for the phone, he noticed a note sitting on the top of the desk: Lyle Timski asking to see him. He shoved it away. Cradling the phone with his shoulder and neck, he opened the address book to the S section and dialed 617—Boston.

"Bud? Bud Stessin?"

"Speaking."

"This is Mitch, Mitch Stevens."

"Well, for Chrissake. Where the—?"

Mitch cut him off. "Bud, I don't have time for amenities. I want to ask a favor. I need some information and I have to get it fast."

"Hey, whoa, wait a minute."

"I'd appreciate your getting—or getting someone else to get—some background material for me on a guy named Harvey Troupe."

"The real-estate developer?"

"You know him?"

"Do you folks in New York know who Donald Trump is? Sure, I know him. Let me see what I can copy for you from the morgue."

"I need more than that, Bud. I need someone to dig into papers he's filed with the state and city, make a few phone calls to some banks, check out his credit rating."

"Aha, you're up to something, aren't you, Mitch?"

"Yes, and you and the *Globe* will get first crack at it before any other paper outside of the one I'm temping for in Southborough—Southborough, Vermont. I'm filling in for Ham Johnson at the *Courier*. I promise you that."

"Okay, you're on. Give me the specifics you're after."

Mitch rattled off a series of questions. "That's it, Bud. Put a rush on it, willya?"

"Hey, listen, Mitch—"

Mitch hung up and started to dial another long-distance number from the S section of his address book. Area code 212—New York City.

"Larry Stengrin here."

"I need a favor, Larry—no questions asked," Mitch said. "I need to find out about a guy who used to be on the force."

"I'm off of police now, Mitch. Behind a desk now. I hardly ever get out anymore. Call it a promotion but I'm an editor—and it's dull as hell."

Nat & Yanna Brandt

"Does the name Handler ring a bell?"

"Handler? Handler?"

"Bill Handler? William McCoy Handler?"

"Oh, Mugsy Handler! I sure do know that name. What do you want to know?"

The buzzer on Mitch's intercom rang. Asking Stengrin to hold for a moment, Mitch pressed the intercom button.

"Ernie says he needs to see you, Mitch," said Maxine. "I told him you were closeted in your office, but he said to tell you it was urgent."

"Okay, I'll be right there."

Mitch switched off the intercom and returned to Stengrin's line. "Larry, I've got to run. Do me a favor. Jot down what you remember about Handler, will you? And anything you might have on him in the *Post* morgue—xerox whatever you think would interest me. I'd really appreciate it."

"You ever going to tell me what this is all about?"

"And send it along to me here—that's the Southborough *Courier,* High Street, Southborough, Vermont—as fast you can." Mitch didn't wait for Stengrin to speak again. "Thanks," he said, hanging up.

ERNIE'S CIGAR LAY in shreds in the tin pie plate he used for an ashtray. As Mitch approached the copy desk, the copy editor tossed a sheet of copy down the table in front of him without saying a word. Mitch picked it up. It was an editorial on the importance of permitting the zoning variation for the Britfair outlet. There was no name on the copy, only the words "MUST RUN" written by hand across the top.

"Where did this come from?" asked Mitch, though he guessed he knew where.

Ernie's thumb pointed in the direction of the publisher's office.

"I'll be right back," said Mitch, taking the copy with him.

He walked back to John Haye's office. Jessie wasn't at her desk—it was all tidied up and neat—and the door to Haye's office itself was locked. An ad rep came by. "They both just left, Mitch," he said. "Haye went up to Montpelier. I think he gave the rest of the afternoon off to—"

"When's he due back?" Mitch asked brusquely.

"Tomorrow, I think. Tomorrow morning. I—"

Mitch walked off, the copy folded like a baton under his arm, his eyes narrowing. He returned to the copy desk. "I'm going to hold on to this for now, Ernie," he said. "Run what I wrote about the state gaming law that was on the sked."

"Hmmm."

Lyle Timski called to Mitch from across the newsroom. Mitch glanced at his watch, then waved the reporter on, striding toward his office at the same time. He held the door until Timski entered, then he closed it behind him.

"Okay, quick, what's on your mind, Lyle?"

"Robin says she can't cover the School Board meeting next Wednesday night and she wants me to do it for her."

"So go ahead," Mitch said quickly, searching for the profile notes through the ad dummies and news galleys that had been dumped on his desk. "It's okay with me."

"But I can't, Mitch. That's why I asked to see you. If she asks, could you please assign Rog to it?"

Mitch stopped his search and looked up. "What the hell's so important about next Wednesday night?"

"It's when I usually go to my AA meeting. I really don't want to miss it."

"Is that where you were headed for last night?" Mitch

asked, his curiosity aroused. "I saw you going into the Unitarian Church as I was driving by."

"Yes," Timski answered. "That's where we hold our sessions. Every Wednesday night. It's an important commitment. I don't like to miss a meeting."

"I saw you entering the side door with a woman." The woman's face flashed across Mitch's mind again. He could literally feel her name on the tip of his tongue. "Can you tell me who she was?"

"I'm not supposed to tell anyone," the reporter said.

"What's the mystery about?" asked Mitch. "You have something to hide?" he added lightly.

Timski looked hurt. "Mitch, I was candid with you about my being in AA. I take it very seriously. We're not supposed to talk about anyone we meet at the sessions."

"That woman is in AA, too, right?"

"Yes."

Suddenly her name came to his mind. A troubled soul. That was what Mitch had sensed when he met her.

"Let me ask one question, Lyle—all I need is a yes or no answer—but it's very important that I verify what I think my memory tells me. I've only met her once, but wasn't that Elizabeth Haye, our publisher's wife?"

Timski looked uncomfortable.

"Lyle, I'm not asking you to breach a confidence. I just need to know for myself that it was indeed Mrs. Haye. Hell, anyone else in town seeing her entering the church would have put two and two together right then and there."

"Okay, none of us tries to hide our problem that way. Yes, it was Elizabeth. She's a wonderful, sweet lady—almost like a mother to me. She convinced me to stay on in Southborough until I got straightened out. She's very supportive."

"So she's probably been in AA for a long time," Mitch said rhetorically. "Do you think she's told her husband about you?"

"Oh, yes, I know she did. She persuaded me to let her tell him. And he's let me know through her that as long as I do my job it's no business of his."

"Well, you have no worry that way, Lyle," said Mitch. "You're a good worker, a good reporter. You're really good enough to be on a much bigger paper."

"Thanks," Timski said. "I appreciate your saying that. But I feel comfortable in Southborough for now. I don't think I'm ready for a move yet."

This time it was Mitch's turn to shrug his shoulders. "That's your business. And I didn't mean to put you on the spot about Elizabeth Haye. Something came up on a totally different matter and I wanted to be sure I had the right woman."

Timski nodded that he understood. "I should get back to the typewriter," he said.

"Do that—and thanks," said Mitch.

"You want the door closed?" the reporter asked as he got up to leave.

"No, it doesn't matter now."

Mitch found Rachel's note about John Haye: "Married to former Elizabeth Bent, daughter of a Vermont congressman, 1954. One child, girl, died in infancy . . ." Mitch recalled vividly being introduced to her the afternoon of the concert at the Mont Vert Music Festival. And what he now understood was her forlorn aspect. He also remembered seeing her afterwards by the table Yuri Putzgarov had pushed over at the trustees' party—the table on which had sat a bowl of "virgin" punch.

The mind plays funny tricks sometimes, Mitch thought. I knew I knew her. He smiled lightly to himself. Well, that gets that bugaboo out of my craw. He was reaching again for the profile notes when his intercom rang.

"There's a Larry Stengrin asking for you, Mitch," said Maxine.

"Put him on."

"Mitch?"

"You really are moving on this one, Larry. What've you got?"

"Bubkus, Mitch—you know bubkus, Mitch? Nothing. The police files on Handler are closed like it was a case of national security. And our own files here at the *Post* are at this very moment being microfilmed for posterity."

"Shit!"

"But I asked around, 'cause I remember the guy and my memory of him isn't what you might call praiseworthy, but I didn't want to rely on my feeb—"

"Larry, dear friend, please," Mitch pleaded. "What do you remember?"

"Okay, okay, I'm getting to it," said Stengrin. "There was a police scandal back in the seventies—around the time Nixon resigned. In fact, just about at the same time, so it didn't make as many headlines as it might of 'cause Nixon got 'em all.

"It went something like this: There was a riot—well, not a riot maybe, but a fracas on a street up in Harlem. A cop had tried to arrest some street dealer—a white cop, a black druggie. I don't know. Maybe he used too much muscle, maybe the guy put up a fuss. I don't know, nobody knows. But the next thing all hell is breaking loose. The cop is surrounded by a mob, an angry mob, and he's radioing for help and his hand is on his holster. You know, like a showdown is about to occur. And before you know it, three squad cars zoom up, and people start pushing and shoving and yelling and screaming. And Handler—bless his soul—gets out of his car, sees what's going on, gets back in, and hunkers down in the back seat where no one can see him."

"He what?" Handler had told Mitch he had retired after being shot during a supermarket stickup.

"He what? He turned chicken. Don't you speak English up there, Mitch? There must've been three, four cops beaten up by the crowd before the whole fucking precinct showed up. And there, in the back seat of the squad car, they found Handler, shaking like he had the D.T.'s or something. A disgrace to New York's finest."

"Was he fired for that?"

"I don't know from fired or he quit. But he left, as we say, under a cloud. And you know what I remember Phil Cahn turning up when he started digging into Handler's background? Handler had a slew of medals for bravery. That's how he got his nickname—Mugsy—from the pictures they took of him at all of the medal ceremonies. He got into the papers almost as often as the commissioner. But not one medal involved a regular police action. I mean he got cited for saving someone from a fire, and another time he jumped into the East River when an idiot fell out of a rowboat, but not once—never—had he ever even fired his weapon while on duty."

"I've heard of that happening with some cops," Mitch said. "It's not uncommon."

"Yeah, sure, but it kind of says something about Handler when you put that together with his behavior up in Harlem."

"I appreciate your getting back to me on this, Larry."

"I just wanted to check out my memory with a couple of the boys still down in the press room at police headquarters. That's what they remember, too. They said someone afterwards scrawled a big C in chalk on his locker at the twenty-third precinct."

"A big C?"

"Yeah, for Coward."

"Listen, Larry, if you—" Mitch's intercom buzzed. "Damn. Larry, if you hear anything more let me know."

"Sure thing, but what's going—?"

Mitch pressed the intercom button. "It's Mr. Haye, Mitch. On two."

Mitch switched to the second extension. "Mr. Haye?"

"Stevens, I just called Ernie to see if he had any questions about the editorial I had Jessie hand him and he said you had pulled it back. Is that right?"

"Yes, that's correct. We have an editorial on the state gaming law skedded for tomorrow's edition."

"Now you look here, Stevens, I personally wrote that editorial—and I tagged it 'Must Run.' You keep on forgetting that this is *my* newspaper."

"If I may be candid, Mr. Haye," Mitch said, getting annoyed, "it wasn't well written and—"

"That's for Ernie to clean up."

"And I think we have to talk about this whole situation anyway."

"What whole situation? Between you and me, you mean?"

"Something like that. I hear you're due back tomorrow. Why don't we both put this on a back burner until then."

"You're tying my hands, Stevens. I don't like that one bit."

"And you're trying to shackle me. So let's talk and try to resolve all this. Okay?" Mitch slammed down the receiver so hard that he hurt his hand. He winced and looked at his palm. It was red again and beginning to swell. "You're lucky," the fire marshal had said. Jeez, how lucky can you get? One, two, maybe three murders. Someone trying to kill me. Ham's house a ruin. And it's my fault. The publisher spying on me. And me pissed off as all hell. How the devil did I ever get into this mess? Better yet, how the hell do I get out of it?

The intercom rang. "Ernie says he needs you again. There's some emergency going on. He's already flagged down Lyle and Robin before they left for the day."

Mitch started to slam his fist on the desk, caught himself in midair, but too late to soften the blow when it hit the surface. He winced again in pain.

LYLE AND ROBIN were already huddled on either side of Ernie when Mitch approached the copy desk. Ernie, cigar in mouth, was on the phone, making incomprehensible notes with his right hand. He finally mumbled something and hung up.

"That was Rog. He was down at police headquarters. The First State's on fire."

Robin ran to the window overlooking High Street and pushed it open. She hefted herself out on the windowsill so that she could look down High Street toward the bank. "Oh, my God, there's smoke coming out of it in huge clouds. And here comes a fire engine."

"Robin!" The young woman struggled back inside on hearing Mitch's voice. "You and Lyle get down there quick. I want a phone call in five minutes from one of you with the lowdown on what's happening." Robin and Lyle looked at each other. "Now!" The two reporters grabbed some copy paper from the pile in front of Ernie and ran toward the stairwell.

"Ernie, get Henry down there pronto. I want as many

photos as he can shoot—and quick." Henry Peddles, the *Courier*'s staff photographer, was notoriously slow-moving, and accustomed to posed shots, compositions he scrupulously devised for feature stories and the like. The best he could do on sports was to catch the batter being congratulated on getting back to the bench after a home run—forget about the swing, the outfielder chasing the ball to the fence, the batter rounding the bases or even touching home plate.

"He's at that new restaurant out Putney way, getting a shot of the owner and his wife," Ernie said.

"Call him back," said Mitch. He reached for the phone. "Where did you say Rog was—police headquarters?" Ernie nodded. Mitch dialed. "And get Rachel in also wherever the hell she is." A voice answered his call: "Police, Officer Harding."

"Hi, I'm calling from the *Courier*. Is Roger Barrows there?"

"Yep. Want to talk to him? But you better make it fast. This place is starting to jump."

"Rog, hightail it back to the office as quick as you can. I need you here." Mitch dropped the phone back on the receiver without waiting for the reporter's response.

"You wanted me?" Rachel, her face flushed, came up to the desk.

"Hang around. We got a fire at the First State and we may need you. Oh yeah, where the hell is the report on Eagleston's death?"

"I left it on your desk, along with the profile material."

"Well, I can't find it. Bring me your copy posthaste!"

Rachel didn't move. She smiled awkwardly.

"Rachel, for Chrissake. Just play it straight. Did you forget to make a copy?"

"I'm sorry, Mitch." She added quickly, "But I remember everything that was on it. It said that he was a diabetic and that he died of heart failure. Apparently, it's not that uncommon. Did you have anything else in mind?"

Ernie called out: "I got Henry, he's on his way."

"Where's Abe, for Chrissake?"

"He said he'd be late. He had to go to the dentist."

"Rachel, you handle the phones on the desk. And Rachel," Mitch spoke softly, "You don't need to play games. You're doing good work. If you make a mistake, don't be afraid to admit it."

Mitch turned to Ernie. "Where's that page one dummy? We better start thinking right now what we want to keep and what can go." He and Ernie studied the front-page layout.

The phone rang. Rachel reached for it quickly. "It's Lyle, Mitch, for you."

"Mitch, it's getting out of hand. The chief has already put out a call for help."

"Anybody hurt?"

"It looks like everybody was out of the building when it broke out, but the smoke is so heavy that a couple of firemen are already sprawled out on the sidewalk getting oxygen."

"How bad is it?"

"It's threatening the whole northern end of the block. But at least there's no wind to speak of."

"Okay, you and Robin stick with it. Figure on doing the lead story. Tell Robin to handle the color. We'll want a sidebar from her. I've got Henry coming down your way. See to it that he gets some good shots in without futzing around too much. And call in whenever you get a chance to keep us appraised. We're going to hold the press until we hear from you and get a better fix."

"Gotcha," said Timski.

As Mitch hung up, Rachel was answering another call. She held her hand over the mouthpiece. "Mitch, it's Wilbur Sway, the pharmacist. He's calling from home and asking for information. He just got a call from a store owner that the bank's on fire."

"Tell him we don't have any details so far, but that the fire company's called for help. And Rachel, from now on why don't you handle all those calls yourself. We'll feed you whatever information we get. I think we're going to get a lot of calls tonight."

Roger Barrows entered the newsroom. "Wow!" he said, "you should see what's going on down the street. The police have it all cordoned off. There must be three–four fire engines lined up against the curb."

"Rog, Lyle already phoned that there've been some injuries to firemen. Get on the phone with Southborough General and find out how they are. We'll want a story about all those injured and how serious their condition is. And feed whatever you find out to Rachel. She's manning the phones for queries."

Mitch looked over to Ernie. "I didn't even hear one fire engine go by."

Ernie, who had already said more than Mitch had ever known him to say in one day, muttered.

"What?"

"Air conditioning."

Mitch nodded. Until Robin had opened the window, all the windows in the newsroom were shut tight, the air conditioners whirring, all other sounds suppressed. It was like working in a vacuum.

"Want me to stay?" It was Maxine Long, a thin white cardigan draped over her shoulders.

"Maybe you better in case I have to send Rog or Rachel out," said Mitch. "Do you mind? Maybe you can help Rachel with the phones."

"Not at all. This is what my mother told me ages ago that newspaper work would be like—and it's the first time it's happened." Mitch laughed. He scanned the newsroom. Rog and Rachel were both on phones, Rog scrawling away busily on a pad in front of him. Ernie was redoing the headlines of several stories that were being moved from the front page to inside the paper. And Abe was just coming in now, nursing a swollen cheek. Mitch smiled. He liked the excitement of a late-breaking story. Let's just hope, he reminded himself, that we don't have to hold the press too long—that will cost overtime and foul up the deliveries.

The situation reminded Mitch of the time a blackout had plunged Manhattan into a scary darkness back in the 1960s: working by candlelight, the jangle of phones the only usual sound that night, the copy being messengered to a friendly newspaper in New Jersey, where it was set and the paper put together. That was the kind of crisis it was difficult to cope with in a small town such as Southborough. The other kind of crisis—some momentous event occurring just as the paper is being put to bed or the press is slowly gearing up to maximum speed—that at least is manageable, even when, as on the *Courier,* typewriters rather than word processors are the norm, and the type is still set by hand. With the world falling apart at the last minute, it's possible to squeeze in a paragraph or two on the front page and figure on catching up with the story the next day—or stop the presses, shoot a reporter to the scene of the event, get a good rewrite man ready to take down his account over the phone, push through the copy in short takes, slap a headline on it and not care whether it fits perfectly, replate and get the presses rolling again as soon as possible. A matter of hours, only on a big paper a missed plane or train delivery screws up the suburban run so that the paper's phones are busy all the next day with readers' complaints, and, to top everything off, there's a whopping overtime bill. With luck, that doesn't happen but once every one or two years. On the other hand, it's also exciting.

All thought of the soreness from the skid burns forgotten, he picked up the direct line to the composing room. "Mickey?"

"Hey, what's going on up there?" asked Peabody. "We haven't seen any copy for the last half hour."

Mitch explained about the fire. "So pass the word. I'm ordering the presses on standby until the fire in the First State Bank is under control."

"It's your money," the compositor said.

The hell it is, Mitch thought. Wait'll Haye gets the bill. "We're sending up some sub heads for the stories we moved already and I'll come along to remake some of the pages in a little while. I think we can figure that most of page one will be given over to the fire."

"Okay," said Peabody. "I'll keep everybody here until we can close."

"Good. We'll feed you the copy in takes once Lyle and Robin get back. I'll keep you informed."

And now it was up to Lyle and Robin. Mitch had done everything possible as an editor, covered all the bases he could with the staff he had. He had alerted everyone that required alerting, had Ernie and now Abe reworking the rest of the paper. Truth was, he told himself, I really should have someone at the hospital itself, with a photographer. He wished he had a couple of rewrite men so that Lyle and Robin could stay by a phone near the fire, calling in their stories. But without additional staff, all he could do now was wait—when Lyle and Robin reported back in would depend on the fire.

"It's for you, Mitch," Rachel called out. "Lyle."

"Mitch? Listen, every old wooden building on High Street is threatened by the blaze and fire companies from as far away as Keene are either here or on their way."

"Okay, you stay with it. I'll tell you what. We'll handle it the way we handled the professor's death. I'll get to a phone with a set of earphones and you can call in your story to me. But Robin will have to come back to the office with hers."

And so the night went, Mitch acting as rewrite, Lyle the legman. The fire had begun well after the bank had closed, though not too long after the tellers and office managers, the daily count in, had filed out of the building. Most other shops on High Street were closed by that time, too, and the downtown area, busy as it might have been during the day, had reverted to an empty, sleepy state, deserted by everyone but the few handymen who lived in lone rooms above some of the stores. The serenity was shattered for nearly four hours as fire companies from other communities, midstate and upstate, as well as across the Connecticut River, raced into Southborough to contain and fight the fire. Which they finally accomplished, though the bank was left a smoldering ruin and neighboring buildings were scorched. And so the *Cou-*

rier, like many of the citizens of Southborough, did not get to bed until well after two o'clock in the morning. And that meant the press rumbled on until after three o'clock.

Mitch could feel its vibration as he sat in his office, a lone lamp lighting his desk. Ernie and Abe had already packed it in. Robin and Lyle had gone home after punching out their stories—Lyle, an enterprising eyewitness account he had rushed back to write to accompany the lead he had phoned in to Mitch; Robin, a sidebar on the companies that had joined in battling the blaze. Rog, Maxine and Rachel had stayed around late, too. Maxine and Rachel had spent the night answering queries from worried store owners and bank customers as news of the fire had fanned across the county. (The inquiries, Mitch understood, were a throwback to the time when most people telephoned their newspaper for information, believing it was on top of things; radio and television stations now assumed that role in most cities.) Rog, meanwhile, had compiled an up-to-date list on the condition of the firefighters overcome from smoke and taken to Southborough General Hospital. Their names and condition were boxed on page one. Ernie and Abe had split up the coverage for editing, while Mitch, once the lead story was out of his typewriter, had re-dummied page one and the jump page for the fire stories, and then—his palms smeared with Vitamin D ointment provided by Maxine and covered with gauze—had stayed beside the ink-stained compositor's bench downstairs, moving stories around, rewriting headlines that didn't fit their new spaces, as the normal deadline for the paper came and went. All in all, a good team effort. And Mitch had a hearty thanks for everyone who had chipped in.

And now, sitting at his desk, too worked up to be tired,

the adrenalin still flowing almost in rhythm with the press below, Mitch tried to relax. A horn honked in the street outside. Mitch had opened the window as the night had cooled. He went to it to look out, but High Street, its pavement glowing wet from the fire hoses, was deserted. He couldn't see the bank—it was a block away—but again he smelled the terrible stench of burned wood, metal and plastic that he associated with the burning of Ham Johnson's home.

Suddenly, with a whine, the press wound down, the run over. In a matter of minutes, the *Courier*'s two delivery trucks, backed up now at the platform at the rear of the building, would be loaded and off on their rounds, the pressmen would swab down the big, oil-coated press and the day would finally be over.

A shot rang out. Instinctively, Mitch ducked. Then, slowly, he went to the door and peered into the darkened newsroom. Another shot rang out. Mitch swept around toward the window in his office. Another shot. He ran to it, hugging the wall alongside it, and carefully looked out. On the street below, a grimy, open-backed truck was belching black smoke from its exhaust pipe. Mitch heaved a sigh. The stench from the bank fire had triggered his fear and he was drenched in sweat. He had repressed the whole nightmarish experience at Ham's house, publicly making light of the fact that he had narrowly escaped. Now his sense of smell was betraying him. He felt chilled and listless. He had been operating the last few hours on a burst of adrenalin and now felt totally drained.

Was it coincidence, he suddenly thought, that it was Bert Lester's bank that had been destroyed tonight?

FIFTEEN

Mitch walked into the small dining room at the Colonial House. His eyes smarted from the glare of sunlight that burst in from a window overlooking the back garden. His body ached from lack of sleep. Squinting, he saw Rachel seated at a table in the far corner, studying a menu. He hesitated for a second and then walked over and sat down next to her.

"Morning." He looked at her and realized that she no longer made him uncomfortable. Well, either I'm senile or I'm not as scared of pretty young things as I am of what's going on in this town.

"Good morning, boss." They were both silent for a moment and then Rachel looked up at him. "Mitch, could I get personal for a minute?"

"Sure, Rachel, what is it?"

"I thought a lot about the way I've been acting." She went on, with some difficulty. It was the first time Mitch had seen her this much on edge. "I realize that I've been coming on to you." Mitch felt himself blushing but he didn't stop Rachel. "It's something I've always done, it's my way of dealing. I know it sounds corny, but you've made me realize that I don't have to." Rachel tilted her head to the side. "Oh, Mitch, I've embarrassed you. I'm sorry, I really didn't mean to."

Mitch chose his words carefully. "Rachel, I'll be honest with you. I almost didn't ask you up here because of the way you behaved in class. But you've got a lot of talent, and, hell, now I'm glad I did ask you. Let's leave it at that." He picked up the menu. "What're you having?"

"Bob. Hi, it's Mitch. Did I catch you too early?"

Mitch turned slightly from the wall telephone and smiled at Rachel, who was just leaving the dining room after finishing breakfast.

Grant mumbled back something about being up already.

"I won't keep you," said Mitch, speaking softly into the mouthpiece but trying not to sound conspiratorial. "I just wondered if you knew a way that I could contact Stanley Lay. I know he's busy and out all day. But I need to reach him."

"Is this about that property I told you about?" Grant asked.

"Yes. I need to clarify something."

"Anything I can help you with, Mitch?"

"No, I think it's in Lay's province. Do you know how I can get ahold of him?"

Grant asked Mitch to wait a minute. "Here it is," he said, coming back on the line. "His wife ordinarily keeps his log and handles the paperwork. Their number is . . ."

Hugging the phone against his shoulder, Mitch jotted down the number. "Thanks, Bob. I'll get back to you eventually."

He dialed again. Lay's wife answered. Mitch explained that he needed to contact Lay right away.

"He's over by Razorback Mountain this morning," she said. "He started out early 'cause he's got so much to do. Wait a sec and I'll find what he wrote down."

In another minute, Mitch had the directions to the property where Lay was working. He started for the front door. His car was wedged between two other cars in the gravel parking lot alongside the inn. Mitch squeezed into the door and turned on the ignition. Another sleepless night had convinced him that he had to take the initiative and get some evidence that he could then take to the police.

He backed slowly out of the lot and onto the road, turning as he did so away from Southborough in the direction of Razorback Mountain.

MITCH WAITED FOR the backhoe to come to a halt with a grunt. "You have a minute, Mr. Lay?"

"Why it's Mr. Stevens, isn't it?" Stan Lay gripped the side of the yellow cabin as he stepped down. "How did you find me out here?" he asked, taking a handkerchief from his back pocket and wiping his nose. A gust of wind made the cloth flutter. Lay looked off into the distance. They were on top of a knoll. To the west was Razorback Mountain, from which, on a clear day, you could almost see the one hundred miles away that the scenic-view stop along Route 6 advertised. A thickening roll of black clouds was moving steadily and inexorably toward them. "It's going to rain," the engineer said without waiting for

Mitch to answer. "What you want? I got to finish this hole 'fore it pours."

"I came to see you about permits," said Mitch.

"Ah, you want to *speed* the process on that land I tested, is that it?"

"It's not any good, is it, Lay? I mean, it can't possibly pass a perc, can it?"

"Now, don't you get discouraged. I can promise that you'll be able to build on that property. You'll get your permit, you'll see."

"But it won't be legal, will it?"

Lay squinched his eyes. "I said you'll pass. What more do you want?"

"I'll get the approval the same way that SkiLand did, won't I? Section 4–03–A3. I mean, who's to know?"

"I gotta get going." Lay reached out to hoist himself back into the backhoe cabin.

"I can prove you falsified the information on the permit," said Mitch.

Lay lowered himself back to the ground. Turning, Mitch saw that he had a monkey wrench in his hand. "What's that to you, mister?"

"I just want to know who put you up to this."

"You got some goddamned nerve. I'm not telling you anything." Lay advanced menacingly toward Mitch, who stepped back instinctively.

"It's not you I'm interested in," said Mitch. "I just want to know who you dealt with for SkiLand." Off in the distance a jagged flash of lightning shot from the sky. A rumble of thunder echoed across the mountains. "A name, all I want is a name."

"Look, I don't know what yer talkin' about. Now, get outa here, I got work to do."

"Mr. Lay, I don't want to threaten you, but unless you

help me, you're going to wind up as an accessory to murder."

Lay looked bewildered. "Murder, whaddaya mean, murder? Are you crazy or somethin'?"

"Murder—at least two of them. Attempted murder—of me. Arson. Fraud. Bribery. You want me to go on, Lay?"

Lay's mouth dropped open. For a moment, he was absolutely still. "Murder . . . who was murdered?"

"Vera Tolvey, Yuri Putzgarov, probably Telford Eagleston."

"Vera, murdered? But I thought that paper of yours said it was a hunting accident?"

"We didn't have proof then. We do now."

Lay turned away. "Christ Almighty, murder. He didn't say nothing about anyone getting hurt. It was just a perc test, a perc test, goddamn it. Nobody was to get hurt. No harm done."

"Acessory to murder—that's what they'll call it. You'll be implicated along with everybody else once the story gets out. All the police will have to do is get the perc tests redone to pin down your involvement. They'll find out soon enough that yours are phony."

Lay searched the darkening sky with his eyes. He turned suddenly to Mitch. "You're crazy. Why the devil should I say anything? You can't protect me. I'd just be hanging myself."

"I can promise you that we—the newspaper—would put in a good word with the police and the court. I'll personally testify on your behalf. Your cooperation would be bound to be taken into consideration." Lay hesitated. "Otherwise," Mitch added, "you'll be implicated right up to your eyeballs. A name, Lay, a name. Whom did you deal with?"

Lay licked his lips. "Okay, okay." He glared at Mitch. "But you'd better keep your part of the bargain." It was a hollow threat, they both knew, but Lay needed to say it. "The guy was—"

A crack of thunder drowned out the name, but Mitch had caught the first syllable and, watching Lay's lips, could figure out the rest. A huge drop of rain splattered on his shirt, then a machine-gun burst of raindrops, just as a roll of thunder drowned out Lay's next words.

Mitch ran back to his car as the rain began to pummel the ground.

"Do you know if Haye is in?" Mitch asked Maxine as he walked by her desk on the way into his office.

"Not yet," she replied. "Jessie's been looking for him, too. There's a Fed Ex package for you. I left it on your desk."

"Let me know when he gets in," he said, entering the office and closing the door behind him. He tore open the thin red, white and blue cardboard envelope. Inside was a sheaf of papers with a note attached:

Mitcho, old boy—
    Herewith copies of the descriptive covering letters attached to a number of Troupe's prospectuses (prospecti?). The prospectuses themselves are too voluminous—and unnecessary—to copy. Note the name of the holder of the second mortgage on each venture. Each is a corporation whose name corresponds to a much earlier venture. You wouldn't make the connection unless you studied all these papers at once, and since they cover a period of 10–15 years, I guess nobody has ever thought or bothered to.

Am no financial wizard (like some others around a certain poker table that I know), but it seems to me he's taking in with one hand and giving out with the other. What happens if any one of the ventures hits a down period and the holder of the first mortgage forecloses, a not unknown occurrence these days? The assets of one corporation depend on the assets of the next, and so on down the line. If anyone ever calls his hand (to pick up the metaphor), he's in deep shit.

Am dying to use this material myself. Troupe has been trying to get the City Council here to approve plans for a "model" urban business-residential complex that would destroy the fringes of a historic district. The dear old Globe is opposed to such desecration. When can I go ahead?

Yr hmble svt,
Bud

Mitch opened the bottom drawer of his desk where he had stashed the profile notes and clippings. He was about to add the package from Bud, but instead, on an impulse, he took out her research and began to leaf through the clippings he hadn't had time to look at.

There must have been more than thirty news clips in the Bert Lester file, stories about his becoming president of his uncle's bank, his fight against sex-education classes while on the School Board, how he led the United Fund's most successful drive in 1983, being elected president of Kiwanis, his idea for a Development Board (with, attached to the clip, a *Courier* editorial supporting it)—all routine stories. Only Lester's reaction to his bank's being downgraded by Standard & Poor was unexpected. "We won't sit still," he was quoted as saying. "That's not our policy. We will fight to get business and industry into Southborough. That will be our priority. The people of this town are entitled to and can expect the highest level of banking—top interest rates, low mortgage terms—from First State, or we might as well close our doors." There was an undercurrent of desperation in his concluding remarks, though on the surface they sounded optimistic: "I wouldn't want to live and work in Southborough unless I could do better, both for my business and for the town."

Again Mitch wondered whether a man such as Bert Lester would resort to murder to protect his career. If his bank was foundering . . . ? If it had extended itself unwisely to support the SkiLand project and now was helping to underwrite the purchase of the land where the Britfair outlet would be located . . . ? Would he have set fire to his own bank . . . ? As an insurance ploy? To divert suspicion?

Mitch picked up the weighty file of news clippings on Haye. If what he had figured out about the publisher was true, he already knew all he had to know about him. Mitch put Haye's file aside and began to sift through Brad Cummings's instead. Rachel was right about Cummings's love for politicking. There he was, beaming, in so many photographs—with the 4-H, at the local fair, in costume for a Fourth of July re-enactment, picketing Vermont Central for lower electric rates—that Mitch raced through them. He stopped when he came to an old crumbling clipping from a 1970 *Courier* feature: "Vietnam Hero Describes Ordeal." Cummings, according to the article, had been cut off from his Ranger unit for a week, surrounded on all sides by Vietcong. He had gone days with virtually no sleep, constantly on the lookout, at one point out of rations and reduced to catching rainwater in his helmet for sustenance. "I vowed then and there," he told the *Courier* reporter, "I'd never, ever, get myself into a situation like that again. I learned a major lesson that time and it's deep within my soul. You have to learn to trust yourself above all other people and never lose sight of your objective, survival."

Survival. Cummings's back was also up against the wall; his store was dependent on the SkiLand development for survival. It was supplying all the appliances, a hefty order for a business on the verge of bankruptcy. If anything went wrong . . . ? And what about his political status . . . ? What would it look like if he couldn't keep his head above water? Mitch tapped his fingers on the top of the desk. What the hell did it all mean?

The intercom buzzed. "Jessie says Mr. Haye is in now, Mitch," said Maxine. "He can see you whenever you want."

Mitch walked back to the publisher's office. Jessie Cummings offered an embarrassed smile as he passed her desk.

"That was a nice job you did on the bank fire. The paper looked terrific," John Haye said magnanimously as Mitch entered his office. "Will you please let everyone know how pleased I am. No, better yet, I'll write a memo to the staff."

"They'd appreciate that," said Mitch. "Look, I have to talk to—"

"Was there a lot of overtime involved?" the publisher asked.

"You're going to get hit for a big bill. Right down the line. I needed everyone. If you're too bus—"

"What about compensatory time?"

"Sure, I'll offer it," said Mitch, getting increasingly edgy. "I'll spread the word around that now's a good time to take time off. Look, I—"

"Sit down, will you, Stevens. You're making me nervous."

Mitch was standing in front of Haye's desk. Outside the publisher's window, the Connecticut River moved sluggishly along, barely a ripple on its surface. In stark contrast was the traffic on High Street on the other side of the *Courier* building. Cars filled with gawking families jammed the downtown area, rubber-necking their way by the burned-out hulk of the bank.

"That's better," the publisher said as Mitch sat down. "Now, what's on your mind?"

"I think we have to talk."

Haye's eyelids lowered ominously. "Where do you want to start?" he said. "*My* editorial?"

"No," said Mitch. "Something more fundamental. I've given this a lot of thought." A lot of sleepless thought, he could have said. The car's backfiring—the "shots" that had scared him—had brought Mitch back to the reality of the murders. He had tossed and turned in his bed at the Colonial House during what was left of the night, running over again and again the flurry of coincidences and his suspicions. He had finally decided to trust the publisher because of his wife. If Elizabeth Haye was in AA, Mitch reasoned, then she knew Yuri Putzgarov was a member, too. And Mitch was certain that she would have told her husband, just as she had told him about Lyle Timski—especially once she learned that Haye and Putzgarov were involved in a business deal. And if that were true, then Haye would have been the last person to try to make the violinist's death look like a case of drunk driving. Yes, you could make a case for the possibility that, after all, Putzgarov was an alcoholic and might have relapsed. But why even raise that point at all? Why create suspicion that would have prompted the police to test Putzgarov's blood, as they should have in the first place? No, Mitch was sure, it wasn't Haye. He'd have known better than to raise the issue.

"I want to talk seriously to you about what I've found out so far, what I think are a string of incidents too extraordinary to be coincidental."

Haye looked puzzled. "What are you getting at, Stevens? You sound like you're trying to scare someone." He sneered. "Is this another way to circumvent my wishes on the Britfair zoning request?"

The publisher's tone annoyed Mitch, but he was too tired to respond in kind. "Listen to me for five minutes and then we'll talk about whose will is going to prevail. I'm tired of being spied on, and I'm tired of your jumping on my ass. Just hear me out. Okay?"

Haye spread his hands placatingly, but there was an ironic bite to his saying, "The floor is all yours."

"First of all, I saw Stan Lay this morning and he—"

"Who the hell is Stan Lay?"

"He's the engineer who handled the SkiLand property perc test. He told me that Bill Handler had approached him about fixing the SkiLand permit. He said—"

"That's it, Stevens." Haye stood up. "Get the hell out of my office."

"But don't you understand? The whole deal is linked with the mur—"

"You heard me. Out." The publisher picked up a silver letter opener and pointed toward the door with it. "You've caused nothing but trouble about the resort and the Britfair venture. I've had enough of your meddling, you sonovabitch."

Mitch stood. "You don't know what you're saying."

"*You* don't know what *you're* saying. I don't like your

inuendos, Stevens. I don't like your smartass New York ways. And I'm not going to tolerate unfounded, hearsay remarks from you."

"They're not hear—"

"Out! Now! You got one reason being in this building and only one reason—and that's to see that the *Courier* gets out every day. You butt your nose into anything else and I'll, I'll . . ." Haye groped to finish the sentence, his face red with anger. "Get the hell out!"

Mitch left, slamming the door behind him. Going past Jessie Cummings, he could hear Haye's voice, still angry, over the intercom on her desk: ". . . me your husband and find out where Harvey Troupe is. Right now!" Jessie winced at his tone of voice and tried to smile at Mitch, but she was too upset to manage more than a fleeting upturn of her lips.

Mitch stomped back to his own office, so angry himself that he almost bumped into Rachel, who was crossing the newsroom to the copy desk. He wanted to get away from the humiliation he felt after the way Haye had spoken to him. He wanted to be alone, to think what his next step should be. The police? Did he have enough yet for the police?

"Mitch, thank God you're back." Maxine was perturbed. "It's Mr. Johnson. He's had a relapse. I was phoning as usual to talk to him and see how he was . . ." She swallowed hard. "A nurse answered. He's in an oxygen tent. They wouldn't tell me more over the phone. I—I—I . . ."

"It's okay, Maxine, it's okay." Mitch took her hands in his. "We'll get up there right now. Okay?"

He spied Rachel crossing back to her desk. "Rachel! Come on over here and take over Maxine's desk, will you?

We're going up to Hanover to check on Ham Johnson. There's some sort of emergency."

The young intern rushed over. "Is there anything else I can do?"

"Yeah. Tell Ernie to handle the paper. He can call Abe in early if he needs help." Mitch was helping Maxine on with her jacket. "Oh, and you'd better tell Jessie to tell Haye what's happened. I'll phone in when we know something definite." He took Maxine's arm and they headed toward the stairwell.

MAXINE STOOD BY Ham Johnson's bed, her hand clutching the edge of the sheet, her eyes meeting his through the filmy plastic tent that covered him. Mitch watched from the corner, where he stood with a bearded young doctor.

"It's not unusual," the doctor was saying. "I'm sorry you had to come all this way, but we have it under control. Pneumonia isn't unknown after an operation like Mr. Johnson had. All that lying around tends to allow water to collect in the lungs."

Mitch nodded, too sleepy to respond.

"I'll check in on him later on my rounds," the doctor added, starting for the door. "But he'll be all right. Don't worry."

Maxine had dragged a chair beside the bed and was talking quietly to Johnson, who was resting his head on its side, looking at her intently. Mitch saw the trace of a smile pass over his lips. Ham was going to be all right.

Mitch checked his watch: almost seven o'clock. He went over to the bedside and put a hand on Maxine's shoulder. He told her what the doctor had said. "Visiting hours are over in half an hour, Maxine. You can come back again tomorrow."

She looked up at him, relief in her eyes.

"We'll grab a bite on the way back to Southborough."

Maxine nodded and turned back to Johnson. His eyes went toward Mitch and he smiled.

THE DRIVE BACK to Southborough had seemed to take forever to Mitch. He and Maxine had stopped briefly at a fast-food restaurant near Hanover and had eaten while driving down I-91. A bright moon, orange at first, had risen and soon bathed the ribbon of highway in an eerie light. They could see for miles. "Moonlight in Vermont," she said, her spirits revived by being with Johnson. She began to hum the tune.

Mitch drove to the parking lot at the *Courier,* now deserted except for Maxine's car. She bent over and kissed him on the cheek as she said goodnight.

HEADING LEISURELY THROUGH downtown Southborough on his way back to the Colonial House, Mitch pondered whether his knowledge of Handler's involvement with Lay in the perc tests would be enough to get the police, the state police if not Southborough's, to begin an investigation. Maybe, he thought, I ought to go speak to Tiny Adams tomorrow, see what he says. He hitched up his glasses and rubbed his eyes with a free hand. He was too exhausted to think any further. I'll sleep on it, and decide in the morning.

Rounding the last bend in the dirt road that led to the Colonial House off of Route 6, Mitch could see that the innkeeper had left the porch light and a light in the living room on for him. Otherwise, the inn was dark, though its white clapboard side glowed eerily in the moonlight.

As he drove up, the headlights from a car parked on the verge across the road from the inn came on suddenly. It was, Mitch saw as he slowed to turn into the parking lot, a Cadillac—John Haye's car. He suddenly became alert. What was Haye doing at the Colonial House?

Mitch pulled over by the entranceway and stopped. The publisher had gotten out of his car and was standing in its headlights. His bulky figure was outlined by the strange halo they caused.

Warily, Mitch got out of his own car. He stood by its door.

"Stevens, is that you?"

Mitch acknowledged Haye with a slight wave of his hand.

"Wait up. I have to see you," the publisher said. He started to cross the road toward Mitch. Mitch began walking slowly toward the publisher. The two men had almost reached each other in the middle of the road when suddenly a shot rang out. The blast echoed off Mayors Peak.

Both men dived to the ground as the dirt at their feet was violently gouged. "Where the hell did that come from?"

"Keep down!" Mitch ordered, crawling on his stomach toward Haye's car. "Let's get out of the light behind your car."

Haye followed Mitch, the heavy-set publisher breathing so heavily that Mitch thought he was gagging. Mitch propped himself up by the front tire. "Get behind the other tire. It'll shield you." His mouth was open, his breath coming in gasps. "I think the shot came from further down the road, beyond the inn."

"Did you—?"

"Shh," said Mitch. "I hear something."

The sound of a car engine grew louder. Mitch leaned against the door of the Cadillac and slowly edged himself up until he could peer through the side window.

"Don't be crazy. Get down," Haye whispered urgently.

Mitch ignored him. He saw a car screeching to a stop, and in its beams was yet another car parked off the road, its lights out. Mitch saw someone bolt out of the newly arrived car without turning off the engine or the lights. He rose to his full height, trying to spot the figure, when suddenly another shot rang out.

Mitch ducked instinctively, looking desperately at Haye as he hugged the side of the Cadillac. But there was no whine from the bullet and nothing had been hit. "For Chrissake, stay down," the publisher said as Mitch edged up the side of the car again.

The figure from the newly arrived car had dropped to its knees. There was a piercing scream.

"Come on," said Mitch.

"Wait! Don't! You might get shot."

Mitch trotted toward the car down the road.

"Mitch, for Chrissake, there's a murderer out there somewhere. That's what I've come to tell you. Come back!"

Lights coming on inside the Colonial House added brightness to the scene, making Mitch easy to identify. He ran on, however, without trying to keep within any shadows. Haye was still shouting at him, but the words never registered in his mind. The publisher rose heavily from the ground and started to run after him.

The figure on its knees, shimmering in the glow from the headlights, was holding a body in its arms and moaning.

Mitch halted when he saw who it was. Haye, lumbering up behind him, stopped also. "Oh, my God," the publisher said, trying to catch his breath. "But it can't be. It's impossible. It's Jessie. She's not the one."

Jessica Cummings's face was splattered with blood, her eyes staring wildly, her body limp in her husband's arms. Brad Cummings was rocking her body back and forth, crying softly.

"But it's Brad who's behind all this," said Haye. "He said as much to us tonight. He said he had to do it, that he was protecting all of us."

The selectman looked up at them. Tears were rolling down his cheeks. He opened his mouth to speak, but no words came out.

"He confessed?"

"And he threatened to implicate us in the murders if anyone went to the police. He said we were all in it together."

"What the hell prompted him to do that?" Mitch asked.

"I told them—Brad, Troupe, Bert, Handler, we all got together at Brad's place—I told them what you said about Handler. All hell broke loose."

"But why would he shoot his wife?" asked Mitch, perplexed. "That doesn't make any sense at all."

Haye stooped down by a shotgun that had fallen near Jessica Cummings's body. Cummings had gently lain his wife back on the road and was keening over her softly.

"It's an old one," the publisher said, moving the weapon from side to side to catch the best light from the headlights of Cummings's car. "It looks like a late nineteenth-century shotgun from Brad's collection. I'd guess it has a Damascus barrel. They were made of iron and steel ribbons twisted and wielded together. If you're a hunter you'd know better than to use a modern smokeless shell in it. The barrel's too soft for the pressure." The publisher stood up with effort. "The second shot backfired on her. She killed herself."

Cummings looked up at them. He ran a blood-stained hand through his hair. "She must've overheard what you said about Stevens," he said to Haye. "She got in her car and ran off. I, I didn't understand until I saw the gun missing from its brackets on the wall."

"She was laying in wait for you to come home, Mitch," the publisher said.

Mitch stared down at the dead woman. "What could she have hoped to accomplish?"

"She was trying to keep you from talking. I guess she was afraid you'd ruin Brad and his business."

"It's over, Cummings. You know that, don't you?"

The selectman was grief-stricken. He started to say something, but broke into sobs instead.

SIXTEEN

THE PUBLISHER SAT in Mitch's office, legs crossed, tapping his fingers impatiently on the armrests, waiting as Mitch and Timski, bending over Mitch's desk, studied a galley.

"Kill these two paragraphs," Mitch said, pointing, "and then add your shirttail. That should do it. If you need more space," he continued, standing erect and handing the galley to the reporter, "tell Ernie to crop more of the photo."

"Gotcha," said Timski. He offered a smile to Haye and left.

"Everything in order?" Haye asked.

"I've got Lyle, Robin and Rog doing sidebars. I'm about to sit down and write the main story myself," Mitch said.

The publisher looked sour. "This is going to leave Southborough with a black eye, a blotch it's going to take some time to erase."

"The town will survive," Mitch said matter-of-factly. "The people here have that kind of resilience."

Haye smirked. "You have it all down pat, don't you? Just another story to you, eh? In and out quick."

"You're in the newspaper business," Mitch shot back. "You should know."

"I don't like you, Stevens. I never did. But that's beside the point." The publisher uncrossed his legs. He sighed. "To be frank, I was prepared to argue with you about running the whole sordid mess, but even before I came in here I knew I was wrong."

"It'd be impossible to suppress a story like this. And irresponsible."

"Of course. I know that, for Chrissake. And it's not the route I want the *Courier* to take. Though I don't think we're going to be able to afford any new machinery around here." Haye snorted. "Actually, it's probably the biggest local story we've ever run. Can you imagine that!"

Mitch looked at Haye, his tone softening. "I'm amazed at how well you're taking all this, considering your stake in it," he said.

"You know something, Stevens? I still plan to run for governor. Hell, it's my newspaper that's blown this up. I can figure on getting some of the credit. But that's not what's important." He leaned forward, wagging a finger at Mitch. "This town still comes first with me, but I think we've all learned that there are ways of doing things and ways of doing things. I want you to follow this right down to the end. Every fact, every scintilla of wrongdoing."

Mitch nodded approvingly. "Tiny Adams says he's called the state attorney general's office over the SkiLand percs. He wants to see both Lay and Handler indicted. I've asked him to go easy on Lay; after all, he did help me. And he had nothing to do with the murders. I promised to testify for him, it's the least I can do.

"I've got to admit they were clever about it," Mitch said. "While we were waiting for the police to come, Cummings told me the whole story. Usually, when a perc test is being done on a major commercial property, a state review engineer from the Natural Resources Agency comes down to oversee the test and make sure it's being done correctly. That's the usual procedure, but it can be circumvented. Handler and Lay rushed the perc test through and then notified the state that they did it in a hurry because they wanted to complete it before the land froze. Winter was coming on. That's not unheard of. By the time the state engineer did show up, the land, of course, was hard as rock and there was no way he could double-check the results, so he just accepted them. There was no reason not to."

"My God. The audacity!" said Haye. "I really had no idea about all these shenanigans."

"Lay also put in the permit that there were no wells within a thousand feet of the property on any side. A lie, but the state engineer wasn't about to spend the time to check it out. They usually don't. It was all so easy."

"Are you going to publish everything that Cummings told us?"

"We were there. We were witnesses."

"I suppose there was no reason to lie to us at that point," Haye agreed. He hefted himself slowly from the chair.

"Well, the professor's daughter was right. You know she came to me for help, begging me to help her prove her father was murdered. It was hard to believe at the time, but she was right. His death just seemed a coincidence."

"How many coincidences are too many?" Haye laughed ironically. "You were certain I was spying on you, remember? That was Jessie trying to protect Brad. She tried too hard, didn't she?"

"You know," said Mitch, "that she was the one who set fire to Ham's house. She was trying to destroy all my notes—and me in the bargain. Or at least get me injured and out of the way."

A shadow of sadness passed over Haye's face. "I had no idea how desperate Brad Cummings felt, or how much of his desperation he communicated to Jessie." The publisher paused and looked down. "It's hard for me to say this, but somehow I feel ultimately responsible for what happened."

Mitch was surprised. Haye was the last person he expected to admit a mistake. "What do you mean?" he asked.

"You know the old cliché where the boss says, 'Gee, I wish we could get rid of so-and-so,' and he's intentionally vague about what he means by 'get rid of'? His overeager associates then go and do the dirty work and the boss is in the clear. As you may recall, it happened with Nixon. When I complained about Vera and her demands for a bigger commission, Cummings must have taken that as a license to kill her. Once he started, he just couldn't stop.

"And," Haye continued, heaving a weary sigh, "he was damn clever about it. Frankly, Mitch, if it hadn't been for your annoying prodding, the police would never have examined Yuri's car, or tested his blood for alcohol. Cummings was counting on their accepting the whole thing as routine. And damn it, he was right."

Mitch shook his head in wonderment. "Cummings admitted to me that he had monkeyed with the steering mechanism. He followed Putzgarov, and when he crashed, Cummings poured a bottle of whisky all over him to make it look like a drunken-driver accident."

Haye shrugged his shoulder and started for the door. He paused, his hand on the doorknob. "By the way, Ham phoned me this morning. He insists on coming back in a couple of weeks despite what the doctors say. I don't know what to tell him. What do you think?"

"Give me some time to wrap all this up. We're bound to have followups. Then we'll set a date for my abdication. Maybe he's trying to rush things and shouldn't."

"It's entirely up to you, Stevens," the publisher said begrudgingly. "I'll try to stay out of your way." He absentmindedly picked up a bottle of paste and studied it. "I appreciate what you've done—not for me, Stevens, for Southborough. You were right to pursue this."

"And I appreciate your acquiesence in publishing the whole story. I hope it won't cost you the governorship. I mean that."

"The governorship's besides the point. At least I have nothing to be ashamed of—and neither does the town."

"And neither do I." The two men shook hands.

BRAD CUMMINGS ADMITS TO THREE MURDERS AND FRAUD; DEATH OF SELECTMAN'S WIFE SPURS SKILAND INQUIRY

State Probe of Resort Development Asked by Local Police; Britfair Zoning Bid Withdrawn

In a startling development touched off when Selectman Brad Cummings's wife Jessica killed herself by accident with an antique shotgun, Cummings was arrested last night for the murder of three people and confessed to engineering the killings in order to protect his interests in the SkiLand resort.

Police Officer George Adams said that Cummings

had implicated real-estate agent William McCoy Handler and civil engineer Stanley C. Lay in a scheme designed to bypass the state requirements for perc tests at the multi-unit condominium and store development near MayorsPeak.

Handler, who is being sought for questioning, has been missing from his home and office since last night.

According to Adams, Cummings said he had shot realtor Vera Tolvey last fall. Her partly decomposed body was discovered on property adjacent to SkiLand several weeks ago. It was believed at the time that she had been the victim of a hunting accident.

Adams said Cummings also admitted tampering with the car of Yuri Putzgarov, the noted violinist, who died in what appeared to be a car accident last week, and to substituting a sugar solution for the insulin taken by Professor Telford Eagleston, a diabetic. Like Putzgarov, Eagleston was involved in the campaign to develop SkiLand. He died two weeks ago from what was then believed to be a heart attack.

Cummings's confessions came on the heels of his wife's death. She had inserted two smokeless shells into the century-old shotgun and fired the weapon late last night near the Colonial House.

Whether she had aimed the weapon at anyone in particular was unclear. In the vicinity of the inn at the time were John N. Haye, publisher of the *Courier,* and Mitchell Stevens, the newspaper's acting editor.

IMPACT OF CONFESSION WIDE RANGING

There were various developments following Mrs. Cummings's death:

—Southborough police asked the attorney general's office to launch an immediate inquiry into the SkiLand development. (See p.4.)

—Harvey Troupe, SkiLand developer, said he would ask the Board of Selectmen to withdraw a proposal for a zoning variation that would have permitted Britfair Enterprises to erect a major store and warehouse in the vicinity of SkiLand. (See p. 4.)

—The Board of Selectmen will meet in emergency session tonight to consider the implications of Cummings's arrest. (See Column 3, p. 1.)

—A new organization of local residents calling themselves the Southborough Citizens for Clean Government and led by Dorothy Cahill will sponsor an open forum next Wednesday at Southborough High School on the future of the community. (See p. 5.)

—Soil Engineer Stanley C. Lay announced through his attorney that he would consider testifying at any state hearing or legal proceeding in return for immunity.

SELECTMAN SAYS WIFE WAS SHIELDING HIM

Mrs. Cummings, 39, was a native of Dummerston. She and Selectman Cummings were married in 1970, shortly after his return from Vietnam, where he had served as a Ranger and for which he had received the Bronze Medal.

Distraught at his wife's death, Cummings said he believed she had been trying to prevent information regarding allegedly fraudulent perc tests at SkiLand from becoming public.

According to Cummings, Tolvey and Putzgarov were silent investors in SkiLand. Eagleston was a supporter of the project because he thought the development would be beneficial for Southborough.

Both Eagleston and Tolvey apparently discovered that perc tests on the SkiLand property had been falsified. Cummings said each threatened to expose the truth—Eagleston "as a matter of principle," Tolvey for reasons of "blackmail."

Cummings admitted before several witnesses that he had murdered both Eagleston and Tolvey "to keep them from talking."

He said he arranged the car-accident death of Putzgarov because of the violinist's "greed." Putzgarov, Cummings explained, suspected that Tolvey had been murdered and had sought a larger share of the profits from the SkiLand venture.

Prodding by the *Courier* staff prompted local police to investigate the circumstances of Putzgarov's death and led to the conclusion that his car had been tampered with.

In tears at the scene of his wife's death, Cummings, witnesses reported, said he had . . .

IT WAS EARLY morning and Mitch was still at the office. He had felt the need to see the paper to bed himself, to make sure every last detail was the way he wanted it. Even now, as late as it was, as tired as he was, he was finding it difficult to think about going home to bed. His eye was caught by an envelope lying on his desk. Oh, my God, Mitch thought, there's the police report on Eagleston's death. I knew it was here somewhere. He looked it over. The report was routine; there was no hint of suspicious circumstances. Well, thank God Cummings confessed, because there really was no hard physical evidence against him. How easily Brad almost got away with three murders.

As much as he tried to hide it from himself, Mitch was

going to miss the action. For a long moment, the thought of leaving caused him almost physical pain. So Ham was right, after all. He did want his job.

SEVENTEEN

MITCH HITCHED HIS legs atop the desk, crossing them at the ankles. He leaned back, the phone to his ear. "Ham? You okay?"

"I'm getting out tomorrow, thank the Lord." Johnson mumbled something Mitch couldn't make out. "Sorry, it was that damn physical therapist. They keep me hopping."

"Ham, I spoke to Haye and none of us sees the need for you to rush back here."

"Well, frankly, Mitch, I don't think I could *rush* anywhere, but I don't want just to sit at home. I spoke to the surgeon and he thinks I ought to be able to come in part-time in maybe two weeks—if I feel all right."

"It's still early in the summer, Ham. I can stay on into early September, if you want," Mitch offered. "It'd be no sweat. I'm enjoying myself."

"So I've heard."

"I hope," Mitch said, "that I haven't screwed up things for you with Haye."

Johnson laughed. "I'm not the same animal you are. He's eager to have me back. At least that's what he told me this morning."

"Well, just in case, I'll plan to stick around until you're sure of yourself."

"That'll be fine by me. I'm going to be bringing a private nurse back with me for the first two weeks."

"That'll be no problem. Bob Grant has found you a three-bedroom house on Combs Hill. I'm going to move in and get things ready for you this afternoon. Val's going to help me. She's taken a three-day break to be with us. There'll be plenty of room for all of us—unless you don't want me hanging around."

"Well, she's not that pretty," Johnson joked. "Shh. Here she comes now to give me a bath. I'll be seeing you."

Mitch strained forward to put the phone back. He rubbed his right shoulder to ease a slight muscle spasm. He had not been able to shake off his depression of last night. His stay in Southborough was coming to an end. It was only a matter of weeks before Ham would be back in the office and then only a matter of days perhaps before he would no longer be needed. Mitch looked at the hopper on his desk. The copy for two stories lay waiting for him. Through the doorway he could see the copy desk. Ernie was leaning over a piece of wire copy, his cigar trailing a slow wisp of smoke toward the ceiling. Robin had stopped by Lyle's desk and was talking to him, her hand resting gently on his shoulder. Maxine was handing Roger Barrows some letters. Rachel was facing a typewriter, working earnestly on an obit.

He was going to miss them all.

* * *

"Well, what do you think?" Mitch glanced at Val uncertainly. "It's not quite as nice as some of the other places I've seen, but the view is okay, and we'd have privacy."

They were standing in the middle of a meadow. Val turned slowly. Off to the north, in the distance across a winding dirt road, was a barn and silo. To the west and south, trees. To the east, on the slope of a hill, stood an old, two-story Victorian gingerbread house with a widow's walk.

Seeing Val's eyebrows go up slightly as she took in the rundown house, Mitch said, "It's not too close. A couple of trees will mask it."

"How many acres did Bob Grant say there were?" she asked.

"Three."

Val shrugged her shoulders. "I don't know, Mitch. It's not quite what I wanted. I mean, it's lovely in a way, but it just doesn't ring any bells. You know what I mean?"

Mitch nodded. "Changing your mind about having a place like this?"

"No, not at all, honey. Why should I?"

"Because of what happened—the murders."

"Oh, that doesn't bother me at all." She looked inquiringly at him. "What about you? Still want to live here?"

"In Southborough?"

Val nodded.

Mitch gazed off in the distance. "I've had a lot of fun up here. Well, fun is not the right word, is it? I've just enjoyed being back in harness so much. It felt good running that little paper. It was exciting. I didn't realize how much I missed the business."

"I don't think you've answered my question," she said, touching his arm lightly. "You still want to have a place to come to here? Or should we look elsewhere?"

"Like where? Farther north?"

"Maybe. Then again, maybe closer to New York."

Mitch reached for her hand. They began walking back to the road where their car was parked. Val stooped to pick some black-eyed Susans and Queen Anne's lace. She held the bouquet of wild flowers loosely as they reached the car.

She turned to Mitch, a wicked gleam in her eye. "How come this sweet little town becomes the murder capital of Vermont the minute you hit town?"

"Just lucky, I guess." Mitch winced. Val's question hit a nerve. Would he really be happy here without the mayhem and murder of the last few weeks? When it was just business as usual? He honestly didn't know the answer.

They drove in silence toward Williamstown along I-91. As they crossed the border, leaving Vermont, the first thing Mitch noticed was the sign that greeted them:

MASSACHUSETTS GUN LAW VIOLATION
MANDATORY ONE YEAR JAIL SENTENCE

Mitch chuckled. "What's so funny?" Val asked, a quizzical look on her face.

Mitch leaned toward her. "Maybe next summer," he said conspiratorially, "I ought to stay with you in Massachusetts. It'll be safer and—" His hand reached across to her thigh.

"You keep your eyes on the road, Mitchell Stevens," Val said, slapping his hand. "You're the designated driver."